AXLE'S BRAND

Death Chasers MC Series
Book 3
by
USA Today Bestselling Author
C.M. Owens

Axel's Brand
Death Chasers MC Series
Book 3
By C.M. Owens
Copyright © 2017 by C.M. Owens

Fate is just a made-up word used to give us hope or absolution. We find hope when we believe bad things happen to us for a reason. We find absolution when we feel as though the wrongs of our past were just fate's twisted design to bring us to our present, and all of it was out of our hands.

Of course, I sort of changed my mind after meeting Axle. The man with scars and haunted, cold eyes. The man who only warmed when he was around me. The first man I felt wouldn't cost me my life. The first man I ever believed to actually be honorable, despite the fact he's a ruthless criminal.

Then fate intervened. Life got complicated. Shit happened. And I sort of fell harder than I thought possible.

The first time we met, I was in my pajamas and cowering on the floorboard of his SUV, hiding from my very insane brother. Lovely first impression, I assure you.

The second time we met, I was literally skating around a bunch of corpses, because I'm slightly crazy like that. Long story.

Obviously, my second impression had just as much impact as my first. Because he fell head-over-heels in love with me in that instant. Kidding. That last part is complete bullshit. Axle is far more complicated than insta-love nonsense. Which is one of my favorite things about him.

Everything about us was perfectly complicated and wonderfully disastrous. It's what every girl dreams of... as long as they're as crazy as I am.

And I'm just crazy enough to hold on, because I don't mind being the psycho chick in roller skates flipping fate the bird. It's just one of my quirks. Turns out, I'm Axle's brand of crazy too.

Life should be really freaking interesting. Or catastrophic. I guess it depends on how much madness you can embrace.

*Adult language

*Sexual content

*Violence

*Not fit for someone who loves rainbows in books. Never mind. There's a rainbow in here. ;) <3

3

As always, this is for the readers, who are pretty fucking amazing.
<3

Where to find me:

Instagram: @cmowensauthor

Twitter: @cmowensauthor

Facebook: @CMOwensAuthor

There are two Facebook groups, the teaser group, and the book club where you can always find me hanging out with fans and readers.

Sign up for my newsletter and get no more than one email a month with new release information and/or a list of my fave books from other authors and deals. (No spamming from me and no one else will get your email address from me.)
https://madmimi.com/signups/425568/join

PROLOGUE

2 years ago…

"I'm just saying, vajazzling is the new bikini wax. Girls have more bling down there than rappers have on their teeth nowadays," Ezekiel says, grinning over at me. "What about you, Maya? Do you vajazzle?"

I roll my eyes, settling down on the comfy couch of the lounge, darting a gaze across the street where our parents are having their meeting. Through the floor-to-ceiling windows, I see them shifting around, my father smiling as he shakes the hand of Ezekiel's father.

Kendra's father is next, taking his turn to shake my father's hand. It's not the friendly handshakes that have my attention. It's the tension in all their bodies. I can tell something is wrong.

"Maya?" Ezekiel prompts.

"You should take her silence as an admission of guilt," Carlisle says, smirking over at me as I turn my attention back to the group.

Ingrid bursts out laughing as I give him a horrified expression. "How did you know?" I ask seriously.

Ezekiel and Carlisle both give me stunned, gaping looks, until I crack a grin and wink at them. "No, I don't have bling on my vagina," I finally tell them, rolling my eyes. "I barely make the time for a bikini wax because I get tired of probing fingers down there."

"No probing fingers; just probing cocks then?" Kendra volleys, giggling.

"Exactly," I deadpan.

As they all break out into laughter, I turn my attention back to the window. Only a street divides us. My parents are up three floors and across said street, but I can see them clearly through the glass from here.

1

Anyone in this building can. Not that they mind, since no one knows who *they* are. But I still don't like seeing them so exposed.

Something feels wrong.

Or maybe I'm just living in a constant state of paranoia lately.

Something has felt wrong for a while.

"Where's your boyfriend?" Kendra asks as she sips her cocktail.

"Thomas is in Manhattan with some of his old college friends tonight. I didn't bother telling him where to find me, because he's rather annoying when he's drunk," I answer with a smile to hide my annoyance.

I honestly have no idea where he is, but I'd rather not say that aloud. Our relationship is…unhealthy most days. Toxic on others.

"What about Lathan?" Ingrid asks me, her laughter tapering off. "Where's he?"

Just as I see my mother sit down by my father, I once again look at my friends.

"My brother is absent. As always. He's been an ass since Father made it official that I was the next in line for the Family. So I didn't tell him where we'd be tonight."

"He's known that his entire life," Ezekiel states dismissively. "Your father didn't want the Family split in half, and Lathan is too hooked on drugs to be a leader."

"I'm aware. But hearing it made official has sent him into a tailspin. More drugs than usual. More girls than usual. More everything and less attendance. I haven't seen him in weeks."

"So he's icing everyone out," Carlisle surmises.

"Not Father. He spoke to him today, but he only told him of the meeting he had to attend, and Lathan apparently hung up on him during the conversation. Father was trying to get him to go to rehab, and asked him to come by after he got back from the meeting. Didn't go well."

Ingrid blows out a breath, about to say something, when suddenly the building we're in shakes hard. The floor rattles beneath us, as noise — just a steady, ear-splitting, undefinable noise — tries to deafen us.

Windows shatter, and Ezekiel tosses me to the ground, his heavy body coming down on top of mine. It's all a blur of motion, nothing making sense.

Screams sound like distant echoes, and I manage to peer up as the building stops moving. My eyes go to the mostly shattered windows, and my heart leaps out of my chest.

I don't know when I get up.

I don't know when I start screaming.

I don't know when I start fighting against Ezekiel's hold, or when he even starts holding me back, preventing me from falling to my death in a quest to save my parents.

It's like it all went black for a second, and suddenly I was at the broken windows, staring in disbelief at a room my parents couldn't have escaped.

Ezekiel is still holding me back as I scream, trying to reach for the burning building across the street as the fire rushes from the room, chasing the outside air.

A second explosion triggers, and I'm launched backwards, the heat and pulse of it so strong against me that it knocks the breath from my lungs.

I blink, wondering when I got back on the ground, wobbling as I stand back up. Ezekiel is unconscious beside me, and Ingrid is slowly lifting herself off the floor, a cut on her head.

A ringing is constant in my ears, making everything else background noise. I see Carlisle's lips moving as he comes to me, shaking my shoulders, but all I can do is stare past him and across the street at the destroyed top half of the building.

The building where our parents were.

As the first tear falls from my eyes, Carlisle shakes me harder, blocking my view as he moves his body to be completely in front of me.

"Not here. Not now," I hear him say, though it still sounds like he's at the other end of a tunnel speaking at me. "Don't cry. Not here. We can't let anyone see us weakened."

Ingrid is batting tears out of her eyes, helping Kendra up, as Ezekiel slowly pushes to his feet.

Hollowed out, I meet Carlisle's gaze again, steeling myself, turning cold like we need to be, even as my heart breaks behind the shield of ice.

"Phillip Jenkins," I whisper, knowing exactly who is responsible for this.

Ingrid takes a step closer, her jaw tensing as she meets my gaze and adds, "Will die."

CHAPTER 1

Maya

Six months ago...

One hour ago, I was in my apartment and settling down for a night of binge watching movies with pizza, beer, and popcorn after just getting settled in Halo.

Now? Now I'm the girl who's freaking out and hiding in the back of a big SUV, and I'm the girl who is silently begging an unknown guy to let me stay hidden as he glares at me with cold eyes, a tense jaw, and indecision in his posture.

This entire thing went south faster than expected.

I guess that's obvious, given my current predicament.

Scars line this guy's face, and he looks freaking terrifying with that glower in those icy eyes too pale to be called blue. They're almost a light gray, creepy but also intriguing.

But for some reason, I also feel safe in his presence. Because I've lost my mind, most likely, and am desperate to feel as though I might be safe again.

I'm so screwed if he doesn't let me stay hidden.

His muscles flex as he finally shuts the back door, not saying anything to anyone as he hides me from sight. He stays close, letting me see him through the side glass, even as I stay as close to the ground as possible.

I have no idea where we're about to go. I have no idea who he is. But right now, that tattooed bad boy with scars is my favorite version of a dark angel, because he may very well be saving my life.

CHAPTER 2

AXLE

She's staring at me with those eyes that scream for help while her lip trembles. Fuck my night. Why is there a girl hiding in the back of our ride?

Then a sick feeling tightens my core when I realize why she's probably hiding. Fury rides through my veins as I shut the door on her, concealing her from sight, when I hear the fast approaching footsteps of our prospective clients.

I shouldn't have opened the door, but I heard a noise. Now all I want to do is put a bullet in Lathan for what he *might* have done to her.

"Did you assholes see a girl run through here?" Lathan asks, wiping some coke away from his nose.

Junkies. We don't do business with junkies.

"Nope," I lie, absently noting how Snake cuts his eyes toward me.

"Fuck!" Lathan roars, slamming his fist against the punching bag in his massive garage that is in the middle of no-damn-where. "Find her!" he yells to three guys who run into each other in their haste to follow orders.

"It's like watching the Stooges," Snake muses from my side.

"It's like watching junkies," I grumble. "Thought someone vetted them."

"Herrin set this up," he says with a shrug.

We watch as Lathan goes on a tantrum, kicking shit, punching random things, and finally throwing things around.

"We need to head out," I yell to Lathan, who doesn't even acknowledge me.

"No way are we fucking doing business with them," Snake says quietly as Lathan actually flips over a table. "Ever."

"Definitely not," I agree, but for an entirely different reason.

"Find her!" Lathan roars again.

"You know she's in the backseat, right?" Snake asks.

"Yep."

"Just checking."

He goes to get in on the passenger side, while I take the driver's seat. This was a waste of two fucking hours of my life that I'll never get back. Herrin is sure as hell going to hear about it, too.

As soon as we're out of the garage and halfway down the street, Snake addresses the stowaway.

"You owe him money or something, girl?"

A heavy breath comes from the backseat, and some of the tension eases out of my shoulders. I hadn't even considered that she might be a junkie—even though she doesn't look like one. My mind immediately always goes to the worst thing that would leave a woman cowering in fear.

"No," she says from the floor very quietly.

That has the tension notching back up.

"Start talking if you want to keep riding," Snake goes on.

She blows out a heavier breath while the rustling sound behind me lets me know she's getting up. My eyes stay on the road instead of glimpsing at her as she makes herself comfortable in the backseat.

"Lathan is psychotic," she grumbles.

"Ex of his or something?" Snake pries.

"Sister," she confesses, allowing all the tension to leave my body with that word. At least I hope he didn't cross that fucking line.

7

"Why are you hiding from him?" I ask, hearing her breath hitch at the sound of my voice.

"Because he's psychotic," she says again, forcing my lips to twitch. "Lathan blew through his trust fund and now he wants mine. Long story short, he had his thugs bring me to his place tonight, and the conversation ended with a gun pointed at my head."

There's more annoyance to her tone than surprise, so I wonder if the gun pointed at her head statement is a euphemism.

"I'm almost positive he was planning to kill me tonight," she goes on. Her tone is flat, almost as though it's no surprise.

Fucked up families everywhere, it seems.

"So what were you guys doing there? Buying? Selling? Working for him?" she asks us.

Snake and I both snort derisively while shaking our heads.

"We're not junkies or dealers," I tell her, listening to the way her breathing hitches at the sound of my voice again.

What's her deal? People freak out over the scars, but not my damn voice.

Irritated, I tighten my grip on the steering wheel. I assumed all the terror in her eyes when I saw her cowering on the floorboard was because of her fear of Lathan. Now I half wonder if it was just the sight of me that had her shivering in fear. Wouldn't be the first fucking time that's happened.

"So what were you doing there?" she asks.

"Our business. Not yours," I tell her curtly, ignoring the sound she makes this time.

"Sheesh. Sorry. Just making conversation."

"You need better conversation skills," Snake points out as we ride out of town and head toward Halo.

"Where are we dropping you?" I ask her.

Fucking eh. Why does she make a sound every time I speak?

"Wherever you're going, that's where I want to go. I can't go back to my place. Lathan's goons got in too easily, and I don't trust him not to just repeat the performance. I doubt I'll get lucky enough to escape twice."

The sky thunders and lightning crashes in the distance, reminding me why we took the SUV in the first place. She'd been shit out of luck if we'd taken our bikes.

"Can't go home with us, sweetheart," Snake drawls.

"Yes. Yes I can," she says quickly.

She doesn't make a sound when he speaks. Just me. Guess the *monster* is scarier than the pretty boy with some ink.

I keep my mouth shut the rest of the way to Halo, but Snake continues to argue with her the second we hit the town line.

"No, you can't," he says, sighing heavily. "Our place isn't for pretty, sweet girls with junkie brothers. Promise."

"I'm not stupid enough to think you guys are legit or anything, which is why I want to stay with you. You could probably protect me. I can pay you. I have a lot of money, hence the reason Lathan wants me dead. Not that he can touch my money if I die."

"Then he doesn't want you dead. He's trying to scare you into handing everything over," Snake points out helpfully.

"Regardless, I can't go home. I can't check into a hotel either. He has guys everywhere. And I can't leave Halo."

"Why can't you leave Halo?" Snake muses, asking the questions I can't, since she doesn't like the sound of my voice.

I feel her eyes on me, and it makes me tenser than I already am. Not sure why she's getting under my skin like this. Probably because of the fear in her eyes... The way she looked like she'd sell her soul for just one more breath.

I've held a breath like that myself once upon a time ago.

"Because," she finally says, "I just can't."

"Well, we *just can't* let you into our clubhouse."

"Oh, so you're a motorcycle club," she says in surprise, causing me to cast a sideways glance at Snake.

He curses himself before staring out the window and zipping his lips, putting the burden of finding out where to take her on my shoulders.

"Where do we drop you off?" I ask her, this time hearing a soft sigh pass her lips.

"Wherever you're going, I'm following. I'm not ready to die just yet."

Rolling my eyes, I turn on the street toward the warehouse, and Snake cuts his eyes toward me.

"We can't take her there," he hisses.

"We can't leave her on the street. We'll let Drex deal with this, since Herrin's the one who set up that meeting to begin with and didn't do any of his homework."

"You seriously want to let Drex around her? Next to Rush, he's the worst person to speak to a woman."

My eyes flit up to the rearview to see a dark set of eyes staring right at me. Fuck. Her bottom lip is drawn between her teeth, and she's staring like she can't look away. Guess she's never seen a face like mine.

Annoyed, I look back at the road, even though I still feel the heat of her heavy gaze on me.

"Drex is the best one to get rid of her," I say dismissively.

CHAPTER 3

Maya

I'm not sure who Drex is, but I don't want to know. My body is still trembling, my hands are shaking, and my heartbeat is in my ears. I hate fear. It stinks and makes me feel like someone I'm not.

It was naïve to think I wouldn't need immediate protection, when I knew the risks coming to this place. Lathan, however, is a little better than I credited him, and caught wind of my arrival in Halo before I even slept one night in my new bed.

Now this…

Is it stupid to ask some random guys with scars, tattoos, and guns to take me home with them? Yes. It's incredibly stupid. But it's by far dumber to go anywhere my brother might find me. And he *will* be looking for me. If I'm going to die, I'd like to at least die at the hands of a stranger, rather than my unhinged flesh and blood.

I was lucky when they pulled up, because it distracted Lathan long enough for me to get out of the locked room he'd shoved me in. My lock-picking skills aren't a waste after all.

Then, to top off my luck, I was able to sneak into the garage while they talked off to the side. I managed to slip into the back of the SUV, undetected.

Lathan was so high it doesn't surprise me that he never saw me slip out to where they were. I thought the model guy noticed me, but he never acted like he did. Until he got in the vehicle.

"Can I ask your names?" I ask the two silent guys up front as we slow to a steady crawl in front of a massive warehouse right in the middle of town. This is their clubhouse? Talk about no discretion or privacy.

It's tucked away between more buildings—nothing at all like I would have expected.

"Snake and Axle," the model says, not telling me which is which as they get out.

I hop out and follow, running close behind the one with scars whose voice sounds like sex to my ears. I've never wanted to fuck a voice more than I want to his. Yeah, I'm a crazy girl, but damn. It's all deep and rough, almost as though he's trying to seduce you with mundane words and succeeding without effort.

"I'm Maya," I tell them, even though they don't seem the least bit interested. "Maya Black," I mutter under my breath as I sigh.

A door opens for them, and a guy with a beard and a bald head looks at me with surprise.

"Picked up a stray?" he asks.

"Drex's problem. Lathan is a junkie," the model tells him.

Still not sure which one is Axle and which one is Snake.

"Damn it. I told him he had to investigate these guys," the bald guy growls.

"Herrin set it up. Not Drex," the model adds before walking farther into the warehouse. "But we're making Drex deal with the stray."

I continue following like it's my right to just bust up in their warehouse, and I move close to the side of the sex-voice guy as my breath catches in my lungs. There are people everywhere, and it looks like we're walking into the middle of a party.

Loud music is blasting in the center of the room as girls dance for the guys, climbing in and out of their laps. I'm fairly positive that someone is fucking against the wall. I won't look close enough to be certain.

I've been in the middle of plenty scandalous parties, but it's a different breed here. Everyone is rough and...some are dirty...

In my element, I can rock these parties. However, this is not my element. I'm in pajamas to top it all off.

Feeling incredibly uncomfortable and like the new girl in school, I lean against Mr. Sex Voice, who jerks away from me like I've just slapped him.

When I look up, he's glaring down at me, keeping at least a foot between us. I'm tempted to sniff myself and see if I stink or something.

In the light, I see his scars so much better. One gnarly scar runs the length of his face on one side and curls under his bottom lip. It's deep, and it had to be painful. Some smaller ones are also on his face, marring what would be flawless perfection.

He cuts his gaze away from me and stalks off, leaving me on my own as a few whistles break out and eyes swing my way. I inch a little closer to the model guy, who is getting a drink.

"Are you Axle or Snake?" I ask him loudly to carry over the music.

He turns toward me with a coldness that wasn't there earlier.

"I'm not interested, if that's what you're hinting at." His eyes drop lower, like he's appraising me and finding me dissatisfactory before his eyes meet mine again. "My girl would tear you apart for even trying. She has pretty claws."

My eyebrows go up in surprise. Surely I'm not giving off a flirty vibe, considering he's not my type. Never been much for the blindingly gorgeous kind.

"I was just making conversation," I grumble, repeating what I said earlier.

He returns his attention to the party, ignoring me, acting like it's *my* conversation skills that need work. My eyes flit around the room, looking for the one who abandoned us. It's too chaotic to really tell if he's anywhere close, but a blonde-haired girl walking toward us has my attention when she flashes a big smile.

She looks vaguely familiar, but I have no idea why.

"Hi," she says brightly, bouncing close to the guy at my side.

His arm drops around her shoulders, and he kisses the top of her head.

"Hi," I say back lamely.

She continues to smile while looking around, and I awkwardly stand in place.

"You came in with Snake?" she asks, glancing between us.

At least I know who Snake is now.

"I needed to escape, and Axle and Snake happened to have wheels," I explain, remembering what Snake said about her claws.

My eyes dart down to see her perfectly manicured nails, and I wonder if she's ever actually been in a fight.

Her eyes brighten, and her sweet smile grows. No way is this girl a fighter.

"I'm Sarah. Snake's girl. You really shouldn't be here dressed like that. The guys...are a little rough here."

I glance down at my skimpy pajamas and shrug.

"I can handle my own—"

"Says the girl who cowered in our backseat from her brother and begged for our protection," Snake cuts in.

"Play nice," Sarah hisses, gently elbowing him in the ribs.

Snake just grabs a beer from the bar behind us and starts drinking as he pulls Sarah closer to his body. He doesn't know anything about me, so I understand that the circumstances are misleading, and it's not like I can explain the truth of the situation.

"Why do you need protection?" she asks seriously.

It's hard to hear her, but I still manage.

"Long story."

She darts a glance at her boyfriend just as he gets called away. I take notice that more eyes are on us now, watching me with undisguised curiosity.

I guess I stick out, considering I'm wearing a small camisole and very short, thin pajama shorts. I have on zero makeup, my hair is barely brushed, and I have on my ugliest sneakers to top it all off, since Lathan's goons barely allowed me enough time to grab shoes at all.

Not my best first impression.

"You're in deep shit, aren't you?" Sarah asks, losing the bright look in her eyes as it changes to something a little colder.

"Yeah. A little bit. I can't go home right now, so I'm trying to convince Axle to let me stay. I didn't realize…this is a little more than I was expecting."

I gesture around to the wild party, noting all the guns I see. Guns don't make me nervous, but when they're attached to a bunch of drunk brutes, that's when anxiety creeps up.

Sarah shakes her head.

"You need to stick close to me, but you can't stay here. There are some guys here who don't wait for consent."

That didn't even cross my mind. My stomach tilts when I think of how stupid it was for that to *not* cross my mind. My father always kept his men in check, so even though I grew up in a similar — slightly more refined — environment, it wasn't as unsafe as this one.

The guys there wore Armani, but they still packed the same Glock as these guys have on their Wrangler hips.

"What's going on with you?" she asks. "Maybe I can help."

Not sure how she can help. "My brother wants me dead."

She nods like that isn't completely shocking. "Sucks when people want you dead. Why?"

It'd be too risky to tell her all the details, so I stick to the story I gave Axle and Snake.

"I have money and he wants it. My parents cut him out of the will before their deaths because he was deep into drugs. They left everything to me, and all he had was his original trust fund that is probably gone."

She starts to speak, when suddenly my eyes land on a returning figure, and my stomach flips over. *Dark angel* is an accurate description. I just wish his jaw didn't tic every time he looked at me.

Sarah's eyes follow mine, and we watch as he talks to a guy who is reading the screen of his phone like there isn't a party going on around him. The guy looks up, confused, then they both cut their eyes toward me.

Shit.

Now I have two guys staring at me like they can't stand the sight of me. But my options are limited and I'm a little desperate to stay here. Despite the cold glower, Axle did get me away from Lathan, and he did bring me here.

Axle might be a stone on the outside, but he obviously has a heart somewhere inside that massive, firm, very distracting chest of his.

Right?

CHAPTER 4

AXLE

She's staring right at me as we walk over to her, and Drex curses me again like it's my fault he has to deal with this.

"What's going on?" Sarah asks.

I really wish she wasn't over here right now.

"You can't stay here," Drex tells Maya, ignoring Sarah's question and jumping straight to the point.

The last thing we need is someone else getting stuck in the crosshairs of the impending war we have breathing down our necks with the Hell Breathers.

"I can't leave Halo and I can't go home," she tells him firmly.

"Not my fucking problem," Drex tells her, bored. "Get the hell out of my clubhouse before I let the guys inspect the new merchandise."

"Seriously, I might die—"

"Seriously, I give zero fucks," Drex interrupts, cold as ice as he steps closer to her.

I should have just kicked her out myself, but she's persistent and annoying, and I hate dealing with women. I do find the determination in her eyes a little amusing. She's not backing down. She even narrows her eyes in challenge.

"I want to talk business," she goes on.

Drex snorts derisively, and I smirk.

"We're not selling cupcakes. Understand? You're more likely to die here than at your brother's hand. Now go."

My amusement dies when she looks at me like she's disappointed. I'm tempted to let her crash in my room for the night.

17

We're not working a job, so I'm not using it. It wouldn't hurt anything if she stayed up there.

Then I remember what a sadistic asshole Benny is, and if we go to war, what she could face is worse than death. She's a little too sweet for the bloodshed in store.

"I have money. I can pay for protection."

Drex's eyes light up with humor as he grins. "We don't need money. We probably have more of it than you. Go. Now. Before I lose my temper. Trust me, you don't want to see that."

"I'll take her home," Sarah says, stepping between them almost protectively.

Drex laughs to himself as he walks away, and I leave Sarah behind with Maya. No one will mess with Sarah. She's Snake's girl and he'd kill anyone if they did. Besides, she's part of our crew.

"So the guy was a junkie?" Drex asks me, already forgetting about the girl.

"Yeah. No deal."

"Pop should have vetted him better."

"Herrin's standards aren't as high as yours. You should take over the vetting from now on," I point out. Again.

Drex snorts, looking over at where Sarah is escorting Maya out the doors. I look away when those dark eyes meet mine again.

"Don't bring back any more strays. For all we know, she could have been trying to plant herself in the crew."

Drex is paranoid, but I don't call him out on it. The girl is a scared kitten who has a twisted brother and nothing more.

"I thought if you had to deal with Herrin's mess, you might start cleaning it up," I tell him, letting the corner of my mouth tug up in a taunting grin.

Since he never says anything bad about his father, I'm not surprised when he simply flips me off and walks away. I decide to get drunk and forget about the girl who shivered at the sound of my voice.

I also try to forget about the fact she touched me. It's been a long fucking time since a girl touched me in any way.

CHAPTER 5

"Where are we going?" I ask Sarah as she turns down another road.

"That depends," she says as she trains her eyes on the road ahead.

"On what?"

"On you telling the truth. You were lying about why your brother wants you dead. Trust me, I know a lie when I hear it."

Shifting uncomfortably, I study her profile. How does she know?

"He really does want my money," I tell her, because it is the truth. "And it was all left to me when my parents died."

"Why else does he want you?" she asks, obviously detecting the honesty there.

There's really nothing left to lose at this point, even though I'm worried that the club is helping my brother. They never would tell me why they were there.

But, considering my limited options and the pile of shit I'm already in with Lathan, I tell her the very long, drawn out story as she drives in circles. When I'm finally finished, I expect her to pull over and shove me out of the car before burning rubber in the opposite direction.

People who want to live stay far away from me and all my dangerous madness.

"You look like a sorority girl," she states randomly, quirking her eyebrow at me before returning her gaze to the road.

"You look like a stripper," I volley, shrugging.

She laughs under her breath. "My look is just an act. Your act is pure genius. You're actually a little crazy."

I nod in agreement. "Some call me insane. But now you understand why I need protection."

She cuts the wheel down a road we haven't looped around yet, and she shakes her head. "You don't need protection. You need to learn how to hide in plain sight, and you need expendable goons. Drex's guys are *not* expendable. One Death Dealer dies because of your mess, and they'll all come for you."

I swallow a little nervously. I'm crazy—not suicidal. I don't know a lot about biker clubs.

"I didn't want Drex's guys or assume they were expendable. I've been looking into building a team. They need to be more skilled than just *goons*."

"I'll make some calls for you. You need to adopt a name to work under if you're going through with this."

"I've already formed an identity—a male identity—that will be the one in charge, or so my team will think."

Her grin only spreads. "I'll let you know when I have some expendable goons in line for your little pet project."

I turn to face her a little more fully. "I have a criteria that has to be met before they're hired. And why would you help me?" I ask her, suspicious.

She turns into an apartment complex. "As of now, this is your home. You have access to your accounts that can't be tracked by your brother?"

"I handled that immediately. But he'll still find me if I stay in the city if I don't have protection. *That's* what I was trying to ask the club for. Protection only."

Her smile never wavers. If anything, she smiles bigger. "Oh, that won't be a problem. I'm an expert at hiding right under someone's nose. I'll teach you. It's not hard to learn. No protection needed until the heat starts coming down. Then we'll start resourcing that task out. It's safer to rely on yourself as long as you can."

As she parks her car and gets out, I follow, still suspicious. "Again, why would you help me?"

She stabs the elevator button, and I glance around the empty garage.

"No cameras out here or in the garage elevator. Two cameras are on your floor, but your new apartment is in a blind spot from both of them because of the angles," she says, still not answering my question.

As the doors open, she steps in, and I follow her once more.

"You have the funds to replace all your clothes. Do that instead of returning to your old apartment for your things. Keep the sorority girl look," she adds.

I run a frustrated hand through my hair.

"Why are you helping me?" I ask her again, knowing how dangerous it is to trust just anyone, but desperate enough to take the chance. If she can tell me why I should.

If I go back to New York after already failing, all hell will break loose. It's the worst option.

She faces me just as the elevator starts whisking us up.

"Because you have a lot of money, a lot of contacts in a world that will be of use to me eventually, and it's always smart to be owed favors from someone like you. I help you, then you help me. Understood?"

That I can work with.

"Understood. How much money do you need?"

Her grin spreads again. "Nothing right now. I'll let you know when I need to cash in on my favors. Until then, be thankful I walked over to Snake tonight. Because I'm about to save your life."

As the doors open, I blow out a heavy breath.

"I am thankful, as long as you're not crazy and just jerking my chain."

She laughs again, and uses her keys to push open a door to an apartment. My breath catches when we walk into the large apartment that looks more like a conspiracy theorist's bunker.

Guns upon guns line the walls, along with various other things — explosive things, mostly. Pictures are stabbed to the walls, and notes are taped up everywhere.

She moves to the center of the room, crossing her arms as I take in the chaos.

"Oh, sweetie, I'm possibly crazier than you. But I love my favors, and saving your life earns me a big one. I'll keep you alive. You just make sure your word is good."

It isn't until I start reading the notes that I realize the most crucial detail of who has just brought me to safety. I also realize why she seemed vaguely familiar, though I've only seen blurred images of her until now.

Things just got a lot more interesting.

My jaw is slack, still trying to make sense of everything I'm seeing.

"It is," I say quietly.

It's a small fucking world as I slowly unravel exactly who Sarah is.

She's not Sarah at all.

"Good," she states flatly, lifting her phone. "Because your life depends on that."

CHAPTER 6

Present...

AXLE

"They took all of it," Drex says calmly, although I can feel the inevitable explosion crackling close to the surface.

I sit back, trying not to lose my shit. Never thought I'd want Herrin dead this badly. He was our P. Now he's nothing but a bitch—and a dead man walking.

"Every fucking penny," Rush growls. "How? We moved all the money to five different secure accounts. All of them were new!"

"Pop didn't get to the top by lying down and taking things. And he didn't get there without making numerous friends either. Someone sold us out within the club, and somehow we got hacked," Drex says quietly.

Suddenly, he stands, and the volatile explosion I was waiting for happens as he slams his fist through the wall over and over again. Propping up, I start going through our list of members in my head, trying to figure out who would be the most loyal to Herrin.

Bottom line, it doesn't matter right now, because we're broke. Which means we're fucked.

"Herrin's smart. The best way to break us is to bankrupt us," Jude drawls, sounding bored with the whole thing. He's not been right since the truth came out about Sarah or AJ or whatever her name is.

A lot of shit has happened in six months. Our club split up. Drex and Herrin are on the verge of a war. Snake started using his real name after Sarah—whose real name is AJ—was outed as someone completely different than any of us expected...

It's been a shitty half year.

"We have an order on thirty installs that would help us out, but we need to buy the supplies somehow," Drex groans.

"The down payment should cover the installs," I say, trying to dig us out of this hole.

We went from having more money than we could ever spend to being broke.

"We need at least sixty grand to do the installs. With the feds sniffing around, it's hard to even keep business, much less ask for a down payment. The only way we're keeping business is by not asking for payment until delivery," Drex explains, frustrated.

"Feds aren't sniffing around us right now. They've pulled back to look for AJ," I say. Yeah, even I hear how stupid and desperate it sounds.

"Doesn't matter. Pop is still attached to our name until we prove we're done with him," Drex growls.

"So how much we got between us?" Rush asks, tossing out a wad of cash. "I've got ten grand."

It's not like any of us keep a bank account. That's too easy for the feds to keep tabs on. The vast majority of our funds stayed in the off-shore club account, and we personally kept our payments in cash or invested in things. Most of us just spent the shit, certain there'd always be more when we needed it.

The laundered money went into the other four accounts we recently set up. All five accounts have been emptied the hell out.

"I have maybe fifteen grand," I announce, blowing out a breath.

"I have at least twenty grand upstairs," Drex says, frowning. "The rest of my cash was burned in the damn fire Ben and his followers set to my house."

"Five G's from me," Snake—I mean *Jude* says, tossing out his own wad. "I just spent a fuck ton on my new bike."

Sledge tosses in his offerings, as well as Dash, and Drex starts counting it up.

"It might be enough for the installs, but we need more money to keep the bills paid in the meantime," Drex says, leaning back.

"I'd say we could take some run jobs, but I doubt anyone would risk their merchandise being in our hands with the club dividing, the feds watching Herrin, and shit going to hell," Rush says, his lips tensing.

"We'll work it out, prove we can handle our shit no matter what, and deal with it as we can. We got that meeting this afternoon with more prospective clients that Rush vetted," I add.

Rush runs a hand through his hair, glancing over at me.

"The guys came back without much info on them, but I talked to three sources the club trusts. All said they were legit. I'm still going with you to see if I missed anything. Last thing we need is to get mixed up with junkies right now," he tells me.

"I'll come with too. Make it look good with me being there," Drex goes on. "It's a big deal that could really dig us out of this pit right now."

"So all four of us are going?" Jude asks, arms crossing over his chest.

Drex nods slowly. "Yeah. We need to put in the extra effort and work a little harder than usual until we can bump the funds back up. And we need to keep this as quiet as possible from the others for now. Half of them are already skittish, and as it is, we obviously have a rat. Possibly more than one."

"Some charters are struggling to pick a side right now," Dash chimes in. "By the way, I'll ride out with you to meet the clients too."

It's just the six of us at the table. Dash, Drex, Sledge, Jude, Rush, and me. This table used to host a lot more.

"Most will side with Herrin since he's the P," Sledge says in a gruff tone. "But the young guns will possibly toss away their patches for a chance to come here and move up with Drex."

Drex stands, pushing his chair back, and he presses his hands down on the table as he leans over it.

"We still have the money coming in from our businesses. I'll cash it all out for the time being. I'll have Liza bring the deposit bags here every night from the strip club. The salon is also in my name. I'll have Colleen bring the bags here from it. Someone needs to escort them daily and take different routes. Multiple escorts, actually. Only guys you know you can trust."

His phone beeps, and he pulls it out, looking at it as I turn to face Sledge.

"You know Herrin better than any of us. When's he going to hit? And should we hit first?"

He shakes his head. "You hit first, and the remaining charters will all side with him. If he hits first, you're going to win more love, though loyalties will still be divided. Herrin is unpredictable, so there's no telling when he'll hit. But you can be sure it's coming."

"So we hit first, and we get shunned. We get hit first, and we might win some guys," Rush states dryly. "Great fucking brotherhood we have."

Sledge tenses just barely as he glances over at his adopted son. "What's going on here is a fucked up situation that no one was prepared for. There's not a rule book on how to deal with it."

"Eve is coming in," Drex says before pocketing his phone, and Rush closes his mouth, swallowing down whatever he was going to say.

That's another change. Drex has an old lady now. It's because of her that he finally understood his father wasn't the legend or leader he thought he was.

Our eyes all cut to the door when Eve walks in, and she arches an eyebrow when she sees us.

"Do I have something on my face?" she asks, then touches her face like she's searching for the phantom issue.

When I look away, Drex is smiling at her, and that has me rolling my eyes. He hasn't gone soft, if that's what you're thinking.

"What's the verdict?" she asks, and everyone shifts uncomfortably.

We know Eve isn't a snitch, but giving her details is still a little too worrisome. Well, to everyone but Drex.

"The verdict is that we're about to go scope out those potential clients I told you about. Stay here and upstairs until I get back. Lock the door, too," he tells her firmly.

She flicks her gaze around the table, and her eyes meet his. "Be careful. Herrin is out for you. He could be setting you up."

Sledge is the first to laugh, and I chuckle under my breath. It's funny seeing someone worry over Drex.

He tugs her to him, his grin turning mocking as she lets him manhandle her.

"We know how to vet them," Rush tells her acidly, but she doesn't even pay him any attention. He runs hot and cold where Eve is concerned. More cold than hot. He hated Herrin more than any of us, so he's thankful to her for at least getting this ball rolling.

When Drex and Eve start kissing, we all get up and walk out, because you never know when things will escalate with them, and Drex isn't afraid of exhibition.

None of us say anything as we all go to our temporary rooms within the warehouse to get ready for the ride to meet our newest possible clients.

I collapse to my bed, covering my eyes with my arm as I try to get a few seconds of sleep. It seems like I get less and less of it the older I get.

CHAPTER 7

Maya

"Tomorrow is the third shipment," I tell Sarah as she stares at a knife blade like it's fascinating.

She's been in and out of here a lot lately, and I don't know what's going on.

"My team is supposed to contact me when it's done," I go on, expecting her to at least be curious.

She stabs the knife into the table and looks down at her phone when it chimes with a text. I know the different tunes on her phone and what they mean—that's how much she's been around.

"You're ignoring me," I decide to say as I roller skate around in a circle, trying to work out my nerves. I've cleared the large room out to give me room to skate in for times like these.

She looks up from her phone and smirks at me.

"How many favors do you owe me?" she asks.

"I'm sure you have an accurate tab on you somewhere," I tell her, since she's pretty adamant about telling me when I owe her yet another favor, though she's yet to use any of said favors.

"You're about to become a bank," she says as she stands.

I skid to a halt, cocking my head. "Okay. How much do you need?"

Her grin only grows. "Not me, love. I'm using the favor for some old friends of mine. You remember Axle, don't you?"

My stomach flips a little at just the mention of his name. Not that it should. He wouldn't even glance at me like I was anything more than a nuisance.

Girl needs self-respect.

"Barely," I lie, batting a hand.

She rolls her eyes before grabbing a few pistols, and starts to shove them into the holsters on her body. She's dressed in all black. Again. Including pleather leggings—she makes them hot. And a corset. Totally hot.

Me? Not so hot.

I'm in roller skates with my hair in twin balls and my 1970's pink socks that stop at my thighs, while I wear my pink Bubble Gum Girl T-shirt and little white exercise shorts.

We couldn't be more opposite.

"Thought they had more money than I do," I finally say when she stares expectantly at me.

Those are pretty much the words Drex Caine—yes, I know his name now—said to me that night.

The guns she straps on all the time used to make me wary. I've learned Sarah is somewhat unhinged—even more so than me.

"They had plenty of money. But shit went down. The club split in half after Drex and Herrin went toe-to-toe. Long story short, all hell broke loose, and Drex finally saw his father as the shitty little weasel he really is. Now Herrin has stolen their money. They need a bank until they get back on their feet. I have a guy who might be able to steal their money back, but that could take time."

I spin in a tight circle on my skates before pushing off and getting closer to her. She eyes my socks for a second before looking up at me.

"I said sorority girl was a good look. Not Bubble Gum Betty."

"This is my unwinding attire. Tonight is tense for me. Anyway, I'll give you however much you need, and you can take it to them."

Her expression goes blank, no emotion showing.

"I can't. You'll have to be the one to give it to them, and you'll have to convince them to take it."

My lips purse. "You have a boyfriend on the inside, and in case you've forgotten, they ran me out of that place. If they need money, then they shouldn't need convincing."

She starts putting on some ammo holsters that hold spare magazines, and I cock my head. That's new. She doesn't usually do that when she leaves.

My distraction is interrupted when she speaks again.

"You'll offer them a job they can't refuse. Not a loan. It can't be me who offers it. Jude left me—"

"I thought his name was Snake," I interrupt.

Her stony expression cracks, and I see the pain in her eyes. "His name is Jude. Snake was just a nickname. I was the only one allowed to call him Jude, and I only called him that when we were alone. Now he takes that special thing away by having everyone call him Jude. It's just one of the many ways he's letting me know we're really over."

Her face hardens again, and she angrily shoves on a few more holsters that take up her forearm. She bends her arms like she's testing their flexibility or weight, and then she picks up a few knives and starts shoving them into her waist holster.

"Why'd you break up?"

Her hands pause their jerky movements, and her face stays hidden by her blonde hair as she exhales heavily.

"Because I did the one unforgivable thing."

"You cheated?" I guess.

Her face stays hidden as she shakes her head, finishing up her dangerous attire.

"No. Worse. I lied."

I frown at that. "Everyone lies."

She looks at me grimly. "Trust me when I say there's nothing worse I could have done where Jude is concerned. His past is really fucked up, and lying is at the core of that."

"What'd you lie about?" I ask, unable to help myself.

She peers over at me. "I told him I was Sarah, and he fell in love with her. Then he found out I was AJ, daughter of Phillip Jenkins, and he didn't love AJ. It's that simple. Hence the reason I still prefer to be called Sarah unless I'm executing people."

"It's not that simple. You're still the same person, just under a different name."

She straightens, and her eyes flick down to my roller skates.

"You can shoot straight, right?" she asks abruptly, lifting her gaze again.

Apparently we're finished talking about her ex and her lost identity.

"Yeah...why?" I ask slowly, tensing a little.

"I'm cashing in on another favor. Time is too limited to bring about a group of goons and vet them to make sure they won't sell me out before I do this, so I need your help. Just point and shoot. I'll handle the hard work," she goes on.

Shit. Shit. Shit.

"You want me to—"

"Start making good on those favors you owe," she finishes as I skate toward a chair that has my shoes in it. "And leave the roller skates on. You can move faster on them."

My mouth falls open as she struts toward the door in her combat boots, and I skate out into the hallway behind her.

"What are we doing?" I hiss as I slide into the elevator with her.

She stabs a button before cracking her neck to the side. "Don't worry. I have the hard part," she assures me. "I just need you to take out the stragglers—which may or may not be necessary. A girl in roller skates doesn't look too threatening, and you can chase them down easily enough."

"Damn it, Sarah. Tell me what we're doing! Why am I shooting someone?"

"Because you owe me," she says simply, her gaze flicking to me. "And your life depends on helping me save the man I love from walking into a death trap."

She grins like she didn't just say that last sentence.

"I'll explain the details of your next favor on the way," she adds.

• • • •

When I woke up this morning, I had one thing on my mind. Going to a warehouse in the middle of Nowhere, Texas was *not* that one thing.

Waiting outside, listening to the sound of rapid gunfire spitting inside the warehouse was also not on the docket for today.

Wearing roller skates on less than ideal concrete was so not on today's freaking agenda!

Pop. Pop. Pop.

The sound of gunshots continue, and I clutch my gun in my hand. Maybe I even tremble a little as I watch the rear exit Sarah told me to keep an eye on, praying no one walks out, because…death and all that.

Death doesn't bother me in the abstract. I can sentence someone to death…but actually causing death with an actual weapon? I haven't popped that cherry, and I'm not so sure that I want to do it in roller skates.

I'm hiding by a massive, disgusting smelling dumpster also, because it's that kind of day.

I'm starting to wish I'd at least shot one person in my life so I'd know how to deal with this, but I haven't. Unlike Sarah, who is a freaking retired assassin. I have teams for a reason, damn it!

I need alcohol to deal with this day.

33

A few screams sound from inside the warehouse, and the gun rattles in my hand. That's a lot of gunfire. And she's only one person. What happens when that army of guys comes out here and decide I'm next in line to die?

Nope. I'm not leaving her. No worries.

I just wish I had picked a different outfit to die in. I can't even remember what panties I have on, other than they have to be white. My shirt isn't the best to tell the world this girl was once awesome. And roller skates? Who wants to die in roller skates?

The gunfire stops suddenly, and my heart thumps in my chest as I wait for any sign that tells me Sarah is alive.

Something buzzes against my right breast, and I squeal a little and jump, almost busting my ass in my skates, before I realize—that due to the lack of pockets on this ridiculous outfit—I put my phone in my bra.

I juggle it out, seeing the text is from Sarah.

SARAH: Come on in. I need some help.

I take a deep breath, swallowing down the nervous knot in my throat, prepare to be a badass, and skate like a demon toward the back bay door. An unplanned rebel yell tears from my throat like I'm Tarzan's female counterpart, as I charge through, skating under the half-closed door.

But I skid sideways and to a halt when my eyes almost fall out of my head, looking around in disbelief at the scene. Sarah is standing before me, clutching her side, and her eyebrows are lifted in quiet mockery.

"I need you to gather all their phones. I'll be way up front, waiting for the guys to show up. And take all their cash, too. Bring it all to me when you're finished, Jungle Girl."

The shaky gun gets lowered to my side as I slowly relax.

I see dead people. No, that's not a *Sixth Sense* joke. There's a lot of dead people in here. Good thing I'm not squeamish.

Tearing my eyes off the remains, I look back at her to see her giving me an exasperated expression. "Now, Maya."

She turns and walks away, and I put my gun down as I start going from corpse to corpse to pick pockets like a total creep.

I feel like I'm at the ground level and trying to work my way up instead of being born on top.

Sarah pushes a button on a remote as she limps toward the front, and music blasts loudly, scaring the shit out of me as I pick up a phone. I do a total cartoonish skate walk, jazz hands flailing in the air, desperately trying to keep my balance, but an embarrassing scream escapes me when I crash to the ground.

Well, to a body that breaks my fall.

"Sorry," I tell the dead guy whose vacant eyes stare back at me. I pat his chest appreciatively while pushing back up to a crouched position.

"This. Is. Not. My. Day," I groan, then grimace as I look at Dead Guy. "Guess your day is worse than mine, huh?"

I almost don't hear it over the music when Dead Guy's phone starts ringing in his pocket. I grab it, looking at the name on the screen. Rush? I have no idea who Rush is.

Not that it matters. Dead Guy can't answer the phone right now, because he's…dead. I'm sure you didn't need that explained.

Instead of answering the phone, I go about the carnage, doing my grunt work as instructed. If this is how Sarah wants me to pay back the favors I owe, life is going to suck.

I've racked up quite the favor bill in the past six months.

CHAPTER 8

AXLE

We roll up to the warehouse, our bikes rumbling as we take in the scene. No one is outside like they're waiting to announce us. The doors are shut, even as music *thumps* from inside. I glance around, growing suspicious.

"Rush, you sure these guys are good?" Drex asks, already thinking the same thing I am.

Rush walks his bike up alongside mine, his eyes scanning everything around us. "I asked three of our sources. All vouched for these guys to be legit. But I don't like this. Someone should be outside."

"Call Jude and tell him and Dash to circle around back," Drex says to Rush, who nods.

As Rush calls them and starts relaying the message, I look over at Drex. "All our sources need to be re-vetted. A lot of them were strongly tied to Herrin, you know?"

He nods slowly, eyes not moving from the front of the warehouse.

"Didn't really think about that being an issue, since I'm twice as lethal as Pop. But yeah. Now it's definitely crossing my mind."

"I'll go in first. This is my mess. If anyone needs to take the risk, it's me," Rush tells us. "My guy isn't answering his phone."

"We go in ready for anything. Leave the bikes here," Drex orders.

I'm off mine first, walking toward the warehouse as I cock my gun. Rush joins me at my side, his own gun drawn. Feeling exposed in the empty parking lot, I look around again, searching for any movement.

The music grows louder as we approach, and I realize what's playing. *Let the Bodies Hit the Floor* is blaring when Rush opens the door, warily peering inside.

"Son of a bitch," he hisses, shoving the door all the way open and rushing in.

Drex curses, and we both follow him in, guns drawn in front of us, but my eyes widen when I see the massacre. Five guys are dead at our feet, bullet holes and blood plumes littering their chests. And every one of them has one execution style shot in their forehead too.

It looks like they were trying to escape and all ended up in a heap by the hallway and door.

"What the—"

Drex's words stop short as I look up, seeing another bout of feet sticking out past the corner, and we walk over, noting the same kill style here, too. That's when my gaze swings up, and I see a blonde sitting on top of a SUV, her head banging as the song plays on.

Her eyes collide with us, and a slow smile spreads over her face.

Sarah. Or AJ. Or whatever.

Life has gotten confusing with all the motherfucking name changes lately.

She lifts a remote, and the music goes silent instantly.

The warehouse is massive, so I have no idea how many more bodies we'll find or why Sarah decided to go on a killing spree.

"What the hell?" Rush bites out.

Sarah slides down the windshield to the hood of the SUV before scooting off it altogether. Rush draws his gun, aiming it at her, and she lazily moves her finger to the trigger of the gun she's holding beside her leg.

One hand is clutching her side as she limps toward us, blood seeping through her fingers. "There's only one guy I'll let hold a gun on me for longer than a few seconds without me killing him for pissing me off." She levels Rush with a crazy-looking stare. "You're not that guy."

Slowly, Rush lowers his gun.

"What the hell, AJ?" Drex asks, pinching the bridge of his nose in exasperation.

"You're welcome," she answers with a cold smile. "Your daddy set you up. Evidence is recorded. I wired the place a few days ago when I found out you'd be meeting here. But only found out this was the plan in time to get here before you and save all your lives."

My lips twitch as she stares down Drex, waiting on some appreciation.

He blows out a breath, his hands going to his hips as he looks around. "You could have just called me and gave me a head's up."

"Or you could say thank you for me handling this and all of you walking away unscathed. It'll send a message to everyone else that you don't fuck around, and they'll be less likely to take Herrin up on his offers in the future."

My eyes drop to her side. It's not bleeding profusely, but she's definitely been hit.

"How bad is it?" I ask her as Rush kneels down, examining one guy on the ground.

"I'll live. Just a nasty graze. I've had worse. You guys need to vet your incoming clients better." Rush glares over at her, about to defend this mess, when she adds, "But I have a job for you that you can trust."

She sags against a beam like she's in need of support.

"Let's get you to a doctor," Drex says, taking a step toward her, but she waves him off.

"I have to get out of town for a little while. You owe me several favors." She grimaces as she bends over and picks up the backpack from the floor. "You're going to take her up on her job offer, and you're going to let her stay with you until I get back."

"Who?" Drex and I both ask as Rush kicks the dead guy at his feet.

"I've gotten fond of the weird girl, so it's about to be your main priority to keep her breathing. But like I said, you get something out of it too," she goes on, not making any damn sense, before her gaze shifts to Rush. "He's not dead."

"I noticed," he says, peering over at her. "Thanks for leaving one for us to use against Herrin."

She shrugs, but before she can say more, Dash is walking toward us, his head cocked in confusion. "Dude, there are at least half a dozen guys dead back there, and there's a crazy girl in—"

His words die when his eyes find Sarah leaning against a pole. She smirks at him as she swings the backpack onto her shoulder with her free hand, and then uses the same hand to dig something out of the side pocket.

She launches something small at Drex, and he catches it.

"Proof you'll need to know this was an ambush, along with your lone survivor that I just knocked out real good for you," Sarah says quietly, using her head to gesture to the motionless guy at Rush's feet.

"What're you going to do with all the bodies?" Rush asks, and Sarah chuckles under her breath.

"I don't know about you boys, but in my house, when someone does all the hard work of killing, someone else does all the cleaning. Have fun with that," she chirps.

"Is she like the little psychotic, dark, guardian angel or something?" Dash asks under his breath as he moves back a few steps.

"I really don't like guns being pointed at me!" a feminine voice snaps, tearing all our gazes away as a familiar face comes into view by the SUV.

Jude is behind her, gun pointed to the back of her head, as the girl skates—fucking skates—toward us. I recognize her immediately, even as my brow furrows in confusion.

Very short, white spandex shorts are suctioned to her body. Pale pink socks reach her thighs, along with a pale pink shirt that says something about Bubble Gum. Her hair is in twin balls on her head like she's Princess fucking Leia or something.

And white roller skates.

With rainbow-striped shoe strings.

And she's in a warehouse with massacred bodies lying around, but she's not batting an eye. Her arms are loaded down with phones that she's hoarding at her waist.

It's the single most ridiculous thing I've ever seen in my life.

"Found this...whatever she's supposed to be, picking the pockets of the guys back—"

Jude's words die much like Dash's did when his gaze lands on Sarah.

Sarah tenses, her lips creasing as she looks away first.

"Take care of her," she says quietly to Drex, and goes to pluck cash out of the band of Maya's shorts before winking at her.

Sarah limply starts walking toward the door, not looking back at us as she exits the building without another word.

"What the fucking hell is going on?" Jude demands, his eyes following the path Sarah used for retreat.

My gaze settles on the girl in roller skates, who, despite the gun pointed at the back of her head, does not look the least bit worried about dying. She looks annoyed.

Until her gaze settles on me. Then a slow smile curves her lips. She's definitely fucking crazy. I should have known that the first time I met her.

Clearing my throat, I look over at Drex.

"We're supposed to deal with *this*?" I ask, gesturing to...all of her.

"We owe her," he tells me with a shrug.

"You mean we owe Sarah? For fucking what?" Jude growls.

"Saving our lives," Rush drawls. "Again."

Jude's body goes rigid, and Drex pushes play on the recording device. My eyes flick to Jude as he stares at it while still holding the gun behind Maya. That's starting to make me tense, so I walk over and push his hand away.

He glares at me for a second, but Maya quickly skates to my side, shadowing me like I'm her damn hero now when I move back over to where Drex is. Fucking eh.

This is not what I need.

CHAPTER 9

Maya

Obviously I stick to Axle's side, even as he casts warning glares over at me. I mean, no; he's not the sweetest looking of the bunch. He's the meanest in appearance.

The scars alone are a foreboding tale of a hardened fighter and survivor.

But since he pushed the gun away from the back of my head, it appears he wants me to die the least out of this bunch. And then there's that whole sexy thing he has going for him. Obviously that is clouding my judgment a little.

As they listen to the recorded proof of the plan to ambush them—which I've never heard before this moment—I take the time to study Axle. I also put all the damn phones in a bag that Cold Eyes thrusts in front of me.

But my attention mostly stays on the man I've been curious about since the day I set eyes on him.

He has dark hair that was made to be permanently windblown—and hot. And he's tall. Really tall. Even in my skates that give me a lot of extra height, my forehead barely comes to his chin. His stubble is intentional and lines his jaw, only interrupted by the scars that deny the hair the right to grow, and possibly why he doesn't grow a full beard.

One scar cuts across his lips in a diagonal, and another jagged one stands out too. It's clear that none of these had proper stitches, because they would have healed so much better and less obvious if they had.

I want to reach up and trace the marks across his lips, curious how they feel. But he's like a wolf. They look pretty, but they'll bite your hand off even if you think they're tame. And Sarah informed me Axle is a total bear when he gets touched.

As the recording ends, the cold-eyed one looks over at me. Well, not me. He's tall too, so his level gaze is over my head as he looks to Axle or Drex. Jude's jaw tics like he's furious about something.

"If we'd known what we were walking into, we could have survived," Jude says angrily.

"But we wouldn't have known, because our sources helped Herrin set us up," the cold-eyed one growls. "Which means they would have at least killed one or two of us by catching us unaware if they hadn't already been dead."

Drex eyes me for a second, and I shift a little closer to Axle, careful not to brush up against him since Sarah gave me the "no touchy touchy" advice.

Which is totally a shame.

"She can't just kill a bunch of guys in our territory, even if she is saying she killed them for us," Jude snaps. "She has a war at her back. How do we know she's not dragging us into it with shit like this?"

He gestures around to the carnage called bodies.

Man, for a model, he sure does sound scary when he's pissed. And he looks half crazed right now too. All because Sarah lied? Little over the top if you ask me.

Then again, I'm wearing rainbow shoestrings in my skates around a bunch of seasoned killers. So what do I know?

"Sarah saved our lives," Drex repeats, his eyes still on me. "We owe her. So let's hear the girl out."

With Drex studying me like a science experiment, it's making me uneasy. In fact, I notice everyone's gaze has shifted to me.

That's not intimidating at all.

It's like I was asked a question, but I don't remember hearing it.

The first thing to come to my mind is what shoots out of my mouth. "Sarah's like a cat," I tell them.

"A cat?" the cold-eyed one asks, his tone devoid of any emotion to tell me if he's amused or confused. Or just wants me dead.

Tough crowd.

"A cat," I repeat. "She disappears for days at a time, but always comes back. She doesn't react well when backed into a corner. As pointed out to me by Model Boy six months ago, she really does have sharp claws—metaphorically speaking. And she gifts you dead rodents as a show of affection."

Just to be clear, I point to a few corpses.

To make things worse, I add, "And she's always clean."

No one says anything as I awkwardly stand still in my skates— total badass achievement. "Cat," I repeat quietly for no reason at all as I pick at an imaginary piece of lint on the hem of my shirt.

Shutting up now. I promise.

"Model Boy? Six months ago?" Drex asks, causing my eyes to move back to him.

I toss a thumb in *Jude's* direction. "Model Boy."

Jude glares at me like he might just slice my throat. That has me shuffling even closer to Axle; so close I can feel the static forming between us.

Drex's gaze flicks to Axle, who has his arms crossed over his chest, then down to me.

"She's the girl Jude and I brought in six months ago after finding out a potential client was a junkie." Axle's sex-rumble of a voice has my body doing really inappropriate things at the worst of times.

"That's her?" Jude asks, eyebrows creasing. Then his eyes go flat. "AJ took her home that night. She said the girl was quiet all the way home. Just one more lie."

"She prefers Sarah, unless she's in kill mode," I point out, earning a few silencing glares. Right. Shutting up again.

"So she took her in like a stray?" Cold Eyes asks.

I almost speak, but then remember they don't like it when I speak, and clap my lips shut again. I'm totally not telling them who I am.

"So she's coming with us?" The other guy asks. The guy who found me in the back before Jude stuck a gun to my head. I almost forgot about him, since he's been quiet until now.

Drex rubs the stubble on his own chin before asking, "What job was AJ—"

"Sarah," I interrupt on autopilot, then cringe when his eyes narrow.

Don't make the big, bad biker mad, Maya. Not smart.

"What job was she talking about?" he goes on.

"Think we could discuss that somewhere else?" I gesture to the bodies nearest to us. "I'm not the brains of this operation, but I'd say it's only a matter of time before these guys are supposed to check in and report how many of you they managed to kill. When that doesn't happen, more people with big guns will come in and start shooting holes in us. And our awesome assassin just walked out."

Drex shoots a look to No Name when No Name chuckles and tries to smother the sound. He shrugs. "She has a point."

The guy on the ground near my feet groans, scaring the shit out of me because...zombies. Zombies are totally real and the government hides it, you know.

I almost lose my feet out from under me, but two strong hands clamp down on my arms, steadying me. It's like a live wire shoots through body from the simple contact, and I try to fight the weird reaction.

Axle releases me when he's sure I'm not about to tackle the floor with my face, and he steps away, his hands fisting and opening a few times as his jaw grinds. Apparently touching people also pisses him off. But his touch is still lingering even though his hands are far away from me now.

Drex rolls his eyes and looks over to No Name. *Would it be the end of the world if they made introductions?*

"Grab the live one and toss him in the back of the SUV," he tells Cold Eyes, and No Name goes over to help him.

"Can I ask your names? Pretty sure No Name and Cold Eyes won't work for too long," I say to the guys as they scoop up the guy on the ground.

I'll be watching to see if anyone has zombie bites later. That's one bug I won't catch.

No Name smirks at me. "Who's Cold Eyes?"

I point to the other guy, and Cold Eyes glares at me, only proving my point, while No Name laughs quietly to himself.

"Get on the back of a bike before I change my mind about taking you with us," Drex says, not helping me out with the name thing. He starts to walk away before turning back and adding, "But not my bike."

He glances around at the warehouse for a brief moment.

"Light it up," he says pointedly at Jude.

"I'm good with the SUV," I say as I skate behind Axle, who is putting his finger on his gun's trigger like he's ready for someone to jump out at him.

Don't spook the big, bad, sexy biker.

"Bike," Drex says again, his tone growing annoyed.

Alrighty then. Obviously I don't tell them I'm not a fan of motorcycles, because...well, motorcycle club and all that. I'd hate to offend the trigger-happy boys.

I continue following Axle across the eerily quiet parking lot. As soon as he starts to get on his bike, I start untying my skates, knowing climbing on will be too hard any other way.

Obviously I hurry, since they may very well leave me here to get blown apart by whoever will be coming.

Cold Eyes is coming out of the warehouse, heading our way, when I finally get the skates off and Axle's bike roars to life. I look at him, my skates in my hand, and he mutters something that doesn't look favorable to me before gesturing for me to get on.

He snatches my skates out of my hand, and I climb on, careful to not touch him. But how do I...

"Can I put my arms around you so I don't fall off?" I ask him.

He cuts his gaze over his shoulder at me but turns back around without saying anything. As he starts rolling away, my arms snap around his waist, my reflexes making the decision easier.

His muscles jump and bunch under my hands with the contact, and I spread my legs wider, pressing my front firmly against his back and screw my eyes shut when he suddenly takes off.

My hands tighten on the hard waist I'm clinging to, but I finally peer over his shoulder, seeing we're going a different way than what Sarah and I did. I assume that's to avoid any possible problems that could involve running into the second team of guys who might want them dead.

It takes longer to get to Halo, but I slowly start to relax, my hands getting lazy in their grip on Axle as they drift a little lower. I'm tempted to run my hands all over his body while he's busy driving. But obviously I don't want to die.

Sarah told me a lot about him and this new job I'm giving them on my way over here. She filled me in on her plan that involved keeping me safe and getting their financial situation under control.

All for the guy who doesn't appreciate it—Jude.

Her one warning was that if I fucked her guy, she'd slit my throat. Not that I needed that warning. I'm not interested, and even if I was, I'm not an idiot.

Then she told me all about Axle. Well, all I needed to know, anyway.

Axle's body stays tense. I'm not sure if it's because I'm touching him or if he's on high alert, but he's rigid all the way back to the massive building they call home. They all pull into a large garage or hangar—not sure of the technical term here.

The space is massive and has tons of bikes already in it. The second Axle is parked, he reaches for my hands and quickly tugs them loose, dropping them fast as he stands and dumps my skates to the ground. He doesn't bother turning around as he walks toward Drex.

"We'll find you a room in a few. All are occupied at the moment, so we need to shuffle some things around," Drex tells me, but I'm busy chasing Axle through the doorway after picking up my skates.

Unlike the last time I was here, there's not a wild party going on with people screwing in the corners. Numerous guys with beards or scruff are staring at me like I'm some beast that has four heads as I hurry through the space in my socked feet with my skates in my hand.

"Who's the derby chick?" someone asks, but I don't hear the answer, because now I'm following Axle up a set of stairs.

I look back in time to see Drex taking a seat with the guys, his face serious as he says something, but I return my attention back to Axle as he steps into a room. I charge in with him, and he steps back, eyebrows up, as I shut the door behind me.

"I want to stay in here with you. Not in a room alone," I say in a rush, my heart pounding heavily.

The last time I was here, I was naïve to their barbaric ways with women. Now I'm not.

His expression goes from confused to annoyed within seconds. "Out. And no. *Fuck no*, you can't stay in here."

"I am staying in here, and you're really going to like me. I can do some totally awesome things with my hips when I'm on top, and—"

Something loud sounds from below, like a gunshot, and I try not to react. I'm so far out of my depth. It'd be easier in my town, on my turf, but…not so much when you're not family with the bad guys.

Damn it, Sarah. What have you gotten me into?

Axle's eyes narrow on me.

"I'm not fucking you. Are you seriously whoring yourself out for a room?" he asks incredulously.

Feeling a little brave, I step toward him, my neck craning back so I can look up into his eyes. His expression almost turns angry, but I figure that's just his default look.

"I'm not whoring myself out for a room. You're the only one here I'd touch, and I want to be in here with you. And it could be fun—"

A squeal leaves my lips when he shoves me against the wall suddenly and slams his fists on either side of my head as he leans down to get into my face, caging me in. I hold my breath, my body tingling in silent warning to remain still as those hard eyes lock on mine.

"You think this is a fucking game?" he asks in a quiet but lethal tone. "Privileged girls get bored and want to be bad for a little while, but this isn't the route for that road."

I don't speak, because I sure as hell don't plan to tell him who I am now.

"You think you can fuck the guy with scars because he's the easiest, most desperate one? You think that's your in? Roll up in your ridiculous outfit and roller skates like it's all a fun time? This isn't a fucking game. And you're taunting the wrong guy," he growls. "You're fucking with the wrong club."

That thin line that has been holding me back suddenly frays and snaps with those words. My hands fall to my sides as my eyes narrow on him.

"I know it's not a game, asshole," I bite out.

His gaze doesn't shift, and his body doesn't stop caging mine in.

"Just because I don't have scars all over my body doesn't mean I haven't survived hell too. And for the record, I wasn't singling you out as the weak link because of your scars. I thought those scars meant you were a survivor — the strongest link. Honestly, I'm into you. Or at least I was."

He pushes back and crosses his arms over his chest, still studying me. I straighten my shoulders, my shallow breaths growing a little stronger.

"I know this isn't a game, and I'm so sorry that I don't skulk around and brood like all of you. Even though I'm only twenty-four, I'd bet anything I've lived this life much longer than any of you, with the exception of maybe Drex. Sarah told me you'd never let anyone touch me if I didn't want to be touched. And since you're the only one I wanted to touch, it made perfect sense to be with you and have some fun in the meantime. But fuck you and your dick ways."

CHAPTER 10

AXLE

Listening to her berate me instead of cowering means she's legit about dealing with guys like us before. Her brother is a junkie and dealing drugs, so maybe I jumped to conclusions, but it's clear she's privileged. She has a trust fund, for fuck's sake.

I'm struggling to believe she singled me out as the one she wanted. I'm usually the last resort kind of guy, since I'm not exactly the cuddly, pretty boy type. There's an angle, but I didn't understand it until she said Sarah promised her I'd never let anyone else touch her.

She turns and walks out, slamming the door behind her, and I try to figure out what we missed. I looked into Lathan and her after all that shit happened six months ago, but only found privileged, boring, private school bullshit. Nothing linking her to this world except the trust fund boy turned drug dealer.

The door swings open again, and I try not to smirk when she grabs her roller skates from the floor. She points a finger at me. "And for the record, you have to be badass to wear this outfit in front of guys like you and not feel the need to explain yourself."

She spins and walks out again, slamming the door once more.

I can't help but be intrigued. And a little amused.

Sarah knows something.

I call her, but she doesn't answer. I also get to thinking about Eve coming in during our meeting, worrying it might have been Herrin setting us up. Eve always knows the details of the plans, and she would do anything at all to keep Drex safe.

No doubt she called Sarah and told her about this meeting days ago when Drex wouldn't take her worries into consideration.

We've all gotten cocky. We're lethal, but our names were forged under Herrin's rule. It makes people more afraid of Herrin than us. We need to remember that and start being smarter, so we don't become too fucking easy to kill.

I walk out onto the landing, looking down at the warehouse below from my metal balcony perch. My eyes immediately land on Maya as she sits down on a chair and starts tugging her skates back on.

Every pair of eyes down there—at least twenty or so—are looking at her. I bristle a little, but try to shrug it off.

I glance up, seeing Drex standing on the balcony and staring down too, and I make my way around to where he is.

"Where's Eve?" I ask him, propping up beside him.

I don't miss the fact his eyes are on Maya.

"She's in the shower. I just filled her in on everything," he says, his attention not shifting.

Why does that bother me?

"She told Sarah about that meeting," I point out.

"Figured that much out already," he says quietly. "She was worried about me, and she knew Sarah would take her more seriously than I did. I won't make that mistake again. Eve has good intuition for the most part. And I've gotten too reckless. I can't believe I'm about to say this, but we need to be more cautious going forward. I overestimated our fear factor."

I gesture toward Maya. "Why're you looking at her like you want a piece?" I ask, my tone not as bored as I'd aimed for. The question comes out like an accusation instead of curiosity.

His lips twitch as he shifts his eyes to me. "Trust me when I say I have zero interest in getting a piece from anyone except the girl in my shower with my name on her arm. I'm not looking at Skater Girl like I want a piece. I'm trying to figure her out and what her role is."

He looks back at her, and I follow his gaze, watching as she skates across the concrete floor to the bar and starts searching for something. She's pissed. I can tell by her very expressive face.

It's a good look on her.

My eyes refuse to move from her ass when she bends over, grabbing a glass from the cabinet. It's been a while since my cock jumped at the sight of a girl. Been a while for a lot of things.

"I took this meeting at face value. I trusted the sources we've had for years," Drex goes on. "I'm no longer taking the surface as the entire package. Your girl stood in the middle of a massacre and wasn't at all affected."

"She's not my girl," I say gruffly, clutching the railing in front of me when her tongue darts out to lick some liquor off her finger.

I also bite back a few threats when I see the others take notice. She doesn't seem aware of anything but the task at hand as she pours another shot and tosses it back.

Drex ignores me.

"Eve threw up the first time she saw a guy die in front of her. Your girl was picking the pockets on what I assume was Sarah's request. Despite appearances, she's been around this type of thing for a while."

I tense a little, thinking of how she alluded to as much. She basically said it, actually. It just seems absurd to think a girl in roller skates and a pink Bubble Gum shirt is anything less than *good*.

"Jude had a gun to the back of her head, and she wasn't even the slightest bit scared," he goes on. "That means it's likely not the first time a gun has been at her head, and she knows that just because a gun is trained on you, it doesn't mean you're going to get shot."

"Her brother took her at gunpoint six months ago," I remind him.

"Her brother is Lathan, and Lathan is a junkie," he says, more to himself than me. "A dealer. And a rich boy turned bad. Maybe the world doesn't know who he really is. Neither of them. And there's a reason they'd keep it secret. A junkie must really be scared of a secret if he doesn't share it when he's too high to think."

I watch as Maya pours a fourth shot, downing it with ease, and then her neck rolls around as her eyes close. It's like she's slowly releasing all her tension.

"Sarah apparently likes her," I say quietly. "She told Maya about us—detailed stuff. She doesn't do that usually."

Or didn't. Sarah is a mystery to us these days.

"Sarah loves her strays," he muses. "She took Eve in without question. Saved her life. Put me in debt to her. Eve is loyal to Sarah. Almost as loyal to her as she is to me. And now Sarah wants this Maya girl protected."

He again gestures to Maya as she sways with the music. She doesn't seem to realize that has even more eyes on her now. Dash is suddenly at the bar, and her eyes open like he's just said something to her.

When she smiles, I want to punch my friend in the fucking face.

This is probably not a good sign. At all.

"Sarah is still a sore subject for Jude. I trust her, though. But if Maya has a story, she needs to tell it. We don't have time for surprises," I tell him tightly.

He nods and looks back to me. "Let's find out who exactly Maya is."

I start to walk away, but he turns to go back to his room. When I give him a questioning look, he grins. "Eve's out of the shower by now. I'll be down in a minute...or thirty."

I roll my eyes and walk down the stairs, hearing a loud, feminine giggle erupt from Eve before his door shuts.

Maya has skated around to the front of the bar, a foot of space separating her from Dash as he says something. She turns and leans over the bar to grab the tequila, and Dash leans back to get a look at her barely-clad ass in those fucking short shorts that might as well be underwear.

His eyes catch mine, and he winks at me as I make my way toward him. His smile falls as he tilts his head, studying me. My fists clench and unclench at my sides as I try to get my temper in check.

"Drex wants a meeting," I tell him, glaring a little.

Maya stiffens in front of me as she pauses her shot-pouring. She doesn't turn around as she finishes her task and tosses another shot back.

"Okay," Dash drawls, arching an eyebrow. "About?"

I gesture to Maya, and he grins. "I was trying to talk her into staying in my room for a while. Drex can't free up any rooms, even though he wants to."

My muscles all tense at once, and my jaw grinds. Didn't take her long to go after someone else.

His expression changes, sobering, and his eyes widen fractionally.

"But she turned me down," he says slowly. "She's considering staying in the hangar with the bikes, because she thinks we keep them safer than girls. Not really the worst conclusion ever drawn," he goes on, standing up.

Maya says nothing as she takes another damn shot. Holy shit. How much has she had? And how is she still standing? In roller skates, for fuck's sake.

My hand snakes around the bottle, halting her from pouring more. She stares at my hand with a scowl, but refuses to turn around.

"Set up the room and grab the others," I tell Dash without taking my eyes off Maya.

He walks away without a word, and I press in closer behind her, feeling her shudder. I assume that's from fear, but with her, it's hard to be certain. I can't even remember the last time a girl wanted me—*really* wanted me. If ever. I can't remember the last time I wasn't the only option remaining.

I also wonder if Maya's reasons are only because she thinks I'll keep her safe.

Fuck me. This is not an issue I need to have right now.

CHAPTER 11

Axle presses in closer behind me, not releasing my new best friend — tequila. It's not as strong as I'd like, but that's what happens when you spend years drinking with guys like my father and his friends.

"You have secrets you're about to share," he says against my ear, pressing even closer from behind me. "And you don't have to fuck someone for protection. No one is going to touch you like that. But you could die if you're dragging us into shit without our knowledge. Understand?"

I swallow the lump in my throat, the steady burn of alcohol losing its edge too quickly. I spin around, which causes my forehead to bump the bottom of his chin before I look up.

He doesn't back away, so I stand my ground as well.

"You can threaten me all you want, but when I tell you who I am, you'll know just how stupid it would be to actually kill me."

He steps even closer, and I shudder against him again when I feel the heat of his body touching so much of mine. His hand coils around my hip, tugging me even closer until my chest is smashed against his hard body.

He stares down, while I stare up.

"Thought you didn't like being touched," I bite out.

His lips twitch. "Sarah really did tell you a lot, didn't she?"

"More than you know. She included the fact that you get violent when someone touches you. But she didn't tell me how you got your scars, or if that's why you don't like being touched."

I keep my hands at my side, careful not to touch him as I let him drive this encounter. I'm not stupid enough to think my small arsenal of badassery could compete with the man before me. A man close to 6'3 or 6'4.

He's not big and wide, but he's solid and strong. He's right in the middle of bulky and lanky — in the best possible way. But it also means he's strong and fast instead of big and slow, or fast but weak.

The haunted, light blue eyes tell me he's ready to back any threats he ever makes, and that he'd enjoy doing it.

The most lethal combination that can exist has me pressed against him.

"She doesn't know where I got the scars. Only Drex does, and Drex doesn't talk."

"And the touching thing is related to them? Why are you touching me if you hate it so much?"

He smirks as he continues to stare down at me.

"I don't hate being touched. I just hate being touched when I don't want to be."

He releases me and backs away so fast that I almost fall forward. I didn't even realize I was leaning against him until he stopped being so close.

I blow out the breath that has been trapped for a few seconds and he cocks his head as Dash — *who is no longer No Name* — calls for us.

I look over, seeing Drex disappear into the room Dash is beside. A girl is pressed against Drex, and she gives me a timid, uncertain smile when I catch her staring.

"Go," Axle says, gesturing with his head.

I push off from the bar, and I skate past a lot of curious eyes that have been watching me since I came down here. I continue to pretend not to notice them. Show fear, and predators attack much faster.

Lesson one in surviving in the wild.

As I slide into the room, I notice that Cold Eyes—also known as Rush—is already in there. Beside him is an older bald guy. Drex is at the end, and the girl is in his lap.

She studies me, that timid smile still on her lips, almost as though she's worried for me. As much as I don't want to tell them who I am, Sarah told me this was coming.

It pisses me off that she asked so much from me, but she's done so much for me that I owe her. And since I know who she is and what she's likely doing out there right now, I decide to give her this.

Because what she's doing is searching for Phillip Jenkins—the man I want dead more than anyone else. That's why Sarah took me in.

We're fighting the same war.

The war against her father.

The door shuts as Axle walks in, and he leans against it. Jude is sitting close to Drex, his finger running over his lips as he studies me with a death glare.

I'm on the other end of the table with no one near me, so I take my time looking them over one by one.

"You need to talk," Drex says. "Tell us who you are and why you asked for our protection six months ago."

Never mind; I decide Sarah has asked too much. It's too risky to tell them the truth.

"Lathan is crazy," I say with a shrug. "He'll come after me."

"You have enough money to buy legit security if you're not doing anything shady enough for the legit guys to turn you in," Jude bites out. "Tell us the truth."

Apparently they've gotten smarter over the past six months.

"Lathan is crazy, but he's still my brother. Legit guys would turn him in to the cops, and Lathan owns a lot of them, so he'd come after me twice as hard. Legit guys aren't prepared for criminals."

Heh. I almost convinced myself with that story. I'm an awesome liar.

Drex flicks a gaze toward Axle, and the girl in Drex's lap winces before looking away. Before my mind can send off warning bells, Axle has me out of the chair, and my breath leaves as he tosses me onto the table. My back is smashed flat, and he grabs my wrists, pinning my arms above my head as he glares down at me.

He steps in between my legs as my heart pounds heavily in my chest, and my eyes stay locked on his.

"The truth, Maya. No lies," he says quietly.

I'm not such an awesome liar, after all.

He hasn't hurt me yet, but the threat is clear. He *will* hurt me if he has to.

His earlier warning about me being untouchable in one way didn't extend to life and death.

I don't need to be forced. I'm wise enough to know when the game is over. And it's definitely over. I'm not probing to see if he's bluffing.

"Blackbird," I say on a long breath.

Everyone in here grows silent for a few moments. Axle looks confused as he releases my hands and steps back. I sit up quickly, my back to the rest of the room as I perch on the edge of the table. The only person I can see is Axle, so I stare directly at him.

"My family is Blackbird."

Axle's jaw grinds, and he takes a seat in my vacant chair. I slide off the table in front of him, and I take the chair next to his, casting a wary glance at him, wondering if he's just going to toss me back up there.

When he doesn't make a move, I look around at the rest of the table, who are all studying me intently. Except the girl. She looks adorably clueless.

"What is Blackbird?" the girl finally asks.

"One of the biggest bookie legends in all of New York," Drex answers, looking at me like I'm a lying piece of dog doo on his shoe.

"Let's say we believe this," Jude says bitterly as he leans up. "What'd you do to your family? Because we already know what AJ did to hers."

"I didn't do anything to my family. I'm still on good terms with them," I explain.

They all exchange glances of disbelief.

"I came to Halo because Phillip Jenkins is setting up shop and bringing girls across the border for his sex trafficking ring. And I'm making his life hell by stealing his girls and sending them to safe houses until they can be taken back to their countries-slash-families."

Deadly silence falls on the room. My eyes drift to Axle to see him relaxed in his seat, but his eyes burn through me.

I turn my attention back as Jude laughs bitterly. "Of course you are. Makes sense why AJ sent her here. She wants to drag us into her family's drama by handing us another girl who wants Phillip dead."

"Actually," I say, lifting a hand, "*Sarah* gave me explicit orders not to drag you guys into this mess at all. As of six months ago, my brother thought I was here to locate him, convince him to come home, and try to clear his name—which isn't the case. Phillip is unaware of the plan I have in place. Lathan now thinks I'm back in New York. Sarah aided in that. If Phillip learns of the plans I have and about my place in Halo, I have to leave and take the trouble with me. Because if harm comes to this club because of me, Sarah will become AJ and my worst enemy. Lots of bodily harm threats went along with that speech."

My eyes stay fixed on Jude, but he looks away, his jaw tensing.

"You knew Sarah?" Drex asks, drawing my attention. "Before six months ago? Or are we to believe this all happened by chance?"

"I knew *of* AJ," I say, shifting my gaze to him. "But I'd never met her. We all knew she was Phillip's ghost of a daughter and favorite assassin. Until he betrayed her and she betrayed him in return. Before then, if you saw her and knew who she was, it was because you were her next hit."

I lean forward, rapping my fingers on the table, knowing this breaks all the rules to tell them everything.

"Imagine my surprise when I found her in the unlikeliest of places on a night that I almost died. The devil herself became my ally. I'm her only tie to the Four Families."

Drex studies me like he's searching for a lie, and his arm tightens on the girl in his lap. I'm not completely sure who she is, but I assume it's Eve. Sarah didn't have time to tell me much on the way to the warehouse, but I've heard her mention Drex's girl before.

I just don't know if that is his only girl or not.

"Four Families," Drex repeats, then curses.

"What?" the girl asks, confused.

"The Four Families are what used to be the Five Families," I go on. "There are *Families* all throughout that run underground things. Arms dealers. Drug lords. Gambling rings. You name it. They own the major ports. Have them on payroll so they can import and export at will. The only thing they don't allow is sex trafficking."

"Which is what Jenkins is doing," Axle says from beside me, his voice settling over me like a calming force.

I nod without looking at him.

"Phillip wanted to bring that into our city. My parents argued against it, because they had a daughter themselves. Most of the Families do. Believe it or not, we're not all monsters. We're mostly regular people with skewed morals. You want to gamble but don't have the money to pay it back? Then that's your own fault, and your body parts get broken or come up missing. You want to snort your way into an early grave? Someone has to make money off the blow, and it's your choice to be a fool. But sex trafficking? Not our cup of tea."

"You keep saying it like you're still part of the Families," Axle says from beside me, and my lips twitch as I turn to face him.

"I am. Hence the reason I said you could threaten me all you want, but killing me would be a terrible idea."

No expression is on his face, but his eyes are intense as they take me in. I return my attention to everyone else.

"This is bad. We can't get mixed up in all this when we have enough issues of our own," Dash tells Drex, running a hand through his hair.

"Herrin being our biggest issue at the moment," Rush adds.

"As I said, I don't want you mixed up in it. You demanded answers; you're getting them. None of this has anything to do with you. I just need a place to lie low and conduct this experiment. And you guys can supposedly conceal anything. I need you to make concealed compartments for girls in the vehicles of my choice. It'd save me a lot of time to take them across the Mexican border and get to the ports where we own people. Since it's in Mexican Cartel territory, I need it to be extra savvy and discreet."

The girl slides off Drex's lap, moving in behind him as he leans over the table, his fingers clasping together.

"Why the cars?" he asks.

"Because you need money, and I need a better solution to hiding these girls," I say with a smile.

"But no way we get dragged into this war?" he asks, unconvinced.

"It's no different than you selling to drug dealers who are at war with other drug dealers." I shrug one shoulder. "No one will know I'm here. And if Phillip catches wind of my plan, I'll leave. It's that simple."

He still doesn't look convinced as to why they should even bother.

"AJ wouldn't risk us, yet she sends this shit right into our club," Jude says with an eye roll. "It's too risky. We can't be fighting battles outside of our own."

This time, I lean back in my chair, a cold smile on my lips. Drex is still staring at me.

"There's a reason she wanted us to know, isn't there?" Drex, the only perceptive one, asks. "Why do you want him dead?"

"Because two and a half years ago, when we were still the Five Families, Phillip ordered a hit against the heads of the other four Families who were meeting in secret. He was the fifth, but he couldn't be there because of prison, and his proxy never showed up. The same night, there was a bomb. All the other heads of the Families were killed."

An audible breath leaves almost everyone at the table, as though they're piecing together what I'm saying.

"Phillip expected to be able to take over the ports and run his sex trafficking business without interference, but the Four Families had kids—like me—who have been groomed since birth to take over the businesses. Growing up where anything you do could end up in a death sentence as a consequence makes you a little different from your average person. I'm the sanest one of them all, if that tells you anything."

They all exchange a look, and I smirk.

"Phillip is only alive now because he linked up with the Mexican Cartel. They protected him in prison. They now protect him here in Halo, hiding him as he uses this for a base of operations," I go on.

They all exchange another look, and I know what they're figuring out. Jude is about to storm out of this room if I'm reading him right.

"So she didn't come here to hide from her father. That was yet another lie. She came to find him and kill him," Jude says quietly.

He stands so fast that the chair flips over, and he stalks out of the room just as I predicted. I cut my gaze to Drex, since he's running this club.

"The Four Families are all funding my plan to get rid of Phillip," I tell him, going on like Jude didn't just slam the door on his way to get far away from this conversation. "His guys came here even before Phillip managed to get out of prison. We have an inside person feeding us information about the container drops. If I hit enough locations and steal enough girls, the money he's getting from the Cartels will eventually become more cost and less profit.

They'll cut him out and take away his protection if his problems cost them too much money. It's a slow game, but if it's effective, the heads of the Families will be patient."

Drex looks to Axle, and they have a silent conversation. Axle leans up, his arm brushing mine. I don't pull it away, and he doesn't move.

"That's why Sarah wanted us to know. That's why she wanted you here," Axle says gruffly.

I nod slowly, assuming he's put it all together.

"Like I said, the new heads of the Families are all a little crazy. I'm Sarah's one link to them; her one link to know what's coming before it comes. Because if my slow plan fails, the psycho kids will blow Halo all to pieces to kill Phillip, and the war with the Mexican Cartel will be inevitable."

"And it won't matter if we get dragged into the mess," Drex goes on, his jaw tensing. "Because we'll just be collateral damage along the way."

"Which is why she wants me here. You'll be granted special concessions for aiding our endeavor—living and all that. The Families will go through me before they make any decisions, because they hope my plan succeeds. They're crazy, but even they want to avoid a war with the Mexican Cartel."

I can feel Axle's gaze on me, but I don't turn around and risk getting caught in his freaky eye lock that seems to render me stupid. Drex curses before running a hand through his hair.

"Sarah is actually helping us by sending you here," Axle finally says.

I face him more fully, and I nod. "Yeah. Because if I say run, you'll survive the hell that will rain down on this place. The Families haven't been this poised on the trigger since the eighties. The last time the young ones of that generation took over."

"What about your brother?" Axle asks. "What part does he play in all this?"

I had wondered what business they had with my brother that night. Now I know. He planned to use their special abilities the same way I'm about to. They just didn't know it was for girls instead of drugs.

"My brother will be the one Phillip thinks is feeding the Four Families information," I explain, my eyes locked on his pale ones.

"Why?" he asks, but then I see it the moment he figures it out without me saying it.

"Because my brother is the traitor who set the bomb for Phillip, and now he's working for him."

Something suspiciously close to pity crosses his eyes, but I just look away. I remember not wanting to believe my brother capable of it. Then he held a gun on me and demanded to know what the Families were saying about him. You get more answers from someone when you listen to their questions.

And all the questions he asked gave me my answers.

My brother was the traitor. *Is* a traitor.

I, of course, played dumb and acted like I simply wanted to bring him home, get him help to get off drugs and stuff, and wanted to clear his name from any nasty rumors that said he played a part in something so atrocious.

"My father learned early on that Lathan couldn't ever be the head of the Family," I go on, quieter this time as I look down at my hands. "He acts before he thinks. So I was chosen instead. And Lathan never let that go."

I stand up, because I'm done talking, even though I'm sure they're just getting started and waiting for me to leave so they can dissect the shit storm they've unwittingly stepped into.

I skate to the door before turning around.

"We were all conditioned differently to deal with what we'd one day face. It's not sunshine and rainbows for a Family child. It's also not terrible. My parents loved me, and I never questioned that."

I pause a beat, noting the curious expressions on their faces.

"I grew up with all the kids of the Four Families. But we were the Five Families before Jenkins turned on us. And never did I meet the notorious AJ. He never brought her around. Never groomed her to take over. Her conditioning, if the rumors are true, was the worst kind imaginable. It's amazing she has enough heart to give a damn about you or anyone. But I've seen it. She does care. The only person she'd ever trusted before this club betrayed her. My parents would have never betrayed me. I can't imagine what that's like. So cut her some slack, because she may be the only person in the world who cares enough about you to risk it all to save you."

With that off my chest, I pull open the door, and skate past a bunch of really mean looking bikers. They're a little put off by my skates, because I'm the crazy chick who has the balls to float like a butterfly up in here.

I head straight for the tequila again, spotting Jude already at the bar and downing shot after shot himself.

"I need clothes from my apartment. Shoes would be great too," I tell him.

He glances back at the closed doors, then his hard eyes level me with a brutal stare.

"When I decide to be a fetch-it-bitch, I'll grab them for you."

I smile, and he mutters something about me being psycho before looking away.

"Seriously. I could use a lift, and they'll be a while."

He cuts his gaze toward me again, and he rolls his eyes before pushing away from the bar. He starts to say something, but a heavy hand comes down on my hip, tugging me back.

When my body reacts with little zings shooting through me, I know exactly whose hand it is.

"Don't make this a problem," Axle says.

I open my mouth to speak, but Jude is apparently the one he's talking to, because he answers before I can.

"Keep her out of my face. I think this club has enough friends of AJ's."

"Sarah," I quickly interject, watching as Jude's scowl forms.

"Her name has never been Sarah. Never will be Sarah. She's Alexius Jenkins. AJ. Not Sarah. Sarah was just a lie. *She* was a lie." His words are dripping with venom as he snatches a bottle of whiskey from the bar and walks away.

Axle spins me around, his gaze leveling me like he's about to chew my ass out.

"Stop goading him. He's not himself right now, and he's got a nasty habit of being unpredictable when he's pissed," he cautions.

"He's being a baby," I say with a shrug.

Axle studies me for a moment before taking a seat in a stool, releasing me completely in the process. I try not to feel disappointed that he's not touching me anymore.

He gestures around at all the guys who are loitering in the massive, open space. Couches and TVs are set up, along with a huge dining table. It's like a home-away-from home sort of setup.

"No one here came to be here because they had a perfect life with normal issues. You end up in this place because you have nowhere else you fit in. Nowhere else that lets you kill the demons. Nowhere else where people don't give a shit if you beat a guy to death for pissing you off. These guys don't play nice, and they won't care who you are if you piss them off enough. We all have triggers, including Jude. Sarah tripped that trigger for him."

My eyes connect with his again.

"And what about you?" I ask, cocking my head. "What're your triggers? If I piss you off, are you going to beat me to death?"

His lips twitch, but it's a brief reaction. I silently make it my mission to make Axle smile. I don't think he knows how.

"If that were the case, you'd already be dead."

I do smile, and I can tell he makes a concentrated effort not to let my smile infect him when he looks away and grabs my bottle of tequila, pouring two shots. I let it slide that he didn't answer me on the triggers.

"You know my biggest secret, and I don't even know your last name."

He pauses, the shot glass almost touching his lips as he looks over the rim at me. He tosses the shot back in one quick motion, and he swallows before putting the empty glass down.

"Axle isn't the name I was born with. The name I was given was burned with the rest of my past. It's just Axle."

I bite down on my lip, my eyes flicking over his face, taking in the scars and the beauty. If he didn't have scars to flaw him, he'd be so devastatingly gorgeous that he'd make me sick. It's the scars that make him irresistible.

"That's all I get?" I ask, looking back into his eyes.

Music starts playing loudly, and I look over as a group of girls—possibly strippers, given the tassels—come strutting in. The guys cheer as the girls saunter over to them, already getting to the lap-dance portion of the evening.

Idly, I wonder if Axle is going to take a turn. Then realize I might cut a bitch if that happens.

Probably not a good idea for me to hang around too long. I'm too crazy to be social.

My eyes swing back to Axle, waiting expectantly for him to answer the question. He's an unreadable book before me, all the pages blank, and the cover only hints to a story I want to dive into.

"For tonight, that's all you get," he says, looking away.

My lips curl in a grin as I skate a little closer, and his hand shoots up, steadying me when I wobble. I really want out of these skates, but I don't like walking around in my socks on this dirty floor.

"But you might tell me more tomorrow?" I ask.

His gaze flicks to my lips, and for a really exciting second, I think he's going to kiss me. But he simply shifts his gaze back to mine.

"You're a confusing girl."

That has me smiling all the more. "Did you just call me normal?"

One side of his mouth tugs up in a reluctant grin, and a small bit of triumph swells inside me.

"You're staying in my room," he says as he pours another shot, watching me as he takes it down in one quick toss.

I arch an eyebrow. "Now that you know I'm the head of a Family, you want me to stay in your room."

Something dangerously close to amusement sparks in his eyes, but he banishes it, just like he does all the good stuff. Life like this doesn't offer too many good things. Gotta find pleasure in the small moments.

"I don't see how you're running a bookie operation in New York all the way from Halo. Makes that a loophole in your story," he says, a hint of suspicion in his tone.

This time, I'm the one who is amused. But I don't want to make him feel stupid. Because he's not. He just doesn't understand the way a syndicate works, as opposed to the club he's in where they handle everything themselves.

"I'll never run the day-to-day bookie operation. Smitty handles that—"

"Smitty?" he asks, his eyebrows going up.

"My father's right-hand man, and the man who has saved my life more times than I can count. He's a really rich man because of my family, and his daughters are my goddaughters. His son is like the adopted brother I always wanted, and he's part of the business, though it's a little on the lower end from Smitty. Smitty runs the operation. I only handle the head-of-the-Family obligations. I don't go around busting kneecaps all day, or keep a ledger on who owes us what. I decide things like how to find, destroy, and kill Phillip Jenkins without starting a war."

He leans back, eyeing my attire like it somehow makes me less threatening. I only grin broader. Finally, he mutters something under his breath.

He stands, and I skate along behind him as he starts walking toward the stairs.

"Axle! You going to introduce us to your little friend or what? She's been here all day, and ain't no one told me her name," some big guy calls out, his beard touching his chest as he strokes it.

I'm not fond of that leering look he has.

"Her name is *Off Limits*," Axle says with a smirk, and the guy waggles his eyebrows at me.

"No ink, my man. No ink."

"Drex is the only one vain enough to put his name on a girl's body," Axle says, shooting a look toward Drex, who simply flips him off as he sits down and pulls his girl into his lap.

Does she not ever get to sit in a chair when he's around?

Axle pauses at the stairwell, and I become a little curious about how to go up the stairs in skates. He eyes them like he's thinking the same thing.

"We'll go to your place tomorrow for you to pack a bag."

"What do I sleep in tonight? You okay with me sleeping naked?" I grin, and a few whistles follow that totally lewd remark that I apparently said way too loud.

Axle glances over my head at someone, then gives an eye roll to me before he bends. Without warning, I'm suddenly over his shoulder, my breath heaving out of me as my hands land on his back.

Catcalls and whistles erupt with a few cheers of encouragement. Axle carries me much too easily up the stairs as my head bobs with each step. I don't even look down below after I see the first guy miming a thrusting motion.

Axle's arm is clamped around the bend of my knees, keeping me secured in place as he opens his door and steps through. When he kicks the door shut, I lock it, since I'm sort of eye level with the handle.

He bends again, and I feel all the blood drain quickly, giving me a head rush when he drops me back to my feet.

"A little warning next time, Cave Man," I grumble.

"Take off your skates, but sleep in your clothes. I can only handle so much for one night," he tells me without turning around.

That's not the answer I wanted.

The room is like a hotel room with concrete floors. A bathroom is in the back, and a large, messy bed with black sheets and a black comforter takes up the bulk of the bedroom.

A small dresser rests off to the side, letting me know my clothing will not have too much room. No closet.

"Do you have a house?" I ask him as I sit down on the bed to start taking my skates off. "Or an apartment?"

"Yeah," is his one word response, before he adds, "house."

"Think I'll ever see it?" I ask, trying to start a conversation as I manage to wrangle off one skate.

He quirks an eyebrow as he glances over at me.

"You going back to New York once all this is finished with Jenkins?" he asks me randomly.

Frowning, I finish with the other skate and crawl up the bed, not missing the way his eyes drop to my ass. My shirt still has blood on it from the dead guy I fell on, so I tug it off, despite his earlier objection.

He's looking at me with narrowed eyes when I drop it to the floor, and I smirk at him. "I'm not wearing someone else's blood to bed. And I'll eventually go back." I try not to react to the small pang I feel in my chest. "Even though there's no one left for me there. Hence the reason I'm here instead of anyone else."

His gaze drops to where I'm starting to remove my bra, and he tenses as he turns around and jerks open a drawer. Without facing me again, he tosses a shirt to the bed, and I grin as I pick it up, tugging it on as I toss my bra away.

Then I slip out of the shorts I'm wearing, and peel off my ridiculously long socks. All the while, his back stays turned as he types something into his phone.

"They sent you without any protection? Sounds like they think you're expendable," he tells me.

"I *am* expendable," I say on a breath. "As I stated, I'm not needed to run the business. My name will pass on to Smitty if it needs to, even though he's terrified of that happening. The head of a Family is always a target, and unlike me, his identity isn't so secretive. But unless he's a head, he's not a target. No one kills the right hand man for fear of the unknown head raining down hell."

I shift under the covers, wondering if he's ever going to face me. In all the chaos, I almost forgot that someone is supposed to text me tonight and tell me about the latest shipment of girls and if we succeeded in running interference.

My phone is on the floor. Poor thing spent all day in my bra.

I decide to stay on topic with Axle after I pick it up and see the text that tells me success was mine.

"But if I came down with an entourage, Phillip would have gotten wind of it really early on. Our plan would be shot to hell, and a war would have already started. Phillip hasn't been physically in Halo too long, but his guys have been stationed here since after the bomb. It took us a while to infiltrate them and get eyes near the prize. Once we had someone firmly in place, I came down to be more aggressive with the plan."

He finishes typing something into his phone, and he spins around, leaning back to study me.

"You hate Sarah too?" I ask him curiously.

He shakes his head. "She shouldn't have lied to Jude, but I don't have beef with her. I'm the one she calls when she wants to keep tabs on the club. But I never give her detailed information—only broad spectrum things."

He crosses his arms over his chest as he leans against the dresser.

"Do the other guys know that?"

He shakes his head slowly. "You wanted a secret, so show me what you do with that one."

He pushes away from the dresser, and I suck in a breath when he tugs his shirt over his head. Hard lines of muscle greet me. Several mostly-subtle scars line his chest and abs, but when he turns around to put his back to me, the scars stop being subtle and scream suffering.

Large, angry red and white scars are bubbled across his back in long swipes.

He was mercilessly whipped.

He was repeatedly cut.

He was brutally tortured.

I'm not good at guessing the dates of scars, but I can tell they're old and were never properly treated when they were fresh wounds. His one arm of sleeved tattoos goes across his shoulder and a full shoulder plate on his back completes the sleeve.

I watch as he shoves his jeans to the floor, and bite down on my lip to keep from whimpering when I'm once again on the verge of being a woman. But then I see worse scars there.

The scars on his legs look like a lot of burn marks...as though he was caught in a fire—or set on fire once. The burn marks go up to his thigh on his left side, but on his right, they stop at his knee.

Violent scars mar the flesh there, and no hair is able to grow over the various red and pale patches of poorly healed tissue.

He glances over his shoulder to find me staring, and I look up, locking eyes on his. His lips twitch.

"Not so desperate to fuck me anymore, are you?" he drawls lazily, but the hard look in his eyes says he's anything but amused.

"Actually, I sort of want you more."

His expression goes blank, giving nothing away. Pale blue eyes study me intently for a moment longer before my eyes drop to his boxers and my mouth twists in a very eager grin.

He's totally turned on, if that erection of his says anything. The tip of his cock is sticking up above his boxers just enough to have me pressing my thighs together.

When I lick my lips, he clears his throat and jerks the covers back. The bed dips when he presses a knee to it and climbs in.

Just as I scoot over to be closer to him, two hands grab my shoulders, and I'm shoved back forcefully. I blink, looking to see Axle is glaring at me.

"What?" I ask, wondering why he's keeping his body on the bed instead of coming down on top of me while he holds my shoulders. "You need an engraved invitation or something? 'Maya's hungry, talented vagina cordially invites your big penis to come stay the night.' How's that work for you?"

I can't be less subtle than I've been.

His eyebrows go up, and a ghost of a smile toys with the edges of his lips as he shakes his head. "Stay on your side of the bed."

He releases me, and I huff in frustration when he turns his back to me and shuts off the lamp beside the bed, submerging us into darkness.

I'm sure there's no way I can go to sleep, but that lasts for about five seconds before I close my eyes and get lost in some of the best sleep I've had in years.

CHAPTER 12

AXLE

Want to know the definition of hell?

Waking up with a mostly naked girl right next to you for seven straight days, and refusing to fuck her, because you don't know what her angle is.

Maya loves to sleep in just my damn T-shirt, even though we've already collected her clothes. In fact, her clothes have essentially taken over my room. I bought several damn temporary, pop-up closets to confine her multitude of things.

She's invaded my bathroom, my room, my bed, and my motherfucking mind, and it took less than a week to accomplish all of the above.

The cover is pushed halfway down her waist, and the curve of her ivory, smooth ass is very visible, since she apparently approves of torturing me with her body. Naked underneath *my* shirt.

It'd be easy to push her up onto her knees and put myself out of my misery. Very fucking easy. Too fucking easy. Suspiciously easy.

Inwardly cursing her, I toss the covers off me and adjust myself in my boxers as I stand up and tug on some jeans. I spent an extra thirty minutes in the shower last night just to deal with the never-ending state of arousal I'm in.

But let's face it, fucking her would be a mistake of epic proportions. No girl runs her eyes over my body like it's the best thing she's ever seen. In fact, no girl at all looks at me once my clothes are off.

I realize people think that chicks dig scars, but not on a scale as massive as this. I know that for a fact.

There's usually immediate hesitation, then subtle grimaces—if they're nice about it. Or there's a request to turn off the lights if they decide to go through with it to become a good little club whore.

Never do they tell me they want me more when they see the full amount of disfigured marks—a more accurate depiction than simply calling it all *scars*. Never do they spend seven days trying to tempt me in every way possible.

So what does she want? What's her angle?

I glance back, seeing Maya stir in the bed. It's always like she knows the second I'm out of bed, because she wakes up within a few minutes. Hence the reason I'm rushing through the motions of getting dressed.

I'm trying to put space between us, but with no extra rooms available right now, she's gotta stay with someone. And for whatever reason, I can't stomach the idea of her climbing into someone else's bed and trying to get into their head by using her body as a tempting distraction.

Annoyed and frustrated, I sling open the door a little harder than necessary the second I'm fully dressed, and I jog down the stairs to see Drake on his crutches. His cast has been downgraded to a brace now, and he's getting along better since the car accident that almost killed him.

Drex is looking at a sketch of something, seeming lost in thought. Drake gives me a smirk when he sees me.

"They tell me you have a roller derby girl in your bed these days," he quips, and I cast a bored look at Eve, considering she's the one who tells Drake everything.

Their odd friendship doesn't always sit well with Drex, but it's a sibling thing with Eve and Drake. Anyone else can see that. Which means we're stuck with Drake more than ever before.

Eve looks away, pretending the wall is fascinating, and I redirect my attention to Drake.

"Any word coming through your shop about the failed attack on us?" I ask in deflection.

Drake scoffs. "Since you lot moved me into the building across from you, I haven't heard much of anything. It's become clear I've chosen a side, and you fuckers are going to take me down with you, it seems."

He groans as he hobbles over to a couch and takes a seat, putting his crutches next to him before continuing.

"I remember the good ol' days after Drex's cocksucker daisy. All I had to worry about was inking people."

Drex glares over at Drake, who is grinning at him, and I drop to a chair next to Eve as she props up on the arm of it.

"Some of the guys who are coming in the shop are waiting to see what Drex is going to do. They're not club members, though. They're just nosy Halo residents who know what's going on," Eve tells me, frowning.

"Which means we're drawing too much attention to ourselves," I say on a long, frustrated breath.

"Herrin wants that," Rush chimes in as he walks in with a bag thrown over his shoulder.

"Going somewhere?" I ask him.

"Back to the job I abandoned when I came back to help collect paying jobs. Apparently I fucked that up, so it's best if I go do something I'm good at."

I start to ask questions, when Drex adds, "Any one of us could have been fucked by that setup; not just you." He looks over at Rush, who is tense. I didn't realize this was still bothering the young blood.

"None of us thought our sources would be stupid enough to choose Herrin. Speaking of which, who's handling them?" I ask, looking from Rush to Drex.

"Jude wanted a way to blow off steam, so he's sending the message. Which is why he's been missing for the past two days," Drex tells us, even as he studies the paper in his hand again.

I haven't been around too much, since I've been deliberately avoiding Maya until I have to crash in bed, so it's not surprising that I'm out of the loop. But I need to get my head off her and back in the game.

"What's the job?" Eve asks Rush.

It's just us today. All the other guys are out at their day jobs or shaking down people from other charters to see which way they're leaning. Maya sparked an idea with her tale of mastery. Instead of starting a war by outright killing Herrin, we're going to fuck his world up until no one cares if he dies.

I've been handling some trouble-causing in that respect, so at least I haven't been rendered completely useless. Mostly it's planting the seed of doubt, turning Herrin into the worst thing there is: a rat.

"Rush is watching after my sister," Drex says distractedly.

It goes so quiet that you can hear each breath being taken. Drex looks around, shrugging, and Rush turns and walks out. Drex never talks about his sister. Ever.

"You think Herrin is going to go after her? How could he find her after all this time?"

"I don't doubt that he's known where she was all along, and was saving her as a token piece to use against me. It's best to think the worst and prepare for it right now," Drex goes on. "Most of the club believes she's dead, just like most outsiders. You'd think if people believed I killed my own sister, they'd be a little less eager to go against me. Curious how that isn't the case, which leads me to believe Pop is up to something."

His attention returns to that damn paper he's been eyeing since I came down here.

We hear a bike roar to life as Rush leaves, and I glance up from the chair I'm on to where Eve is still sitting on the arm. She gives me a one-shoulder shrug in response.

"What're you looking at?" I finally ask Drex.

"My design and name for your half of the club, since you can't use Death Dealers anymore," Drake answers, robbing Drex of the chance.

Drex rolls his eyes when I cock an eyebrow.

"He reworked the reaper so that we don't have to deal with too many ink changes to our originals, for all of us who have the tats," Drex tells me, handing me the paper.

When I see the name, I hold back a groan. It's so obvious that it's almost ridiculous.

"If they're the Death Dealers and you want to face off against them, then it only seemed right to call yourself the Death Chasers," Drake says, grinning over at me when I hold the paper up.

"I really like it," Eve says, looking over at it. "And the name is apt. It'd send a statement to everyone. No fear and all that."

Dash nods slowly, like he's taking her words into consideration.

"She's right," he finally says on a long breath. "It'd definitely send a statement, and it'd cause a lot of hesitation to everyone out there willing to double cross us. Especially if you couple it with the massacre AJ left behind in our name."

Fucking Death Chasers. Looks like the misfits have a new name.

"Should be simple enough to fix on the tats."

"Simple?" Drex asks Drake skeptically.

"Simple for me, because I'm amazing," Drake quips as he stands, tucking his crutches back under him. "Come, minion. We have calls to catch. Our appointment book is about to get hit," he adds, winking over at Eve as she flips him off.

She hops off the arm of the chair I'm sitting in, and she goes up to her tiptoes, pressing a kiss to Drex's lips.

I stand as well, and Dash walks over to me. Sledge joins us, coming from out of nowhere, his attention attuned to only me.

"My contacts in New York haven't found out anything yet. But they said the heads of the Four Families are a mystery to anyone not high enough in power. We may just have to trust Sarah on this," he tells me.

"Sarah has been out of the loop just long enough to miss this supposed power exchange. Three years ago she left New York. All of this alleged tale of betrayal and new heads could simply be a wild concoction from a girl we know nothing about," I say quietly, looking over at Drex as he carries Eve out, her legs wrapped around his waist.

As much as I trust Sarah to not completely fuck us over, I don't trust Maya not to have fooled her. It's easy to see why she'd be convincing.

"It does sound crazy, but it almost sounds too crazy to be made up," Sledge says as he glances up at my closed door. "Until we know for sure, keep your guard up."

"And if it is true, you might want your guard up even more," Dash drawls, studying me. For seven days, he's given me that look. "Mafia girls are the craziest breed of all. Look at Sarah."

He smirks, but I just turn and head back to the room to grab my guns.

"Get the down payment from her," he calls to my back. "We're going to need new cuts."

I don't acknowledge him as I take the stairs two at a time. When I walk into the bedroom, Maya whirls around, and my mouth dries.

Why is she in a fucking towel?

Groaning, I take in her dark, wet hair as it clings to her, and she cocks an eyebrow at me when I run my gaze over her from head to toe.

"You finally going to take me up on my offer?" she asks dryly.

I tilt my head, shutting the door behind me. I almost lock it. Almost.

Fucking girl.

"Not until I figure out your angle," I answer honestly.

She rolls her eyes as she goes to pull open the curtain on her makeshift closet. "I have numerous angles. All of which you'd love. There's one angle I'm particularly good at," she goes on.

This is what I've dealt with. For seven fucking days.

It's just after noon right now. It's a long time before I crash in the bed beside her again, and it's going to be harder to avoid her today, since I'm sure Drex will call a meeting/party to introduce the new name.

I can't leave her alone with the others here today. Especially since some more of our charters have dropped their cuts and joined us after Herrin's attempted—and failed—hit on us.

"You like your games, don't you?" I ask in a bored tone, going to the dresser and pulling out my guns, putting them both in their holsters.

"No games. Just figure life's too short to be subtle. Also, I usually always jump in with both feet when I want something. It's called living. You should try it some time," she deadpans.

She lets the towel fall away, and I lean back, against my dresser, watching her as she slips into her lacy underwear. Various tan lines wrap over each other, proving it's a true tan.

I tell myself I'm only watching to prove to her I have control over myself. Again, I've been telling myself this for seven days.

Her perky breasts are just daring me to touch them. Nipples are peaked and ready, as though offering an invitation.

But I can watch without tossing her to the bed like I want to. I've watched her all week. Usually I got to leave for the rest of the day, but I've still watched her all week.

"I enjoy living, but you learn to be suspicious of someone when—"

"When they want to have sex with you?" she interrupts, turning around and putting her back to me. "That's sad. Must be hard to get laid if you always sit around wondering what every girl wants from you."

My jaw grinds as she bends over, showing me her ass through the skimpy shards of lace, as she pulls on a pair of shorts.

"What do *you* want, Maya?"

"Already told you what I want from the club and you. From the club, I want cars and a place to lie low while I conduct my operation. From you, I want orgasms. It's that simple," she answers without turning around. "But at this rate, I'll just take the cars. I'm starting to see you as too much work. I really like being chased as opposed to always chasing."

She spins around as she tugs a shirt into place. The damn shirt has a pink cupcake on it.

A pink fucking cupcake.

How can I take her seriously?

How can I believe she really runs a notorious bookie family?

"Yet you came down here completely alone, and you didn't seem to have a clue about what you were doing," I tell her instead of commenting on that other part.

She rolls her eyes as she starts brushing her wet hair, sitting down on the edge of my bed.

"I'm not going through this again, Axle. You know why I came alone, and yeah, I'm a novice at how to discreetly take down an ex-Family head in a town where I know no one. I was going to take a few months to get it all sorted, take in the lay of the land, and make some new friends who could hook me up with the right people. But Lathan jumped me when he found me much sooner than I imagined. It sped up my need for protection, hence the reason I begged that night."

She looks over at me as she puts her brush down and picks her towel back up, squeezing it around the long, dark strands.

"Either start asking some new questions, or at least get some fresh material to reword the old ones," she goes on.

I check my phone. Again. Sarah hasn't been answering any of my calls or texts to explain this situation to me.

Putting my useless phone away, I lean back, measuring the girl in front of me.

"Something feels off about you," I finally tell her.

"I wore roller skates in the middle of a slaughterhouse. Totally get that off-putting vibe of yours," she says as though she's amused.

Her phone dings on the bed, and she looks down, reading whatever preview is on the screen. I expect her to ask for privacy, but she just redirects her attention to me.

"Last chance, Axle. Do you want me or not? It'll be the last time I ask, because I'm through chasing. Hot as you are, I'm not into wasting time on guys who aren't interested. Girl has to have some self-respect, you know."

I snort derisively, rolling my eyes.

She arches an eyebrow. "I do hardcore Kegel exercises. My pussy is a ninja," she says seriously, waiting for me to respond.

I...hell, all I can do is blink. Half the time I wonder if she even knows what she's saying. It's like she goes for shock factor and wins time after time with me, because I've never met anyone like her.

"I'll see you tonight. There will be a party," I say in deflection, trying not to think of her ninja pussy she's offering.

She looks away like she's disappointed, and starts putting on lotion. I blow out a breath while leaving the damn room.

Drex is back downstairs, talking to Sledge about tonight's party that I knew was coming. Maya stays upstairs as I get a rundown on what Drex needs from me.

Leaving the warehouse, I head to our strip club with Dash, and he goes to start telling guys about tonight's festivities. Liza — Sledge's old lady — pushes a beer in front of me when she sees me at the bar.

"Looks like you need a drink," she tells me with a straight face.

My phone starts ringing before I can respond, and I immediately start walking out when I see who's calling.

"About damn time you called me back," I growl into the phone.

"It's hard to be discreet when you're blowing up my phone like a stage five clinger. I had to turn it off, because believe it or not, you're not my top priority," Sarah volleys.

My free hand fists as I step to the side of the building, barely hearing the steady thump of the music inside.

"I've been calling and texting because—"

"I know. I've heard all the numerous messages and read all the texts. I just haven't had time to respond. Besides, Drex seemed to be cool with Maya. Not sure why you're the one wanting to rip this all to shreds when she's very possibly the only thing that will save the entire club. And the only reason she's doing it so willingly is because she has a thing for you and owes me a huge favor."

My eyebrows go up.

"Sarah, I swear—"

"I've known the heads of the Families for a long damn time, even though they never knew me. I knew their children. I knew when they took over the Families. My father was naïve and arrogant, thinking he could destroy them by killing the heads. Instead, he turned loose a bunch of brilliant psychos who all want him dead for killing their parents."

She exhales heavily like she's exhausted.

"The point is, Maya is legit. Lathan is a serious threat if he finds out she's still in Halo. And her plan could go to hell in a handbasket if she doesn't manage to keep a low profile. Keep her alive, and she'll return the favor. And be nice. She never asked for this. She's doing what she has to, and be thankful she gives a damn about stopping a war."

Running a hand through my hair, I watch as a few guys walk into the club, their eyes shifting to me. I make it my business to know everyone affiliated with us, so it's no surprise that I recognize them.

Nodding, they head in, and I return my attention to my conversation.

"Something is off about her."

Sarah outright laughs. Hard.

I'm not amused.

"Of course there is," she says when her laughter tapers off. "She's twenty-four and is currently running a notorious crime syndicate from the shadows. People get PTSD when they see someone die. People like Maya and I grew up watching both people we knew and total strangers die all the time. It's a way of life for us. You don't come out of a family like hers without being a little *off.* I'd be more concerned if you thought she was perfectly normal."

Sometimes, I'd like to throttle her. This is one of those times.

When I grow silent, she groans.

"She's legit, Axle. You know I wouldn't risk Jude. And I know Maya is telling the truth. I still have friends inside the circles of the Four Families. Very high-up friends. Finding her was like finding the Holy Grail. Count your blessings, because sometimes, life sends you something good to make up for all the bad shit you've dealt with."

"Axle, what the hell?" Dash's voice has me glancing toward the entrance where he's holding his hands up.

"I'll be back in a sec," I tell him as he flips me off and heads back in. Then I speak to Sarah. "You ever gonna tell me what went down between you and your Pops?" I ask her.

"You ever gonna tell me where you got all those scars?" she quips.

My jaw grinds, and she takes my silence as my answer.

"Didn't think so. Take care of Maya. I'll be back soon with a present; then I'll take her off your hands again."

With that, she hangs up, and I pocket my phone while resting my head against the building. What happened to the days when we just drove for hours on open stretches of highway and built some fucking cars? The days where we sometimes kicked a little ass and maybe blew a few holes in people?

I miss those damn days.

Fucking mafia bullshit and girls in roller skates didn't play a part in those days.

CHAPTER 13

Maya

It's late when I poke my head out the door, hearing the music blaring.

Par-tay. Heeey.

I could use a night of drinking and acting like a fool. I'm just not sure that's so safe to do here.

There are a ton of guys downstairs, and also...a lot of women, though they're gravely outnumbered by the dick holders.

I shut the door behind me and walk down the stairs. Another hit will go on tomorrow night, and until then, I need to take my mind off things. If this one goes well, it'll be five successes in a row. That'll hit Lathan and Phillip hard.

Not hard enough, but they'll definitely start arguing. My brother will be under suspicion, if he's not already. Phillip's a paranoid fucker.

Coming down the stairs, I spot Eve as she speaks with another girl. Considering I don't know anyone else, I head over to them. Eve is like a lamb amongst wolves in this place, but she doesn't seem scared. I still don't know her story.

I sidle up to them, and Eve smiles at me.

"You're out of the room!" she says happily.

The girl she's with turns to face me, gives me a body-sweep with a skeptical eye, and walks off.

"Something I said?" I ask rhetorically.

Eve laughs lightly. "That's Colleen. She's big on hazing the new girls. Liza—Sledge's old lady—will be twice as bad." She glances around before lowering her voice. "Everyone not inside the circle thinks you're just a girl Axle picked up. No one knows the real deal, which I'm sure Axle has already told you."

He told me my secret needs to stay a secret, but not that everyone thought I was his. It thrills me a little that he probably hates the hell out of that cover.

I smirk a little as my eyes scour the numerous bodies, and I finally spot him sitting in a chair, drinking a beer as he talks to the guy beside him who is getting a lap dance.

Axle's eyes don't even seem to stray to the half-naked girl. Hmmm. I never considered the possibility that he might be gay. That would explain so much.

And it really freaking sucks.

But he gets hard when he watches me...

"Is that why the girls seem to keep passing him?" I ask, watching as another girl takes a wide berth around his chair to move to a guy near the back. "Because they think he's with me?"

Eve snorts derisively, and I return my attention back to her.

She gestures with her thumb to where Drex is shoving a girl away from him, his eyes narrowing like she's crossed a line. As soon as the girl walks away, he rolls his eyes and resumes what appears to be an interrupted conversation with the bald guy they call Sledge.

"No. The girls don't give a damn who's taken. I'm learning to fight. Eventually, I'll be able to kick their asses and stake my claim and all that. But until then, I have to silently seethe and try to keep from stabbing them with a broken beer bottle or something."

I'd laugh, but I'm confused when I see another girl going out of her way to steer a wide path away from Axle on her quest to Dash.

"So why aren't any of them trying to dance on Axle?" Not that I want them to. My fighting skills are rusty, but I can still hurt a girl if necessary.

I look over at Eve when she doesn't answer, and she worries her bottom lip while shrugging.

"The girls here have a lot of options. And unless Axle directly requests them, they try not to draw any attention from him. I haven't even seen him request anyone since I came here several months ago, but...anyway. He's not... They don't..."

She groans, and I slowly piece things together. "Because of the damn scars?"

She purses her lips. "The girls who've been with him say they're really bad under his clothes. They talk about the guys a lot; I wasn't seeking out this info. Anyway, his legs seem to be the worst. And in case you haven't noticed, they're not here to look beneath the surface. This is a good time for them. Not to mention, Axle isn't exactly very approachable, in case you haven't noticed."

Good. I won't have to fight for his attention if I'm the only one who is into him. Sucks that they like perfect, pretty boys. Because none of these guys are perfect, pretty boys.

"Where are you going?" Eve calls out to me, but I'm already heading up the steps to the room to change.

As soon as I'm locked inside, I strip out of the cupcake shirt and find the sexiest dress I own. It barely covers my ass, which is the point. I'm supposed to look like a stripper.

But only one guy gets a lap dance.

The black dress stops high on my thighs, and the high heels give me a couple of inches of height. I let my hair down from the ponytail, happy to see it didn't have time to get that annoying little ring/bump.

When I'm sure I look scandalous, I turn and walk back out, shutting the door behind me, and strut like a badass down the stairs.

One guy blocks my path on my way to Axle, and I peer up as he leers down.

"Five seconds to remove yourself before I make you wish you weren't a man," I tell him sweetly.

That lazy grin of his flattens to a thin line.

"Excuse me?" he growls.

Sledge is suddenly at my side, appearing from thin air. His name needs to be Ghost.

"Axle's old lady," Sledge tells the guy, whose eyes widen noticeably.

I go with it, and step around him like it's the truth. Axle barely looks up at me when I come to stand right beside him. *Sail* starts playing as if it knew I needed the right mood music to pull this off.

Axle looks away, then his eyes dart back to me again, surprised, as he tilts his head and runs his eyes over my body and leans back. His gaze drifts up to connect with mine again, and he arches an eyebrow as if to ask what I'm waiting for.

His eyes spark with intrigue as I step in between his legs, and he relaxes in his seat as his lips twitch. A few gazes swing my way, but the only pair of eyes that I'm concerned about are the pale ones that are trained on me right now.

I start moving my body to the beat of the music, my eyes still locked on his as he sips his beer, watching me the way he watches me get dressed. The way he constantly watches me is the thing that has kept me chasing so long.

It's also what squashes his sexual preference debate for me.

I move closer, and my legs brush the insides of his. He takes another long drag off his beer, eyes hooded and intense as I continue to move with the music. His gaze dips to where the dress has a long slit down the middle, exposing the sides of my breasts down to my navel where the slit stops.

Since he's not pushing me away, I lean over, grabbing the chair on either side of his head. Our lips are so close that I can feel his breath, and he puts his beer down on the table beside him.

His hands come up, grabbing my hips, and the touch courses through my entire body like liquid fire inside my veins. He lifts me and pulls me down on him until I'm straddling his lap.

I don't know if anyone is watching, and I don't care as I grind against him, finding incredible friction against his very hard erection. My dress rides up, giving him peeks at the black lacy underwear he saw me put on this morning.

His gaze drops to there, to where our bodies are connecting as I continue to gyrate my hips. His hands slide to my ass, and I bite down on my bottom lip as he squeezes it through the dress and pulls me even closer.

I swing my hair over one shoulder, keeping with the whole stripper persona, and glide my hands down to his shoulders. His grip on me tightens as he leans over. His breath whispers across the bare skin of my neck as he reaches my ear.

"Thought you were done chasing," he says in his sex-rumble voice.

I shudder against him, my grip tightening on his shoulders as I tilt my head to the side, completely exposing my neck to him. When his lips connect with the sensitive skin there, it feels like flames start licking over me as heat washes through my body.

I moan as I grind harder, and he sucks on my neck, flicking his tongue there next. The sexy song, coupled with his incredibly sexy mouth, has me on the edge as I press even harder against him, essentially fucking him with clothes on.

His hands tighten on my ass, controlling my movements in his lap, and my hands slide up into the soft strands of his dark hair. One of his hands glides up slowly, raking that heat across me with it.

He grabs a handful of my hair, and a breath escapes me when he uses his hold to pull my head back. But surprise hits me with a wave of desire when his lips crash against mine in a possessive, claiming kiss that steals the last of my air and sanity.

My fingers tighten on his hair, and I pretty much submit and melt against him as his tongue slips between my lips and wrecks me in the best possible way.

I'm vaguely aware of the music still playing, though another song is on. It's like it's just the two of us as I kiss him harder, letting go of his hair as I run my hands down his chest, clutching the fabric of his shirt to keep myself grounded.

His hand slinks under my dress, moving to my lace-clad ass as he grinds himself against me, letting me feel every hard inch of him under me. When I moan into his mouth, he releases a sound of his own—a raw, guttural sound that only turns me on more.

Everyone is probably seeing my ass, but I stopped being shy a long time ago. Modesty is reserved for the normal girls who get to grow up and worry about such luxuries.

It's not for girls who grow up worrying if it's the last day they get to live.

His hand that's in my hair tugs my head roughly as he breaks the kiss, and my eyes come open to see several people watching us. But my lids flutter shut again when I feel Axle kissing the underside of my chin and slowly working his way down the column of my throat.

His other hand slides up to the middle of my back as I lean in to it, letting him kiss his way down to my chest. I'm vaguely aware of someone speaking when Axle's lips stop their descent and abruptly leave my body.

My eyes pop open to see him smirking at me, and I lean forward, ready for more, when he tugs my hair again, halting me.

I look around, noticing a few guys have taken some chairs close to us, one of them being Drex, who is watching someone—probably Eve—across the room.

"I need to talk shop for a minute," Axle tells me as my gaze shifts back to him.

I'm being dismissed?

Yeah, I realize I came out here to act like a stripper, but I didn't expect him to just shove me away the second things were getting good. It's as degrading as it is embarrassing, especially when a couple of the unknown guys chuckle at me.

"Right," I say calmly, tugging my dress down as I awkwardly climb off his lap.

He grabs my hand just as I start to leave, but I shake free and keep walking. Done.

I'm not playing games. No one has time for that. One minute you can be talking to your daughter about the pros and cons of bacon, and the next minute you're being blown to pieces by a bomb set by your son.

Yeah. The last conversation I ever had with my parents was about bacon.

I realized then life was too damn short.

A few guys move out of my way as I angrily head toward the door at the back. I came here for a job—not a guy. A guy just seemed nice to have, since it's rare I actually find someone who is tough enough to handle a life like mine.

Bitch boys don't do it for me.

Pretty boys sure as hell don't do it for me.

Survivors turn me on.

There's suddenly a body in front of me, and my eyes take in the large expanse of a chest that has a black shirt with a white reaper on it.

I crane my neck back to look up at him.

"You're in my way," I bite out.

"I want a dance," he says, swaying a little as he holds up a twenty.

"Not a stripper," I retort, shouldering my way by him when the asshole refuses to budge.

A hand clamps down around my upper arm, and I curse as I'm tugged in reverse, my back slamming into that beast of a body. The bearded jackass bends down, and his long, wiry beard tickles my bare shoulder.

"I said I want a dance. So dance for me, girl."

Oh, I'll fucking dance for you. Then I'll make you sing soprano.

Just as I whirl around, ready to break my kneecap on his balls, the guy is suddenly ripped away. I stumble back, and my eyes widen seconds before a fist collides with the guy's cheek.

I swear I hear something crunch, but the music is too loud to be certain. Big Beard crashes to the ground, taking a small table out as he does.

Axle stands over him, his fist still clenched as he glares like he's making sure Big Beard stays down. All Big Beard does is groan from the ground, loopy from the hit, as blood trickles from his split lip.

The music cuts out, and everyone stares in silence. "In case you missed the memo," Drex says, a smirk on his lips as he walks over to Big Beard, offering him a hand up, "Maya here is a guest of Axle's. Hands off."

Everyone looks from me to Axle, who is still tensely glaring at Big Beard as Drex helps the oaf to his feet.

"Sorry, brother," Big Beard grumbles to Axle. "Won't happen again."

Axle doesn't say a word or look at me, before he walks away, heading back in the direction where I left him.

I swear he's the most frustrating man in the world, because—

Never mind. I just realized this entire thing was to go along with the ruse they've started. To the rest of the club, I'm supposed to be Axle's girl, because no one wants to risk letting them know who I really am.

And I played a part by dancing on him.

And he played a part by punching a guy for me.

Asshole. I almost swooned for no damn reason.

Whirling back around, I walk away as the music cuts back on. Eve stops me before I make it to the door, blocking it with her body.

"Are you okay? Did that guy—"

"He grabbed my arm. No harm, no foul. But you can tell your boyfriend and his merry band of dickwads that I can handle myself. I don't need protection. I've been lying low for six months without issue. And right now, I need to go."

I turn and head up the stairs, not giving her a second to argue, and I change quickly out of the stupid dress and uncomfortable heels. As soon as I'm dressed in normal clothes and my phone is in my pocket, I walk back out.

I spot Eve talking to Drex below, and his eyes flick up to me. I can tell he's about to try and stop me, but I jog down the stairs and burst out the door before he can catch me.

My eyes catch sight of the tattoo parlor just across from me. The alley on either side is too long for me to get out that way before Drex is on my heels.

I don't know Drake well enough to hope he won't sell me out, but I take my chances as I barge in.

Drake jerks a little, a sketchbook in his hands, and his eyebrows go up as I slam the door and lean against it. I blow out a long breath as a slow grin curls his lips.

His bottom lip has two ring piercings that somehow look just right on him. And every inch of skin I see from his neck to his arms is loaded with ink. His inky black hair is styled in spikes on top of his head, and I'm almost certain it's a crime against humanity for a guy to have lashes that dark and long.

"Hide in the back," he tells me.

I really like Drake already.

I dart to the back and shut the door, just as I hear the door to the front jingle as it swings open.

"Did Maya come in here?" I hear Drex ask.

"Maya?" Drake asks, sounding genuinely confused.

"Axle's girl."

So Drake doesn't know who I really am, either.

"Why would the roller derby girl be in here? I'm two seconds from closing up and joining your party."

My breathing echoes back to me as a grin tugs at my lips. It's been a long time since I hid from someone. My smile falls when I remember the last time I had to hide—I was hiding for my life because of my brother.

"Damn it. Tell Axle to get his ass out here. I think Byson spooked her. I told Axle he needed to let the guys know she was his," Drex snaps to someone—doubtful it's Drake.

That has me rolling my eyes for a multitude of reasons. Number one: Byson? Seriously? What sort of country grown, back-asswards name is that?

"He's on his way," a familiar voice—Dash?—says.

"If you see her, call us," Drex says, probably to Drake.

"Aye, aye, Captain," Drake retorts, making a growling sound like a pirate.

That has me grinning again.

As soon as I hear the door shut, I blow out a breath of relief. After a few seconds of silence, I hear, "You can come out now. Life is boring, so come entertain me with whatever drama has you hiding in the storage room."

I twist the handle and walk out, finding Drake still sitting in his chair, working on a sketch. His eyes barely come up to meet mine, and he returns his attention to whatever he's drawing.

"Assholes galore in there. Just needed some fresh air," I lie, taking a seat across from him.

He snorts and shakes his head. "Gotta do better than that. Drex doesn't just come looking for any girl but Eve. There's more to you than simply being Axle's girl."

"I'm *not* Axle's girl. He's actually the asshole I'm mostly avoiding." I prop my feet up, checking out some of the artwork and pictures of tats he has hanging all around the room.

I've never wanted a tattoo before, but if he really did do all this work, I might change my mind. He's a seriously talented artist.

"If you're not his girl, why are you sleeping in his bed?"

I study a very odd daisy that has the word "Cocksucker" written on it. That's just weird. And somewhat random. But I kind of want it.

"I don't know you well enough to give you that story. And to be honest, you'd have to really love drama to even want the story."

I hear the pencil when it stops scratching the surface of the paper, and I look back to see him studying me.

"If you have trouble tied to your name, warn me now. I've already been half killed the last time the club brought in a girl."

I smirk as I get more comfortable. "Eve? The girl from the burbs?"

He adjusts in his seat like he's wary of me.

"Whatever trouble she had, I can guarantee you I come with a hell of a lot more. You sure you want me to spill my secrets?"

He hesitates, then finally he groans as he goes back to sketching. "On second thought, just sit there and look pretty. Secrets just get people shot or wrecked or killed. I'll pass."

"I should probably go."

"They'll be out there. Just wait it out. They'll move their search elsewhere if you're that important to them," he argues.

"Why are you letting me hide in here?" I decide to ask.

He grins as he looks up and winks at me. "Because I love pissing off Drex. It's my favorite hobby."

CHAPTER 14

AXLE

I'm going to kill that stupid motherfucker.

"Find her?" I ask Drex over the phone as I walk back down the alley toward the warehouse.

"No. It's like she vanished into thin fucking air. She not answering her phone? I saw her leave with it."

"If she was answering her phone, I wouldn't be asking if you'd found her," I snap.

Byson is a dead man walking if anything happens to Maya because he scared her. I never expected her to spook so easily after seeing her in that warehouse full of corpses. And certainly not if she really is a Family Head.

Which calls everything she said into question once again.

"Damn it," Drex hisses. "I need to deal with something. I'll meet you back at the clubhouse when I can. Dash is still checking all the neighboring stores and restaurants that were still open. She couldn't have gotten that damn far."

I hang up on him, trying not to crush my phone. Just as I near the warehouse, I hear feminine laughter—laughter I know too damn well to mistake it.

I glance over at the tattoo shop that has the blinds drawn shut, but the lights are still on, and two silhouettes are there.

Apparently I'm going to have to kick Drake's ass tonight, too.

I start to go jerk the door open, when I hear the conversation going on.

"Roller skates?"

"It's...a long story," she says, still lightly laughing. "And one I probably won't ever live down."

"If you and Axle aren't bumping uglies, why're you in his bed? Just a cover?" Drake is asking.

That has me tilting my head in confusion. She's fucking telling Drake this shit?

"Apparently it's just a cover. Which has me feeling like a total jackass after tonight—the really embarrassing situation I already explained. Hence the reason I'm done with the club. I was only here as a favor to Sarah and because I wanted to see Big and Surly again."

Big and—

"Big and Surly?" Drake asks the question my mind was trying to form.

"Axle. The prick who made me feel like a waste of breath tonight. I guess it's my own fault for throwing myself at him and dressing like a girl who was asking for it. But...I don't know. I'm just done. I don't have time for his mind-fuckery."

Ah. So this is what melodramatic is.

It had nothing to do with Byson and everything to do with that damn lap dance I had to stop before I fucked her in front of everyone. The point of the party was to conduct business. Not give a show to every member in there.

Rolling my damn eyes, I start to open the door, when I hear Drake responding.

"If you need a good fuck, then I'm available. And I'll let you dance on my lap all you want to. No business is too important to interrupt that."

Dead. He's fucking dead.

CHAPTER 15

Maya

My eyes do a quick sweep of Drake. Lean. Sexy. Witty. And very easygoing.

He's not a pretty boy, but he looks more like a lover than a fighter. And fighters turn me on more than lovers.

Heh. Maybe that's my problem.

Terrible taste in men.

Before I can turn down his random offer, the door swings open, and Drake jerks in his seat as I squeal and leap to my feet. I'm running on instinct when I race for the back room, but a strong arm sweeps around my middle, ripping me off the ground as Axle ends my hiding time and slams me against his body. I spin around, facing him as I take in his angry features.

My hands grip the black fabric of his shirt as I glare up at him, but his attention is focused on Drake.

I hope I didn't just get Drake into trouble.

I turn and look over my shoulder to see an amused smile on Drake's lips, which has me relaxing, since he doesn't seem concerned. Drake is half the body mass of that beast Axle took down with one punch earlier. It might break him.

Even though he's not too much leaner than Axle, he's not as mean. You can see that without needing insight into the world I've grown up in. Like I said, more lover than fighter, that one.

"Wouldn't hurt a guy on crutches, would you?" Drake asks, gesturing to the crutches beside him.

Axle points a finger at him. "Don't fuck with this one. She's not Eve. She's not some sweet girl mixed up in bad shit. Whatever she told you, you need to forget it. Fast. Because her secrets *will* get you killed if people link you to her."

Obviously Axle thinks I just run my mouth to everyone I meet.

Drake's smile wanes before falling, and I wink at him. "Bet you're glad I didn't tell you my secrets now, huh?"

He looks at me like I've sprouted a second head. "Fucking hell, woman. You'd better not get me killed," he finally says around a long exhale.

"Nah. I'll make sure you live if the time comes for survival measures," I assure him, which has his eyebrows going up in confusion.

Axle seems to relax a little now that he knows I'm not affected by verbal diarrhea, but that arm stays firmly fixed around my waist. His gaze sweeps down to my face as his eyes narrow.

"The hell were you thinking?" he snaps.

I open my mouth to call him a few less than charitable names, when Drake butts in.

"She was thinking you're a cunt tease," Drake says dryly.

I glare over my shoulder to see him sketching again, no expression on his face.

Rolling my eyes, I look up at Axle once more, and find him arching an eyebrow at me in question.

"I think you're a disrespecting prick who likes to make me feel like an idiot when the mood strikes. I also think you enjoy toying with me, though I don't know what purpose it serves other than to be an asshole. That's what I was thinking, because I don't need this right now."

Axle flicks his gaze to Drake as a small chuckle follows that little rant. Axle's obviously not the one chuckling.

"She's feisty. I like that. Most girls just wither and shiver in your presence. Not sure why your cock is on a mission to avoid the pretty kitty." Drake should never try to write poetry.

Instead of saying anything, Axle releases me suddenly, and just as quickly, he bends and I'm airborne. A surprised squeal bubbles out of me when I realize I'm folded over the barbarian's shoulder, and he turns and walks out, careful not to bash my head on anything as he moves through the doorway.

"Nice chat. Stop by any time," Drake says as I steady myself on Axle's shoulder by gripping his back.

I blow a strip of hair out of my face and glare at Drake as the cheeky dick grins at me.

Axle leaves the door open, and he walks us quickly across the narrow street to go inside the clubhouse, where the party is still raging on. As soon as we walk in, howls and whistles erupt.

I expect him to put me down, but he jogs up the stairs instead, as I bobble helplessly on his shoulder. He doesn't put me down until we're in the bedroom, and instead of gently standing me on my feet, the bastard drops me to the bed.

A grunt pops out of me when I hit, and I keep my eyes in angry mode as I stay put.

Does he seriously look amused right now?

Oh, I take it back; I've never held any interest in being the brute force of my family's operation, but I'd totally blow out a couple of kneecaps right now.

"Tonight's party was to keep the guys happy, keep them excited to have chosen our side. It's a very fragile time for us right now, because if we lose too many, we deal with Herrin and an army on our own," he says suddenly, cocking his head as he studies me.

My lips purse as confusion settles in, pushing anger to the corner at the moment. I stare at him, waiting for him to elaborate.

"We're broke. Herrin took everything. It's going to take a while to figure out which guys are double agents and which ones are truly loyal to us."

He moves to the dresser, leaning against it as I sit up and pull my knees to my chest.

"Our sources are compromised, making the vetting process much harder for fear of an ambush with a job. Everything is in disarray right now. We've decided on a name, and when we get the cuts in, that will change the game a little. The second you put on that sovereign show of unity and pledge yourself to a brotherhood, the consequences for playing both sides suddenly doubles. It feels like twice the betrayal."

"You're explaining why tonight was important. Not why you treated me like a piece of dog shit that was stuck to your shoe."

The bastard smiles. *This* is what makes him smile?

Oh, but it's a damn good smile. One that transforms his entire face.

"Because," he says as he wipes the smile away, "you just showed up a week ago. If I treated you too good, people would assume I'm whipped or weak. And as I said, this is a fragile time for us. No weakness allowed."

"I don't see Drex treating Eve like dog shit, and he's the president, right?"

He moves toward the bed, and I shuffle back. When he grabs my ankle, I don't fight. When he jerks me down the bed, I don't fight. And when he spreads my legs so he can come down on top of me, I let him.

He braces his weight with his elbows on either side of my head as he stares down at me. The soft fabric of his shirt tickles the insides of my thighs, making me all too aware of how intimate this is.

I'm not sure why my breaths are so shaky. It's not like it's the first time I've been in this position with a guy.

His gaze flicks to my lips, and his thumb starts to trace the outline of my mouth. I force my body to remain still and not to succumb.

"Eve has earned her place and her right to respect from the club. That's a long story, but it took time. You're the new girl. As far as everyone is concerned, you're just some hot girl I brought in as mine. They can't know who you really are to know why you get immediate respect. And as I said, anything else would be considered weakness."

He stops tracing my lips, and his hand falls away as his gaze comes back up to my eyes.

"They'd be hard-pressed to believe your story anyway. Even if we did trust them all enough to tell them," he adds like a sucker punch.

I shove at his chest, and he rolls off me, cocking that damn eyebrow of his again as he stands back up.

I jerk the covers back, shuffle out of my shorts, and grab a pillow to put in the middle of the bed. "Don't worry, Axle. I don't need you or anyone else to believe my story, and I no longer want to have fun while I'm here."

His face blanks, giving nothing away, and I let him watch—as usual—as I get undressed and pull on one of his shirts that I had already picked out. For the first time since the first night, I leave my panties on.

It's not like that will stop anything, but it's a statement more than anything.

"I just explained—"

I cut my eyes toward him. "You just explained why you treated me like a gnat that needed swatting. Got it. But you still act like I need to keep justifying my intentions. And I don't have time for that. It's me who should be concerned with this club's intentions. I'm going on blind faith in Sarah that this is a good idea…the best place to take cover while I work from the shadows—"

"I haven't seen you *work* yet," he interrupts with narrowed eyes.

I grab my phone and toss it to him. He catches it with one hand, but he doesn't take his eyes off me.

"Feel free to read all the messages. They're mostly in code, but I'm sure a smart criminal like you can read between the lines. Now go. I need sleep. It's been a shitty night, and I need to speak with Drex about getting out of here first thing tomorrow."

He has the audacity to look pissed. "There hasn't been any word from anyone about girls getting—"

I sit straight up and interrupt him this time. "There won't be talk about containers of slave girls getting stolen from the original thieves who stole them first," I state flatly. "You guys are a lot of bells and whistles—muscle and fireworks. But my kind operate on a level that inspires stealth and pure silence. We *own* senators. We *own* governors. We own more than you could know, which affords us a certain amount of leniency. Even a war would go mostly undetected by anyone not caught in the crosshairs. It's why I was shocked that Lathan found me so early on. It's why I had to rush around for protection. It's also why I couldn't bring down any of my men to start working the jobs. The Families have a leak. One in a lot of power. One who told Lathan I was here."

"Smitty," he says immediately.

"It's not Smitty," I grind out.

"How can you be sure?" he fires back.

I look around. "You have rats too, right?" I ask rhetorically, since he just stated as much. He doesn't bother answering that. "Is it Drex?"

His lips tighten, and I can see immediately I've pissed him off.

"That's how I know. Smitty was my father's friend like Drex is yours. Smitty refuses to take the business, though I've offered it to him multiple times. Because he wants me to honor my father's wishes and continue on as the head, even though he still runs the business but doesn't take the title—the title is *everything. That's* why I know Smitty is not the leak. It's too dangerous for him to be the head, anyway, and it's his job if I'm dead. Besides, he knows I'm still here, and Lathan has guys tearing up New York in search of me because he thinks I ran home."

I turn over, jerking the covers up over my shoulders as I stare at the wall.

"Everything we planned had to be changed, and if it hadn't been for Sarah, I'd have been screwed and the entire plan would have gone to hell. A war would have been started. So I adapted. I adjusted. Something you do when lives depend on your actions," I go on.

I blow out a frustrated breath, before continuing.

"Not that you guys understand that. You're all brute power and no finesse. You can't win a war with soldiers. You win a war with the right offensive plan. Otherwise, you just suffer a lot of casualties with no end in sight for when the bloodshed stops."

I hear him moving through the room, and I close my eyes. "Don't cross that pillow. It stays between us."

"Your feelings got hurt and now you're isolating yourself from us. That's it? This temper tantrum is going to get you killed if you try to walk out of here and lie low without help," he says with an edge of annoyance.

I keep my eyes shut.

"It's not a temper tantrum. And your inability to trust is going to get you killed quicker than trusting too easily. I've told you everything. You've told me nothing."

"I told you about the weak state of our club, and—"

"*You've* told me nothing I didn't already know from Sarah. You explained it better, but you didn't share anything new. Because you're incapable of it. I just didn't realize that until tonight."

Because I'm a fool who thinks everyone is like me—ready to live while air is still in their lungs.

I feel him vibrating with fury because I'm using the same dismissive attitude he dealt me earlier. Then he snaps. "I just explained why I couldn't look weak. You're letting your fucking feelings—"

I jackknife into the seated position, my eyes flying open. "Weak? You think you'll look weak? I get that, Axle; I really do. That argument is over. We're onto the part where you still question my every move, and I can't afford the time it takes to deal with something like that."

"You can't afford the time," he says slowly, that edge still in his tone. "You fall into our laps with this ludicrous story, but everything you say shows how disorganized you are, while you claim to run an *organized* crime syndicate."

Taking a deep breath, I clutch the comforter with both fists to keep from punching the arrogant idiot.

"I couldn't grieve my parents the night I found out they died. None of us could. We all had to immediately step into our roles and pretend as though we were cold and callous to stop anyone from seeing how *weak* the loss had left us. We all had a part to play to stop chaos before it started. We couldn't let Phillip win by giving in to our grief and losing our power. Don't tell me about not looking weak. I get it all too well."

My voice starts to crack, but I clear my throat and press on.

"I wasn't ready. I'm still not ready. None of us are. But we have to pretend like we are, otherwise, someone else will step in, and who knows what will happen then. If Phillip is in charge, it'll be like the early years of the mafia all over again, and trust me when I say that will *only* benefit him. He'd have more control over the U.S. than the Cartels have over Mexico."

You know what? I'm sick of defending myself and exposing all my weaknesses to a man who tells me nothing.

"Go away. I'm tired. This day has sucked, and I'm ready for tomorrow."

I drop to the bed again and screw my eyes shut as I jerk the covers back over my shoulders once more. My body tenses when I hear him moving toward me. A *thump* has me tempted to open my eyes, but I'm too stubborn to give in.

I track the sound of his retreating footsteps that sound like he's moving toward the door, and I listen to the telling *click* that assures me he just left.

My eyes open to look at the table beside me, and I see my phone. He couldn't have read the messages, and I'm not sure if that means he's finally hearing me, or if it simply means he doesn't *want* to trust me.

Instead of analyzing it, I close my eyes and pretend to sleep, even though I know I won't fall asleep until he's beside me in bed. Since the explosion, I haven't slept; I've only crashed.

I'll stay awake for days until my body demands I sleep, and I collapse from exhaustion. It's how I've operated. It's the only way I could operate.

Then I came here, and sleep…happened. The nightmares still come, but they're not as bad. Not as painful. The false security could be the effect of having a guy like Axle so close.

Guess I'll find out.

CHAPTER 16

AXLE

I awake with a start, feeling the bed beside me and hitting the damn pillow she put between us instead of her. A sense of panic hits me when I see her side of the bed is empty, and my eyes dart to the clock as I jump up and start stabbing my legs into my jeans.

It's after two in the fucking afternoon, so it's no surprise she's not in bed. She could be any-fucking-where by now. Damn it!

I don't even bother with a shirt as I sling my door open...only to slam to an abrupt halt when I hear *Rock 'N' Roll Train* humming through the speakers as Maya skates backwards, making a large loop around Dash, Drex, and Eve as Drex tries to talk to her.

He's having to yell over the music as Maya spins in a fast, tight circle, her arms straight up over her head.

"You can't leave right now. It's not safe." Drex is saying as she breaks out of her spin and starts skating again, facing front this time, and gaining a lot of speed.

"I have work to do, and all you guys are concerned with is my story. We haven't even discussed the cars I need built, and my guy never sent me a text last night. Which means something went wrong with the last job."

Her shirt has vampire teeth on it with a logo that reads, "Bite Me." Pretty sure some blood is dripping from those teeth. She has on long socks again, only this time they're blood red.

Her shorts are black and barely cover her ass. Fuck me, I really love/hate spandex.

"You still can't leave. We'll go check out—"

"No!" Maya shouts, skidding to an abrupt halt close to Drex.

I start walking down the stairs quickly, cursing the metal steps against my bare feet.

"I'm not supposed to allow you to get involved. This is my show. Not yours. All I need from you are the fucking cars. They're here. Do your genius stuff, and that's your job done," she goes on.

Colleen walks toward them as I approach, but no one notices me.

"You guys need to get quiet. All this music is waking people up, and they might hear you yelling about this."

"She knows?" Maya asks, crossing her arms over her chest as she glares at Drex.

Drex runs a hand through his hair.

"No. She didn't. But you're the one who seems to have forgotten a lot of others have been crashing here."

She drops her arms to her sides and grimaces. "Right."

Maya starts skating backwards again, and my hands dart out, grabbing her hips before she can run all over me. She jerks, and I end up tightening my hold so she doesn't fall and break her damn neck.

When she looks at me over her shoulder, the surprise turns into exasperation as she rolls her eyes and looks back at Drex.

Colleen looks over at me, her eyes widening in her head, as Maya continues speaking.

"Anyway, I need to go check on things," she says quieter. "And you need to remember that I'm not a prisoner."

Maya shifts closer to me when Drex stands, and I put an arm around her waist. Drex's eyes flick to mine. "Deal with whatever it is she needs."

Maya makes some grumbling noise as she starts skating again, pushing away from me. Drex comes to my side as I watch her drop and spin again very quickly.

"Keep her happy. Please. If she leaves and gets herself killed, it may come back on us in a bad way. We have enough shit to worry about," Drex tells me.

"Yeah, Axle. Why the hell isn't she happy?" Dash goads mockingly.

I flip him off and start moving to Maya, but Colleen shrieks, causing me to look over my shoulder at her. Her eyes are trained on my back, because I'm still fucking shirtless, and she's pale as her gaze sticks there.

Maya skates over, putting herself in front of my scars. "Problem, Red?" Maya snaps, glaring at her like she's my protector. "Because if you have a problem, we can discuss it like two crazy chicks any time you want."

Colleen jerks her gaze away, her cheeks heating with color, and I roll my eyes when the guys bite back a little grin. Maya is no one's fucking protector, least of all mine, but she's still staring down Colleen like she wants to slap her or something.

A squeal leaves her lips when I suddenly grab her at the waist, tossing her over my shoulder, then straightening to my full height.

"Are you kidding me? You can't just keep manhandling me any time the mood strikes you," Maya gripes.

"I need to shower and dress if we're going to go find your crew," I answer before making my way to the steps.

Maya just groans, her hands clutching the back of my jeans as her hair tickles my back.

As soon as I barge into my room and put her down, Maya spins, shoving at my chest, while her face burns red from all the blood flow being redirected to her head. I try not to laugh when she struggles to get all her hair out of her face.

"You can't keep doing that. It's degrading. And embarrassing. And—"

I shut her up when I jerk her to me and kiss the hell out of her, feeling my body twist tight the second she moans and melts against me. She can't fake her reactions.

And Maya sure as hell wants me.

Which leaves me damned confused about the complex enigma and what to do with her.

CHAPTER 17

Maya

Axle is kissing me. With no one around. And he's kissing me like he's going to do much more than kiss me.

Which takes a second to sink in.

My hands slide up his bare chest to his shoulders, and one of his hands slides down to my spandex-clad ass, squeezing it roughly as he pulls me flush against him. I keep moaning like he's a piece of chocolate cake sliding into my mouth, acting like a stupid virgin kissing a guy for her first time.

But I can't help it. Kissing Axle is like tasting an adrenaline rush, or feeling a drop from the top of a building. It's as exhilarating as it is terrifying, because he's the kind of guy who could consume a girl with very little effort.

When he starts tugging up my shirt…that's when it finally sinks in what's going on, and I push away. My skates make that easier, since I sort of fly backwards, giving us an immediate three feet between our bodies when he releases me.

He arches an eyebrow as though he can't believe I'm the one stopping things for once.

"Keep her happy means to fuck me, doesn't it?" I ask with a scowl. "Drex just told you, in no uncertain terms, to fuck me into staying put with a smile on my face."

His lips twitch.

"You think I'd fuck you just because Drex wants me to?"

"I think those guys down there are the only ones you'd do anything for. So yes; I do think you'd fuck me out of obligation."

He cocks his head, his lips thinning.

"So I'm a jackass for being suspicious of your motives when you crash in from out of nowhere. But it's okay for you to be suspicious of my motives when I finally decide to quit thinking."

I bristle a little. *When you put it that way...*

No. No. I'm not an idiot.

"You've made it a point not to touch me in private. Then Drex tells you to keep me happy, and you drag me up here like a caveman to kiss me stupid."

His eyebrows go up, and I swear my panties catch fire when a small, sinfully perfect smile quirks on one side of his lips.

"I wanted to do more than kiss you stupid, but feel free to find reasons to halt it. Or feel free to admit you've just been playing a game you never thought you'd win, and now you don't know what to do with me. Whatever you need."

He walks by me, not looking back, and disappears into the bathroom. Cursing, I drop to the bed, removing my skates, as I listen to the shower come on.

"Most complicated man in the history of all complicated men," I grumble.

There's one way to check his temperature on this situation and find out if he's legit into me all of the sudden.

I quickly strip out of my clothes, and I walk into the bathroom, seeing his naked silhouette through the frosted glass shower doors. I lick my lips, wondering why I thought it was a good idea to think I'd be running this thing.

Axle will consume me within minutes if I go through with this. He'll hold all the power. Because it's clear I'm way more into him than he is me.

But for some reason, it doesn't really matter.

I move toward the shower doors, and I see it when he realizes I'm in here. Though I can't see his face or eyes, I can feel his gaze on me as I open the door. I step in and look up into that intense, heated stare, and face him fully as I shut the door behind me.

Holy sexy male. Naked is a good look on him. I've seen him in boxers. I've seen him mostly naked. But truly naked? It's beautiful.

My eyes fall down, and I see a curious scar on his massive beast of an erection. He's definitely hard enough to prove he wants me.

I want to touch the scar that is near the base of his dick, but I'm scared now that I'm alone with him. What if I touch something he doesn't want touched?

"Why don't you like being touched?" I ask him, peering up at him carefully.

The water sprays against his back. His dark hair looks even darker all wet, and he runs a hand through it, making it stick up in a way that I find much too sexy.

"I told you I only don't like being touched when I don't want to be touched," he tells me quietly.

"Do you want to be touched right now? Because I don't think I could survive a hit from you, if we're being honest."

His hands pause and he scans my face. "I wouldn't hit you. I'd just shove you off me if I didn't want *you* touching me. But that hasn't been a fucking problem since you showed up."

He grabs my wrist, and I hiss out a breath as he jerks me against him. My other hand slams against his wet, hard chest, and he studies me like he's waiting for a reaction.

"When I first joined as a prospect, I was still a punk teenager — naïve and horny as fuck. A woman was all over me all night at my first party. It was the first time a female had ever acted like the scars didn't bother her. Acted like I didn't scare the shit out of her."

My hand slides higher on his chest, and he releases my other wrist, using his newly freed hand to gingerly grab my hair and hold my head so that I'm forced to stare up into his pale eyes.

"She fucked me. Took my virginity like a pro. Then stole close to twenty grand in cash from the club after I stupidly asked her to spend the night. Herrin had her by the hair the next morning, and all the guys in his circle were taking turns with her. See? They knew what was coming, so she never made it out the door."

My stomach roils. He sure as hell knows how to kill a mood.

"It was him and five of his closest men, all of them planning to punish her for weeks. So when Herrin told me it was my turn, I grabbed a gun from the counter and shot her between the eyes. Figured that was mercy. They considered it to mean I was a coldhearted bastard. Herrin was wary of me from then on."

I swallow audibly as he stares down at me with unreadable eyes.

"I got my cuts that night, and I haven't been stupid like that since then. So yeah, I have trust issues with girls who claim they want me. Girls who look like you and throw themselves at me."

My hand slides up, touching the scar over his lip. He goes still against me, but I keep touching him. He said he'd just shove me off if he didn't want it.

"I've watched three guys I've dated die because they were too naïve for this life," I tell him suddenly, swallowing against the knot in my throat. "Three men who weren't survivors. They were just guys in over their heads, and that was with my identity being mostly a secret. Imagine if more people knew who I was."

My finger traces over his lip scar again as I continue.

"Your scars don't bother me, because they mean you went through hell and came out on the other side alive. Your scars tell a story. Your scars make you sexy because it means you could handle me without getting yourself killed in the process. I love your scars, because they mean you're strong enough to withstand the worst in life. And my life is toxic. Dangerous. Constantly a snake pit. Even if you're only in it temporarily."

I blow out a breath, feeling his grip on my hair soften, and his hand on my ass caresses up to my back.

"I may not have the outward marks to prove it, but I'm scarred all over too, Axle. Mine are just hidden from sight, because life was hard for me in a different way. People tend to constantly die around me. I lost my family in less than a blink, and I was betrayed by my own brother. So yeah, your loyalty is sexy. Your scars are sexy. *You* are what turns me on, because I feel like you can survive *me*."

His lips find mine in a flurry of motion, catching me by surprise, and my fingers dart up to tangle in his hair as he pushes me against the shower wall.

I moan into his mouth, and his tongue uses that to gain access. For a man who plays hard to get, he sure as hell knows how to kiss.

The thing about Axle is that he's a constant presence that seems to surround me the closer he is. With him kissing me, pressing me against the wall, he feels like he's burning me from the inside out.

It's consuming.

That hard erection grinds against my stomach, which only has me holding back whimpers. This game of cat and mouse has gone on for far too long.

His grip on my hair becomes just shy of painful, because Axle does everything a little rougher. That fact alone has me ready to climb him.

His body is like a wall of lean muscle trapping me to him, as though he's worried I'm going to change my mind and try to run away. He continues to kiss me stupid, and I reach between us, finally grabbing the smooth, tight skin of the part of his body I've been wanting for so long.

One of his hands trails down, and a surprised sound slips free from my mouth to his when he grabs my thigh and jerks it up around his hip. My other foot leaves the ground, and I scramble to wrap it around his waist for stability.

Both his hands go to my hips, supporting my weight with scary ease. I'm not sure how he manages to do it, but suddenly he's thrusting in without warning.

My lips break apart from his as he pulls back and thrusts in harder, burying himself all the way inside me this time. It feels even better than I thought it would, because the size of him drags against my inner walls, touching every nerve-ending.

He seizes my mouth again with his, and I kiss him harder, hungrier, as he continues to drive in and out of me. One of his arms goes behind my back, and his other hand hits the wall beside my head as his thrusts get even harder.

My ankles cross behind his back, forcing his drives to grow shallower, but he still finds a way to grind that pelvis of his against me in the perfect way.

It happens so fast that I don't feel it sneaking up on me until the force of the orgasm is crackling over my body, leaving behind a wave of tingles as my entire body shudders and I cry out.

He drinks down my sounds, still rapidly thrusting in and out, until I'm struggling to keep my limp legs strapped around his waist.

He drops me suddenly, pushing me down until my feet hit the floor, as he breaks the kiss simultaneously. I'm swaying, half dazed and half drunk on the awesome orgasm, when he spins me around, forcing my hands to come up and slam against the shower wall.

The confusion of his actions is temporary when he grabs my hips, lifts me up and thrusts in from behind. I moan from the sensation, and he lowers me back down to my tiptoes, still clutching one of my hips to anchor me to him. His other hand grabs my hair and roughly angles my head to the side so that his lips can come back down on mine, stealing all my sounds again.

His pace quickens, and with the ferocity in his rhythm, I struggle to keep myself pushed back from the wall. I feel like I've somehow unleashed the beast, but I'm not complaining.

Axle is all sharp edges and rough finesse. He's too hard to be a soft guy, which makes him everything I've always needed *and* wanted. There's nothing gentle about him, so I'm surprised when he thrusts in one last time, grunting his release, and his kiss turns almost reverent.

His body shudders against mine as his painful grip on my hair and hip both soften at the same time. Languidly, he continues kissing me even as he pulls out.

I vaguely register the spray of the shower still beating down on his back and misting me. Slowly, I turn to face him, our lips never breaking apart, and wind my arms around his neck.

When my lips feel swollen and raw, he finally breaks the kiss, and I shiver a little when a soft spray of very cool water connects with my leg while he shifts to turn the shower off completely and steps out.

While he's grabbing a couple of towels from the rack, I take the opportunity to admire his scarred back full of mysterious pain from his past, and try to digest what just happened between us, still feeling the undeniable chemistry surging through me. It's never felt like that—connected, intense, overwhelming...consuming.

That's the word I use most to describe the enigma of a man in front of me—consuming.

The burn scars on his legs are the most prominent reminders of what he must have gone through. All the scars couldn't have happened at one time, which suggests a repeated pattern of abuse. Which is what leads me to believe those burns were intentional.

Someone was sick and twisted.

And at one point, Axle wasn't strong enough to fight back.

My powers of deduction conclude it most likely happened when he was a vulnerable child. It's the only explanation as to how someone was able to take on a man like Axle—he wasn't a man yet.

I'd like to see that son of a bitch come after him today. And I'd like to watch as Axle slowly killed him. I'd stay in the room and make sure he stayed hydrated while he made the death last for days.

Axle turns and tosses me a towel, and I blink out of my thoughts as I frown at him.

"Get dressed. We'll go investigate the trouble with your team," he says flatly, as though what just happened between us didn't happen at all.

I didn't expect cuddling or anything, but...this is colder than I imagined, and it totally ices my after-sex buzz that was still crackling through me.

"Yes, sir," I say under my breath, my eyes going down to my body as I start drying off.

There's suddenly a shadow falling over me, and a finger goes under my chin, tilting my head back up. Cold, pale eyes stare into mine as though he's trying to figure me out.

Again.

"You wanted it, so don't act pissed now. I know you got yours," he tells me with narrowed eyes.

Seriously?

"Sometimes, I want to slap you," I tell him, jerking my head away from his touch as I shoulder my way past him, wrapping up in the towel. When my back is to him, I call over my shoulder, "And I'm not pissed about the hot sex. I'm pissed about the asshole who threw me a towel and pretended he felt nothing. Because it's irritating as hell."

With that, I walk out of the bathroom and go to angrily pull on my clothes. However, there's a text that comes through on my phone, and I blow out a heavy breath when I read it.

Fuck this day.

C.M. Owens

CHAPTER 18

AXLE

I have no idea what the hell to do with her.

She's pissed about what, exactly? Hell if I know. Not the sex—that much I know. Now I know, anyway.

Sex has always been cold and detached, a means to breaking things up with my hand and getting something soft around my dick. Never much else.

Club whores have been the status quo for me, and usually they have to get really drunk to take me on. And that's after they've been told to. Never too many volunteers, considering the scars. And the fact they find me too rough—which Maya didn't seem to mind. There's also the small hitch of me killing that one girl.

Somehow, it always gets omitted that she was a thief and that she was about to be ran ragged for weeks before someone else killed her. On Herrin's orders.

I just sped up the process and cut out a lot of her suffering. Motherfucking saint.

Maya? Maya wanted this. Hell, she's wanted it since she saw me. No ulterior motives have been discovered yet, and there was no faking the way she reacted to me.

There's no way to fake the way she kisses me.

There's no way to fake how wet she gets just from my touch.

Hence the reason I have no idea what to fucking do with her.

Annoyed, I walk out of the bathroom after I'm finally dry, and leave the towel behind. But when I step into my bedroom, I see Maya staring down at her phone, her towel still wrapped around her firmly, and her face a blank mystery.

122

"What?" I ask her.

She jerks a little at the sound of my voice and puts her phone down.

"My team was killed last night," she states emotionlessly. "Which means Lathan has wised up to the game. Or Phillip has. They may not know I'm here, but they're aware that someone is definitely targeting them, and now they're more prepared. Or our inside guy sold us out. I won't know until I get ahold of Ingrid."

"Ingrid?" That's a name I haven't heard.

"A Family head who has the inside man," she tells me. "I sent her a message. Just waiting on her to send me one back."

She drops the phone to the bed and moves to go start changing. The second her towel falls off, my eyes rake over her flawless skin, taking it in like I can't get enough.

I've fought her as long as I could. But hell, I'm only human. And she's as sexy as they come. It was inevitable that I was eventually going to take her.

What I wasn't prepared for was how different it would be from anything I've had before. She fucking wanted me. Got off on me touching her. And called out my name when she came on my cock.

That's still fucking with my head.

I'm not used to any of this.

Fucking girl.

She turns to face me as she tugs on a shirt without a bra, and she quickly shimmies into a pair of transparent black underwear.

"It happened when you were a child, didn't it?" she asks, drawing my eyes away from her underwear and back up to her gaze.

I stiffen, not liking this conversation already. This story isn't up for grabs.

"Why do you ask so many questions?"

"Because I like you and want to get to know you. It's pretty common for people to do that when they have great sex. It's better than throwing them a towel and pretending as though they felt nothing," she volleys.

My eyebrow goes up as her eyes gleam with a challenging glint.

"It happened when I was a child," I confirm, wondering why I'm telling her that at all.

"I figured the person had to get you at your most vulnerable age," she says with a shrug, as though it's no big deal. "No way would anyone be able to hurt you now."

Again, I have no idea what to do with her.

I cross my arms over my chest, and her eyes flick up and down my body like she's taking me in, hungrily.

When her eyes meet mine again, she asks, "What was your real name?"

Something inside me turns cold, and I turn, grabbing a pair of boxers to jerk on. I was planning on getting back inside her, since we aren't going anywhere now, but the urge has now been shattered with the questions I hate.

"I don't have a *real* name," I answer, reaching for a shirt and angrily tugging it on as well.

"Everyone has a real name," she says as though she's confused.

As soon as my jeans are on, I pull on my boots, tying them quickly with my back turned to her.

"I need to update Drex on your situation."

"Drex has nothing to do with my situation. Your crew is to stay out of it. I told *you* as a courtesy."

I sometimes think I want to throttle her almost as much as I want to fuck her.

"Drex needs to know what's going on in our town, so as a *courtesy*, I plan to inform him," I bite out.

"Fine," she says flippantly. "But your guys are not to get involved."

Breathe, Axle. Just fucking breathe through the irritation.

I decide not speaking to her as I dress is the best course of action.

"Where did the name Axle come from?" she asks randomly when the silence stretches on.

She's going to keep pressing for answers, but she's not going to like anything she hears. Then, if I see any fucking pity in her eyes, it'll ruin whatever this is that she seems to feel for me.

I'm not sure if I want it ruined or not. Pity fucks are the worst. The damn girl is fucking with my head.

As I stand, she continues staring at me from her corner of the room, still wearing just those damn panties and a T-shirt that stops at her waist.

"The nurse gave me that name. It was the first thing that came to her, since her husband and son were working on building a car. They were greasing the new axle that day when she came into work," I tell her, watching as her brow pinches in confusion.

I start walking for the door, but as soon as I reach for the handle, the too-inquisitive girl asks yet another motherfucking question.

"What nurse?"

"The one who was on call the night I was brought in for the burns on my legs." I don't mention it was the first time I'd ever been outside *that* house since I'd been taken there, and that it was a stroke of luck a neighbor heard me screaming. I also don't tell her what happened that night. The night I was freed and fucked up the worst, all at the same time.

"Why would she need to give you a name? I'm just trying to understand this," she tells me softly.

I hesitate, almost deciding not to answer.

125

Opening the door and not turning around, I quietly murmur, "Because until then, I was only referred to as the Demon's Child."

I hear her breath catch, and I never look back to see her eyes as I walk out, heading downstairs to find Drex and update him on Maya's business situation.

Before I even reach the bottom of the staircase, Drex is already walking toward me, his eyes shifting toward the closed door of my room before finding mine again.

"Maya is the real deal," he says quietly, glancing over his shoulder at the warehouse full of guys who have gathered for a ride today.

We're getting back to basics, boosting morale and all that shit. Some of us joined this club because our lives were too fucked up, and no one else could understand us except for others who lived through their own twisted version of hell.

Some of the guys just joined because they liked to ride and raise some hell. So today, those guys are riding and raising hell, while the rest of us are hanging back to deal with the financial situation.

A financial situation that Maya is about to save our asses from.

"Thought you already assumed she checked out," I tell him gruffly.

"I did assume it. Now I know it. Sledge has a friend in New York who rides with a different crew. They don't know the names of some of the Family Heads, but they do know all the shit she's told us is legit. That bomb and all. And the fact the Families have been too quiet, meaning they're up to something. Another guy says Blackbird is a family operation, and they know for a fact a girl is running the show now. And the girl is a little...wacky."

Definitely sounds like Maya.

"Still doesn't explain how you know for sure it's her," I say, even though I know it's her.

I'm not sure why, but I fucking trust her. She's too genuine...too real. And it's easy to tell from her haunted eyes and bizarre reactions to tense situations that she's not exactly playing pretend.

She's her own breed of fucked up. Just like the rest of us.

"The girl had twenty of Phillip's men executed," Drex says quietly. "Point-blank shots to the head after the bomb."

I tense a little at that.

The fucking hell? Maya? I see her as…well, crazy. Not murderous.

"One of them was her boyfriend at the time," he goes on, quieter still. "Apparently he was a spy for her brother and Phillip."

I swallow a little harder on that. She mentioned loyalty upstairs. She didn't mention why it was so important. I assumed it was because her brother betrayed her. She also mentioned guys weren't strong enough for her. I took that as cowardly, not traitorous.

"That's — we're talking about Maya, right? You think she's capable of killing a guy she was with?" I ask, unable to process that part of the story.

"Not directly, but she definitely issued the order. It was what kept anyone from assuming they were too weak to handle things after the sudden deaths of their parents. It was probably also the reason Blackbird became the head Family in charge of leading this war."

He once again glances up toward the door, and I cross my arms over my chest.

"Still not sure how you know it's definitely Maya."

He looks back at me, eyes bland. "Because the girl who issued the order rolled in on roller skates, tall socks, short shorts, and had braided pigtails twisted in balls. Made her a little legendarily insane when she issued the order to kill them all and round up anyone else still in New York who sided with Phillip. Then she played a Spice Girls' song directly after and skated around in circles while dancing to it, all while they put bullets in the heads of the guys. This reaction is what sent Phillip's operation deep south."

Definitely Maya.

Girl is just as fucking insane as we are. Possibly more so. In a different way, of course.

"The boyfriend was worked over for a few days before he was finally killed," Drex goes on. "That's apparently how they got their information that led to the trail here. It's also how they turned someone in his crew. No one wants to fuck with the kids who've taken over. They're all batshit fucking crazy, and they don't care who knows it."

Not sure why, but my lips twitch. I remember thinking the scared girl in my backseat was too sweet to hang with this club. Turns out, the scared girl was just a resident psycho who enjoys getting to live another day to wreak more havoc in the most bizarre of ways.

I quickly fill him in on the bad news Maya got, and he curses under his breath, trying not to draw attention to us. No one needs to see us frustrated or concerned right now.

The crew is still too fragile for another wave of problems so soon.

"It feels like we're involved in this, even though she keeps promising we're not," Drex says, still keeping his tone too quiet to be overheard.

"Because we are involved. Have been since Phillip rolled into Halo," I point out, feeling an inexplicable sense of defensiveness on Maya's behalf. "At least we know it now. Herrin is involved too, but he's completely unaware. That might be the only good thing that comes out of this. It's not just Halo where Phillip is ciphering women. It's Herrin's town too, and if the feds somehow linked him to all this..."

I let the words trail off, planting the seed in Drex's head. A slow smile spreads across his face when he gets it.

"Then Pop would go down with Phillip if the operation finally gets some federal attention. But what happens if it doesn't get attention?"

"We set him up and let the cards fall however they fall," I say with a shrug. "We've already made him look like a fed rat to a lot of different crews."

He nods distractedly, as though he's thinking it over. His gaze once again flicks up to the room's closed door. I know it's closed, because I keep looking over my shoulder every five seconds.

"How's she taking the loss of her crew?" he asks me.

Apparently I'm a prick for not thinking about that. "I don't know," I answer tensely.

"Don't piss off Blackbird," he tells me pointedly. "You're the only person in here she seems to give a damn about. We need her to survive so that we can get through this shit storm."

"I'm not using her for survival purposes," I say in a clipped tone that has his eyebrows raising and that stupid smile of his spreading.

"Alright then," he says, still fucking smiling. "Then go do your thing. My bad."

"You sound a lot like Drake when you talk and smile at the same damn time," I grind out.

His smile only spreads. Bastard.

"The guys are going for a ride, but they'll be back in a few days. We're going to throw a party. Our morale game needs to be strong," he says, shifting the subject but not losing that damn grin.

"And?" I ask, wondering why the hell I care about a party. I always show up, but it's not like I care to be there.

"And you should bring Maya. Let her get to know people."

I tense again. "You mean some of the other guys?" My tone is flat, but for some reason, the fucker is grinning even bigger.

I'm going to kill him. Or at least remove his legs.

"I mean let her get a feel for the club. You know. In case she decides we're worth letting survive and wants to continue to hang around. She'd make a nice old lady, and you could always clear out some of the furniture to give her more skating room."

Ah. Got it. The dick is mocking me.

I turn around, flipping him off as he laughs to my back, and I stalk back to my room. When I fling open the door, I pause, once again finding myself in a stunned state.

Happens around Maya too often.

She's singing along with a song on her phone while dancing like...a spaz? I'm not really sure if she's dancing, considering I *know* she knows how to dance. Right now, she's shaking her entire body like a wet dog, screaming the lyrics as loud as she can, and I shut the door behind me before anyone comes up to investigate the ear-brutality going on in my room.

Girls Just Want to Have Fun is apparently the song she's trying to butcher. At least I think. She's louder than the music.

And she's still in her panties and T-shirt.

Scrubbing a hand over my face and groaning, I clear my throat loudly. Then realize the Thrashing Song Butcherer can't hear that. So I walk over and press pause on her phone, killing the music.

She sings—or whatever that noise is called—for a minute longer before she seems to register the music is gone.

Her wild hair is shoved out of her face by one of her small hands, and she glances over at me, panting for air as the thrashing comes to an end.

"Care to tell me what the hell you're doing? I thought you'd be a little more upset over your guys that you just lost."

Drex saying that she had her boyfriend tortured and killed didn't worry me until now. She just lost her crew, yet she's jamming out like it's the eighties and school's out for summer.

Now I'm worried I fucked a sociopath.

This girl is a bucket of issues every time I turn around.

She rolls her eyes at me.

"They were hired guns and knew the high stakes coming in. They took the very large salaries and the assumed the risks. I had no personal attachment to them," she tells me callously. "It's not like these were the types who contribute to society. They were expendable."

"And what are we?" I ask her, narrowing my eyes.

Her jaw tenses, but she shakes her head and mutters something under her breath. I think she just called me a bag of dicks. And I'm not really sure what kind of insult that is.

"You're not expendable, or I'd happily place you in the line of fire instead of working on my bug-out plan to keep you safe."

"That's because of Sarah," I remind her. "You wanted to hire us at one time. For the same thing this crew just died for."

She groans. "No. I wanted to hire you for security, jackass. I was still working on who was going to do my grunt work when Sarah stepped in. And even so, I didn't know you then. I just wanted to sit on *your* face."

Just when I think she can't possibly stun me silent again, she proves me wrong. It's like she's a bag of zigs and zags, and I prepare for a zag, only to get hit with a zig, which has me reworking my words and looking like a complete fucking moron much too often.

She grins and winks. "Don't worry. I still want to sit on your face. I'm on birth control, by the way. Thanks for asking before deciding to get off inside me."

This time, I roll my eyes. "I know you're on birth control. I see you take the pill, and I've seen the cartridge on the nightstand multiple times."

Her grin grows. "Well, I'll be damned. Maybe you are interested in learning something about me. Might want to ask me if I'm clean or not."

"Let's skip health class," I say. Before she can come back with another crazy remark to knock us off subject, I add, "So the guys meant nothing to you. What's with the dancing? Or the spaz attack? Or whatever that was supposed to be, mixed in with the paint-peeling squealing you were doing."

"Axl Rose, did you just make a joke?" she gasps.

"Do *not* call me Axl Rose," I bite out, to which she grins.

"That name story would have been so much better if the nurse had been listening to Guns and Roses and Axl Rose popped into her head."

"Different spelling, and completely...fucking stupid." There's sure as hell no pity in her eyes. Which is a relief, but also worrisome...again. Sociopath is definitely on the table. "What's with the spaz attack?"

"Not enough room for me to skate, and I didn't feel like skating around the bearded assholes downstairs, so I decided to destress this way."

"By shaking violently and screaming lyrics?" I ask dryly.

"Not all of us can just sit around and turn sour over all of life's little fucked up disappointments. Shit happens. This is my coping mechanism. Trust me, there's not enough room in here for us both to brood."

She gestures around the small-ish room, and I...I have no idea what to do with her. Still.

"Talk about the boyfriend you had tortured and executed," I say with no preamble, and mentally curse myself for the brash way it comes out.

I'm usually not the one who has to do the talking. That's Drex's role. I just hit people. Maybe shoot them. Sometimes kidnap them to get beaten up. Or killed. In short, I'm the muscle. Drex is the talker. And, God help us, he's usually the brain, too. Which means a lot of people get fucked up a lot of the time.

Fortunately, I'm cool with that. Helps get the anger issues under control when you have a viable candidate to beat down.

It takes me a second to realize Maya has gone stiff. Her eyes are cold and flat, and there's zero expression on her face. It's eerie, mostly because her face is too expressional...normally.

"Tell me how you got those gnarly scars," she deadpans, not an ounce of *anything* in her tone.

My eyes narrow, but her expression doesn't change.

"Why the fuck would I do that? And why are you asking that right this second?"

She cocks her head, and that's when I see something I wasn't expecting.

She's not a sociopath.

Tears are in her eyes.

"Until you're ready to talk about your scars, you have no right to ask about mine. I'm not sure where you dug up that information, but it's not fair to pull my pain out of a box when you keep yours locked away. I don't dig up your information, and I easily could."

It's like I can't do anything right. And I swear I've swallowed more than my foot, because I actually feel like shit.

She's the first person to make me feel that way. Guilt is an emotion I haven't experienced since I was a child...until she came in like a hurricane.

She turns around, and I hear her taking deep breaths, like she's trying not to cry. I make a mental note to punch Drex in the mouth, since I decide to blame this mess on him. After all, he's the one who told me that.

It's not like I have a clue what to do with a damn crying woman in my room.

So I do the only thing I do know how to do, and risk her clawing out my eyeballs.

The second I reach her, I spin her around, see the wet eyes that peer up at me in confusion, and kiss the hell out of her.

She's rigid, tense, and definitely not up for the kissing. I still continue trying, slowly, gently running my hands over her back. My tongue glides along the seam of her lips, trying to coax them open.

Even though her body stays tight, her mouth finally gives in, and she moans into my mouth as I slide a hand into her soft hair.

When she finally softens against me, I relax a little, trying not to think about how good she feels or how easily she seems to get wet for me. Because I'm a little too close to wanting this. All of this.

To wanting her.

And that shit can't end well.

CHAPTER 19

Maya

Five days ago, I was reminded how human I really am. Axle brought up memories I'd rather not think of. Ever again.

Then he fucked me until I suppressed them again, which was definitely appreciated.

Four days ago, we spent most of the day in bed, still forgetting the past, both of us using the other to do that with.

Three days ago, there was a rowdy party. Axle went down for about an hour. I peeked out, but when I saw him chatting with Drex, Dash, and Jude, I decided to stay in the room. It didn't take long for him to join me for the rest of the night.

Which was a surprise, but then it involved a lot of being naked, so I shouldn't have been too surprised.

Two days ago, Axle found me a whole new set of expendable goons to do my bidding. Well, he found me numerous candidates, and I spent the day sorting through the files to find the ones that would work. And I set up the new deal, paying them via wire transfer, and only giving them a burner number to text. They only know my stage name—Tyler Loyd—and what to do.

Pictures are required, and then my actual guy—one of my Family's loyalists—takes over once the girls reach the dock. He's the only Blackbird member they deal with in person, and no one knows who he is. Blackbird is not tied to this operation. At least, not officially.

One day ago, Axle left for most of the day, and I spent the bulk of the day on the phone making private calls to the other heads of the Families, filling them in on everything, then talking down Carlisle when he wanted to fly down and just blow the place to hell.

Fortunately, he's only a co-head, and not a full head. His sister—Kendra—sided with the rest of us mostly sane ones, reminding him that it's not the middle east and we can't just go to war like we own the country.

Today, Axle is wrapped around me, his body tangled with mine. Since he's not a cuddler, I'm betting on him freaking out and jerking away when he wakes up. We sort of fell asleep after the shower we took two hours ago...because I've awoken the beast.

Axle is a lot of pent-up sexual frustration, and he's unleashing it on me. I love it, even if my vagina is begging for a break.

He never holds me after sex. Never does any of the sweet shit I didn't think I wanted.

But I sort of want at least a little sweet shit, damn it.

This is the sweetest thing that's happened, and it happened by accident while we were asleep.

As predicted, the second he wakes up, he stiffens, probably realizing just how entangled we are.

"Spooning won't give you cancer, you know," I quip when he starts to move. "I'm almost positive it won't cause heart disease, either."

He grunts, and I expect him to pull away, but instead, he slides his arms around my waist a little tighter, resting his face in the crook of my neck from behind me.

A slow smile spreads over my lips, and I test the waters, sliding my fingers over his. He doesn't move away, and I think I sigh. Pretty sure it's a dreamy sigh, too.

"We're supposed to be getting ready for the strip club," he mumbles against my neck.

"Yeah. I'd hate to miss seeing a girl with all the same body parts I have as she gets naked in front of you. Sounds like a prize of a night. Sharp objects should probably be left behind for the safety of others."

I almost pinch myself when he laughs. Axle laughs. He knows how!

It's a quiet, barely-there rumble, but it totally counts as a laugh.

He doesn't say anything, so I take it upon myself to fill the silence. "Does Eve not get pissed at Drex for letting another naked girl rub all over him? And does she not get pissed that he *pays* her to do it?"

Another small rumble of laughter has me squirming. It's a really sexy sound. I'm not sure why my body is acting as sex-starved as his.

"No one dances on Drex anymore. He usually fucks Eve somewhere in the club. It's just where we do our business, and we need to put in an appearance from time to time. It's also one of our businesses where we clean our money. Speaking of which, thought you wanted us to do a job."

I yawn, nestling into him a little farther. "I do want you to do a job. But can I make a suggestion?"

I feel him shrug.

"You lost all your money from five accounts very recently. So...don't clean the money. I'll pay in cash, as you should ask all your clients to do for a while, and then you should put all the money in different safes between all of you. You can run your business with dirty cash on the down-low."

He shifts, and I fall onto my back as his face hovers over mine, taking me in with a curious expression.

"Why?"

Reaching up, I let my finger trace the scar on his lip. He doesn't flinch away. Instead, he leans in to the touch like he can't get enough. I really like a loosened up Axle. It's my favorite new thing to enjoy.

"Someone could easily figure out what happens to the money if they know the legit businesses you use to launder it. And someone inside the club might have told Herrin when it was laundered. You put the money in separate safes without telling *anyone* outside your circle—not even Eve—where it is, and no one will touch it. Then, you'll wait on someone to start asking questions. This is the long game—the waiting game. The person who knows you're bringing in money but can't figure out where you're cleaning it will start asking questions. Discreetly at first. Then they'll start nosing a little harder."

He shakes his head. "Herrin had our accounts hacked," he tells me like he's arguing.

"And he'd need to know what accounts to hack," I volley. "You have leaks. This is a solid way to flush this particular one out."

His gaze sweeps over my face, like he's taking me in, and it finally settles on my lips. I know what that means, and I'm smiling like it's the first time again.

"I'll tell Drex," he answers.

"Right now?" I ask, worrying he's about to leave without one more round.

His lips tilt up in that devastatingly perfect grin he never shows for long, but as always, it's gone before I can truly appreciate it.

"Right now, I have to go to a strip club. You really won't go with me?"

It sounds like he actually wants me to go, and that's seriously tempting. But I'm crazy. I might go crazy jealous if *any* girl gets too close to him right now. I totally can't be trusted to keep my composure. And they don't need that drama.

Not to mention, it's not wise for me to risk the exposure. Halo is crawling with Lathan's goons. And while Phillip isn't stupid enough to expose our identities, he'd likely have some of his close inner circle with him who know who we are.

"I'm sure," I say with a one-shoulder shrug.

He drags his lips across my shoulder before he pushes up and climbs off the bed. I take every opportunity to admire his body, so I watch with shameless abandon as he gets dressed.

As soon as he's finished — which is like five minutes later — he picks up his phone and texts someone.

"Eve isn't going tonight," he tells me as though I've asked. "She's working at the shop. Wants to know if you want to hang with her and Drake."

I don't respond right away, but finally nod after I think about it. I guess it'd be good to get out for a while and avoid cabin fever.

I dress quickly while he continues to text. I half wonder if he's texting Eve, and ignore the unimportant twinge of jealousy. See? I'm not completely sane.

Axle walks out first, and I lock the door behind me as I follow him. Lots of bikers are down below, but none of them check me out anymore. Pretty sure that has something to do with Axle knocking that one guy out.

Or the fact Axle normally doesn't have a girl around, which makes me different than the usual fling they suppose the others have.

I like that.

If they knew who I was, it's unlikely any of them would be suicidal enough to touch me.

As soon as we're down the stairs, Axle's arm drops around my shoulders and he steers me out of the warehouse. I'm not sure when he started touching me like this so easily, but I like it.

It's a taste of normal. I've never had a guy brave enough to touch me in public. My father was always…a tad overprotective. Smitty has taken over that role nowadays.

Just as he starts to guide me into the tattoo parlor, a loud motor revs, drawing my attention.

It all seems to happen in slow motion.

I see the guy on the motorcycle seconds before I notice the gun in his hand, or hear the loud *boom* that echoes off the walls of the alley. My heartbeat drums in my ears as I feel myself falling, realizing belatedly that Axle has just shoved me down.

He comes down on top of me as an unbidden cry leaves my lips, forced out of me from the pain shooting through my hands and knees. His heavy weight pins me down as loud gunfire deafens me, sounding too close to my ears.

The guy on the motorcycle jerks, his gun falling as more gunfire registers. It takes me a second to piece together the fact he's being shot.

He falls off the bike, obviously dead by now, but they don't stop shooting. I don't even know who *they* are, other than Axle, who is shooting his damn gun right above me, his body still pinning mine down.

All at once, the gunfire stops, or at least I think it does. My ears are ringing from being too close to the action in such a closed off area, so I could just be momentarily deaf.

It feels like a mountain lifts off my back when Axle pushes up to his feet. Air rushes into me as I take a big, much needed breath, and roll onto my back, wincing when I feel a sharp pain in my side.

Axle bends, his face hard and his jaw tight, as he grabs me under the arms and lifts me to my feet. As soon as I'm standing, his eyes rake over me in quiet appraisal, as the flurry of footsteps racing around dimly register to my temporarily impaired hearing.

I hiss out a breath of pain when his hand touches a tender spot on my face. Sheesh. I'm going to need to take inventory, but at least there aren't any bullet holes in me.

That has me patting down my body and looking at my side that hurts. I breathe out in relief to see my shirt is just torn and the abrasions are left behind from the pavement and not a bullet.

"Just superficial stuff," I tell Axle as he bends, getting a closer look at my side.

My eyes dart to his arm, and a sick knot tightens in my belly when I see the ripped material there and the blood trickling from his shoulder.

"You were shot!"

He bats my hands away when I try to take a look, but I'm persistent. Blowing out a breath of frustration, he lets me look closer at it.

"Just a graze," he finally says.

I look at him like he's an idiot. Technically, *it is* considered a graze. But it's a big freaking graze from a damn bullet!

"You need stitches. And some hardcore germ-killing stuff. And antibiotics—"

"You two hit?" Drex's voice has me snapping my head to the right as he walks up, his eyes hard and lethal.

"We're fine. Where's Eve?" Axle asks him, his hand moving to the back of my neck like he needs to make sure I don't plan to walk off.

"She and Drake are inside."

They both look down the alleyway as Drex calls out, "Get that cleaned up before the cops roll in. They'll give us ten minutes before they send a black-and-white."

The guys at the end walk into the garage, and back out, emerging with bleach, a tarp, and some garden hoses. They begin spraying away the blood before two guys even get the body rolled into the tarp.

Another guy starts splashing around the bleach, and they continue to spray the water, cleaning away the evidence of a dead guy. But there are plenty of bullet casings to prove something happened.

My guess is that the cops don't really ask too many questions as long as there's not a body present.

At least that's how it works at home. Then again, at home, we could have four bodies strung up and there'd still be no questions.

"It was Garren," Drex tells Axle quietly.

I idly notice the Death Dealer cut they've pulled off the guy and tossed to the side.

"Herrin sent him on a suicide mission." Axle's response is just as quiet as Drex's, and I wonder if I'm not supposed to be listening.

Hell, I'm just happy that my hearing seems to be okay again.

"Pop was just sending a message," Drex says. His jaw clenches so hard the muscle along the jawline actually jumps.

"Yeah, and the message is that he can come at us any time."

"Or that he's not afraid to come after you," I point out, then clap my lips shut when Axle shoots me a look I don't particularly like.

"Herrin is definitely afraid," Axle tells me. "He's just a coward who plays like he's fearless. It's easy to sentence someone else to death. If he wasn't a coward, he'd have already rolled up in here himself and opened fire."

I say nothing. I have a healthy relationship with fear and self-preservation, but I'm not a coward. I still don't handle the grunt work on my own. It's just not the *civilized* manner of handling things back home. You have guys for that. You have reach for a reason.

But apparently things work differently with them.

"I say we send a message of our own." The new voice startles me, and I look over my shoulder to see Jude standing there.

Holy crap, that look is scary. He's too pretty to be so scary.

"I'm in agreement with that," Drex says, a cold smile on his lips. "We'll hit the club afterwards."

He turns and walks over to the tattoo parlor, and I bite back the questions I want to ask and the advice I want to give. It's a great show of disrespect to any organization for a guest to butt in and start getting nosy or too helpful. It's also suspicious.

I'm sick of suspicion.

I've already overstepped by telling Axle not to launder their money for a while.

"You two get inside the warehouse and lock up. We're going to go make some noise," Drex is saying as Eve walks out and into his awaiting arms.

I sort of envy how easily they seem to fit together, and remember not to ever be jealous of her again. Even if she wasn't obviously in love with Drex, Axle wouldn't ever do anything to fuck up his friendship with Drex.

I watch as he kisses the top of her head, and find myself leaning back on Axle. "Should I be worried about you watching D?" Axle asks, drawing me out of my thoughts.

The dead guy is gone when I glance over, and I turn to face my favorite brooder as I frown.

"I know you're not being serious, so I'll skip over that rhetorical question. What I would like is for you to tell me that making some noise and delivering a message is you two banging on some war drums and not blowing something up or putting yourself at risk for more gunfire."

His eyebrows go up, and he opens his mouth to speak.

Just to be clear, I add, "Lie to me, Axle. Right now, just lie to me."

Something in his eyes softens, but as usual, he hides any expression behind a blank veil the second he shows too much. The guy loves his mysterious factor.

"We'll be banging on drums and completely safe," he lies.

Taking a shaky breath, I nod in gratitude, and turn to walk back to the warehouse that is safer than the tattoo parlor. Just as I reach the door, he spins me around, and his lips come down on mine, surprising me.

The only time he kisses me in front of the others is when he's making a point of claiming me or something just as barbaric as that. But this...this is how he kisses me when it's just the two of us.

It's real, and it's almost desperate. It always feels so desperate, as though he's making sure to soak it all in before it goes away. I do the same.

He pulls back, his eyes intensely on mine as he straightens to his full, very tall height.

"I'll let you know when we're finished banging on the drums," he says in that sex-gravel voice of his.

A full breath of relief comes out. "Thank you."

He hesitates for a second, his gaze shifting over my face like he's trying to get inside my head, but then turns around and heads to the open hangar. I walk inside, pretending like I'm not already staring at my phone and waiting for this night to be over.

It's a hell of a lot harder to be on this side of things. I'm used to being the one calling the shots, or at least weighing in on what shots get called.

Now I'm sidelined because I'm on someone else's team, and it sucks because I have no control over Axle's fate.

Maybe he should join my crew and leave all this behind so I can keep him safe.

CHAPTER 20

AXLE

Drex pulls the pin on a grenade, and we all hang back, guns poised and ready. He nods at us, and then he twists, launching the grenade as hard as he can.

He turns and sprints, running as fast as he can back to us, and leaps over the trench from the desert to the property line. He scrambles back into it just as a loud explosion crackles through the air.

The top loft of the building blows, all windows breaking under it. I can feel the pulse of it, even from the distance I'm at, and the heat hits me next.

I'm the first to pull my trigger as Drex stays covered, keeping his head down so we don't accidentally shoot it off.

Rapid fire hits the warehouse, punching holes in the metal, sending out telling *pings*. We fire for about two solid minutes before we realize no one is firing back.

Either that grenade killed them all, or the fuckers changed their location to a safer place that isn't in the middle of no-damn-where.

Fuck.

Drex heaves himself out of the trench and comes to join us, a pissed off look on his face that tells me he's reached the same conclusion.

"I want to know why we never heard about a move, and I want to know where he is!" he snaps.

"On it," Dash says, turning his bike around as he revs the motor.

Drex gets back on his bike, and I glance back again, cursing at how easily we could have ended this if we'd just struck sooner.

Then again, it was way too easy for all of us to get this close, even though we did approach from the desert instead of the road.

No doubt they had security protocols in place before they abandoned it.

Not to mention the backlash from the other charters had we hit first. Might have even caused a war. No matter what, we've drawn the short straw, and nothing seems to be working in our favor lately.

We ride back to Halo, everyone pissed and ready for a fight we can't have yet.

Maya was too close to getting caught up in a war that isn't hers. I have no fucking clue how I got her down and covered in time to avoid the gunfire, but I'm thankful I did, even if I did cut her up on the pavement in the process.

It happened too fast for me have really felt anything much, but I was definitely pissed. Still am.

I'm also still bleeding, haven't changed out of my dirty clothes, and now we're pulling up at the damn strip club.

I pull out my phone and text Maya, remembering the actual worry and dread in her eyes when she asked me to lie to her. Not sure anyone has ever been that worried about me before.

ME: Drums are played, but there was no audience to hear it. Another time.

MAYA: That took a long time! I've been freaking worried to death, and there wasn't anyone there?

A slow smile curls my lips before I can stop it. This girl is definitely getting under my skin.

ME: Sorry you worried. We're at the club now. Stick with Eve and Drake, or lock yourself in my room.

MAYA: Don't get any lap dances. I shouldn't have to remind you that I'm crazy.

Smirking, I put my phone away and head inside. The guys are already at our table, and a girl is already getting shoved out of Drex's lap. Pretty sure he's about to make her cry. Girls know the rules with him, but always break them.

Never had that fucking problem personally, so Maya has no reason to be crazy.

My feet slow when I see a Grim Angel approaching the table. I join the party, listening as Nicholas — the P — talks to Drex.

"Never saw a kid more loyal to his pop than you," Nicholas is saying. "So I figure Herrin did something real bad to split up the club the way he did and end up on the opposite side as you. I heard the rumors, and only one makes sense, if you know what I'm saying."

"It's an in-house problem," Drex says cautiously. If he tries to spread the rumor himself, people will question its authenticity — it'd be too forced. But I can tell Nicholas has already heard the right rumor we want to infect people with.

Nicholas smirks. "Understandable. Just wanted you to know that you have a friend with us if you find yourself needing allies. I'll take loyalty over cowardly rat any day, and I've always known Herrin to have a streak of yellow."

After an exchange of parting pleasantries, they clasps wrists, shaking once, and Nicholas gets up, leaving us behind.

The night dissolves into business talk after that. Dash ends up doing shots from a stripper's breasts and Drex ends up smoking while lost in thought. I make a few calls, seeking out more work for our crew.

Putting in an appearance is showing everyone we're not backing down or afraid of Herrin.

By two in the morning, I'm sick of putting on said show.

Liza, Sledge's old lady, who runs the club for us, is talking to us about the messed up message Herrin sent, and the fact it cost Garren his life. It's the same thing as normal, and usually I have no problem with it, but tonight, I'm just not interested in conversation.

"I'm ready to head out," Drex says, standing up and leaping over the back of the seat.

Fucking finally.

Liza looks over at Sledge, and I try to dismiss what she says, but it has my blood simmering a little too close to the surface.

"That new girl you guys have at the clubhouse needs to go." She's deliberately saying it loud enough for me to overhear. Liza regularly oversteps her boundaries when we bring in new girls. "All this trouble started happening once she blew in. First the setup, and now this. She's almost as much trouble as Eve, and I know Drex tends to overlook all that."

"The setup was before her," Sledge says, casting a glance at me before looking back at her and giving her a grin. "Don't you worry about the girls laying those boys. They're harmless."

I snort derisively, and Sledge winks at me over Liza's head when I turn to look at him. She doesn't have a clue just how dangerous Maya is, but it's safer for her if she doesn't know. Drex is wishing Eve hadn't been in there now, because he doesn't even want her to know.

The ride home is boringly uneventful, and as soon as my bike is parked, I'm heading toward my room. I don't even bother turning around when I hear Jude call my name, because I'm taking the stairs two at a time.

Not sure why I'm worried about her not being here, but for some reason, the feeling is there, and it's gnawing away at me unexplainably. I unlock the door, walk in, and breathe out in relief when I see her sleeping on my side of the bed.

After shutting and locking the door, I strip out of my clothes and slide into bed on her side before pulling her to me and kissing my way down her neck.

I feel it the second she wakes up and her hands slide up my back, like she's searching for my scars and making sure the right man is on her. That leaves an uneasy feeling in my stomach, but my mind returns to the right place when her lips search out mine and kiss me like she's been waiting for me all night.

After tossing back the covers, I shift until I'm between her legs, and smile against her mouth when I realize she's already completely naked.

Her legs move until her knees are pressed against my sides, and her nails dig into my back like she wants me closer. My cock glides between her legs, feeling her slick and ready for me. It slides right in without any guidance, and Maya's breath hitches as I hold back any of my own sounds.

Sinking deep inside her, I feel encased, gripped, and too damn good. It's the first time in my life I've had a girl waiting in my bed when I came home, and it's the first time I can remember never wanting to give something up.

CHAPTER 21

Maya

After living in Axle's little warehouse room for over a month, I'm definitely going a little stir crazy. Skating around the warehouse below only happens when the guys not in the inner circle are out on rides.

It gives me a break.

Soft lips find the back of my neck as I read the latest text from the latest takedown, and I lean back on Axle.

"Your brother is trying to figure out who's fucking up his operation," he murmurs against my neck, sliding his hand over my stomach and pulling me back against his chest. "Just heard about it yesterday when one of his guys came to ask Drex if he'd heard about anyone new in town."

I stiffen. "One of Lathan's guys came here?" I ask tensely.

"No. They sought him out at the salon when they heard he was there with Eve. You don't just roll up at a clubhouse unless you're invited or stupid."

I grin at that, relaxing against him.

"What'd Drex tell him?"

He drags his lips to the other side of my neck, kissing a trail down the curve, working his way to my shoulder as he pushes my shirt out of the way.

"Told him he hadn't heard of anyone new in town, but that Halo was ours anyway. And Lathan had no right to be operating so close. The guy lied and said he wasn't operating out of Halo, and scrambled off, high as fuck and tweaking the entire time."

Definitely sounds like Lathan's people.

His lips leave me abruptly, and I almost fall backwards when he's suddenly not there for me to lean against anymore.

He stands, fully clothed for a change, and I cock my head as he grabs a pair of my sneakers and tosses them to the bed.

"Put those on. We're going out. You've been caged up in here for too long," he says randomly.

"If Lathan's people are sneaking around here, then—"

"Shoes on, Maya. Meet me downstairs in five."

He turns and walks out, and I stare at the door when it shuts. I'm really not used to being bossed around, and I have no idea why I simply put my shoes on like that isn't what just happened.

Even guys who didn't know my identity didn't have the balls to boss me around.

Axle is a different breed of man altogether.

Putting my phone and a credit card in my back pocket, I tell myself that it's merely curiosity propelling me forward to find out what he's up to instead of being dominated by him. Yep. Not one bit of submission in my body.

I tell myself this all the way down the stairs where Axle, the smirking bastard, who probably knows what I'm thinking, is waiting on me near the bar. Drex is drinking a bottle of water across from him, and Jude is lying on top of the bar and throwing a baseball up and catching it on its way down.

"You wanted me to come be boring with the rest of you wild ones?" I muse, slipping easily next to his side, and peering up at him with scrutiny when he just continues to smirk.

Jude casts a glance at me before rolling his eyes and resuming his task of tossing a ball straight up and catching it.

Reckless danger going on here, people.

Axle says something to Drex that I miss, and then he turns, grabbing my hand and guiding me toward the door.

"Where are we going?" I ask, still following like a follower.

"For a ride," he states flatly.

"Is that smart?" I ask, jogging to get to his side instead of trailing behind, still holding his hand.

"It is if no one can see our faces. We'll look like some randoms just taking in the sights as long as we use one of the spare rides, since mine is too well-known."

I start to argue as we step into the massive beast of a bike hangar that only has a few bikes in it today. He drops my hand and goes to grab two sleek, solid black helmets off the wall that are equipped with darkly tinted visors on the front.

Okay then. That'll do.

He hands me one, and I take it, tugging it on a little forcefully. Snugly hidden from sight, I follow him to a black Harley with chrome fixtures.

Nice. Glad to see this is just a *spare*.

Wordlessly, he takes a seat, helmet on already. I imagine his eyes are staring at me impatiently, but they're completely hidden behind the tinted glass of the visor.

Finally, I take his hand, using it as a balancing tool as I climb on back, sitting with my legs spread around his hips as close as possible, since the saddlebags on this thing are huge.

The damn thing is so obnoxious when it roars to life that I might squeal a little. Not that you can hear the sound over the damn loud-ass thing under us.

As soon as my arms wrap around his waist—tightly—he shoots out of the hangar without warning, not bothering to crawl out like I expected. My grip tightens even more, and I clutch his middle as I peer over his shoulder at the roads he's crossing, driving us toward the edge of town.

As soon as we're on an open, car-less stretch of highway, I stop tensing and just start enjoying the ride. A stupid, pointless, and somewhat confusing grin spreads across my face for no reason at all.

I'm not supposed to like motorcycles, damn it.

But in this moment, I love everything about it. The freedom. The openness. The fresh I taste when I lift the front of the visor. The feel of the wind against my skin.

The bugs fucking suck because they feel like stray hail slapping me.

But I can deal with the occasional insect collision right now, because the positives outweigh the negatives.

My ass is numb way too soon, though, and my legs are cramping from holding this position for so long. It feels like we've been riding for days instead of hours.

Fortunately, Axle parks us just outside a hotel. A nice one, by the way.

Hello, room service. I've missed you.

He pulls his helmet off, and I follow suit, grinning at him even though my head is a little gross and sweaty.

"A hotel? Trying to get lucky?" I quip.

He huffs out a small laugh as he undoes one of the saddlebags and pulls out a backpack I didn't know was in there. With a curious eyebrow arch, I watch as he tosses the backpack on one shoulder and clutches the helmet with his other.

"I figured you could use some time out of the warehouse, but you're not safe just anywhere. I'd take you to my house, but it's not any safer right now with all this shit going on with Herrin." He gestures toward the hotel without looking at it. "So this is our only option."

A grin spreads over my lips as I waggle my eyebrows.

"So you're angling for sex *and* a blowjob."

He rolls his eyes, walking by me.

"Never had one of those," he says conversationally.

I laugh, shaking my head. "Your jokes are seriously terrible. You need to stop trying to make them."

He looks over his shoulder at me as I follow, and his brow furrows. "I wasn't joking."

I actually stop walking just because it takes all my concentration to focus on the nonsense he just said. And was serious about.

He pauses at the door, seeing I've stopped walking.

"Coming?" he asks, still acting as though what he said was no big deal.

"You've seriously never had one?" I blurt out.

Bored expression on his face, he walks back to me, waving off the guy at the door who is holding it open for us.

"Not sure why that's so surprising to you," he says gruffly. "A random party girl took my virginity just to steal money from the club. The status quo has been the occasional club whore since then and an immediate STI test in case the condom failed. The girls might get theirs, but that doesn't mean I'm ever their first choice. In case you haven't noticed, what I lack in appearance, I do *not* make up for in charm. The last thing they want to do is get their faces that close to the worst of my scars—on my legs—and suck cock. And I don't ask for it. Sex works to take the edge off, and that's all it was ever about."

He studies my expression, his lips thinning.

"I'm going to stop telling you shit if you start showing pity. I like the fact you don't pity me, so don't—"

"It's surprise," I interrupt. "Not pity. I'm not just to *take the edge off*, am I?

My eyes narrow expectantly as my hands go to my hips.

He smirks. "There hasn't been an edge since that first night. We both know that."

He turns and walks away, and I grin at his back as I skip behind him, following him through the door.

"I'm sort of happy about the fact I'll be the first girl to suck your dick," I state bluntly, loving the way he always seems stumped by the things I say.

However...I forget we're in a snazzy hotel lobby when I toss that line out. Loudly.

An elegantly dressed woman gasps, staring at me in horror, before dropping her fancy store bag to the ground. Several other eyes are also staring at me like they can't believe I just said that.

Axle simply looks at me with zero expression on his sexy face. "Pretty sure the entire hotel didn't need to be informed of that," he tells me blandly, not rattled by me anymore, apparently.

He walks on to check us in, while I ignore the woman still gawking at me with reddened cheeks puffed out on her face.

Sheesh. Talk about sucking dick and people act like you just made a terrorist threat.

I sidle up next to Axle just as he gets the key cards to our room, and I follow his lead to the elevator. Much to her dismay, the red-faced woman joins us on the elevator, practically hugging the other side across from us like dick-sucking might be contagious.

I grin up at Axle, who merely rolls his eyes at me. The hand not holding his helmet reaches over and squeezes my ass as he draws me to be in front of him.

I'm a little surprised when he bends and starts kissing me, both of us ignoring the indignant gasp from our elevator companion. Our lips don't part until the elevator doors ding with arrival, and Axle draws back, glancing over at the woman.

"Enjoy the rest of your ride," he drawls, and the poor woman turns about three more shades of red as she scoots to the back of the elevator when she finally stares directly at his face and the scars there.

Unaffected, Axle turns and struts out, clasping my hand along the way, and I grin back at her and wink.

He guides us to a room, releases my hand to dig out the card and open the door, and we both drop our helmets just inside the door as soon as we're inside.

He drops the backpack that I can only assume is carrying an extra change of clothes, and I go straight to the room service menu.

"I take it you're hungry," he says, sounding amused.

"Room. Service. You have no idea how obsessed I am with someone bringing me food, and I actually collect those tiny little condiment bottles. They're just so damn cute," I tell him without looking up.

Well, I finally look up when he doesn't say anything back.

He's just watching me, eyebrows up in confusion.

"What?" I ask.

He shakes his head, a small smile playing on his lips.

"Just when I think you can't surprise me any more, you prove me wrong."

"My tiny condiment bottle collection stuns you more than me being excited about popping your oral cherry?"

With a completely serious expression, he retorts, "I think you're still just trying to sit on my face."

My grin grows, and when his smile starts to spread like it's contagious, he turns his back and starts unzipping the backpack.

"Timing is still off, but that joke was almost funny," I say, laughing to myself as I resume reading the menu.

I know all the things Axle likes to eat—steak being one of them—so I call in my order, using one of my burner credit cards as payment.

When I finish, Axle is climbing up on the bed, dropping to his back as one of his arms snakes around my waist with comfortable familiarity.

"The guys are working on your cars today. My part is already done, but I'll help out with theirs when we get back tomorrow," he says as I turn to face him, lying down and pillowing my head on his arm.

"Do you think I ordered enough food?" I ask, not wanting to discuss anything outside our bubble right now.

No motorcycle club and no Blackbird can exist in this little bubble. Just for today.

He arches an eyebrow as he looks down at me. "I think you ordered enough food for ten people."

I laugh under my breath. "You get more tiny condiment bottles the more food you order."

His laughter catches him off guard, and he turns his face away as his chest shakes with the effort it takes to stop laughing.

His attention comes back to me, eyes sparkling with amusement. It's nice to see him out of the clubhouse and not wound up so tightly. He's relaxed here, not having to put up any shield or keep his surly reputation intact.

I kiss a path along his jaw as he lazily runs his fingers through my hair.

"Thank you for this," I finally say when I'm close to his ear.

He just makes some noise because he obviously can't act like he appreciates the gratitude. Grinning, I kiss his cheek sweetly, and his hand tightens on my hip.

Axle isn't used to sweet gestures, hence the reason I do them as often as possible. I'm not used to sweet gestures either, and this is probably one of the sweetest.

It's a little annoying to spend all your time in one room or with a bunch of bikers, never having a moment alone with each other. And I need a day off from my reality as well.

He's successfully suspended reality.

I climb over him and across the bed to go open the curtains. His room in the clubhouse has no window, so I soak in the sunlight while I can.

C.M. Owens

After a few minutes of me just standing there, smiling out at the city view, Axle moves in behind me, wrapping his arms around my waist.

"We could always dance right now and take this over-the-top with romantics," I offer with a smirk.

He groans from behind me. "You're going to make me feel stupid for this if you keep on."

I, of course, just grin.

At least until he starts swaying behind me, his hold causing me to sway in time to whatever music he may or may not be hearing inside his head. Then my heart does a little kick in my chest.

After a few minutes of songless swaying, I turn in his arms, and his lips come down on mine in a soft, devastatingly sweet kiss that contrasts so much with his usually harsh nature.

I'm a little high on him by the time he pulls back, his eyes flicking between mine as he just stares at me. I love it when it feels like he's trying to get inside my head.

"I was thinking that was damn sweet from someone so hard-natured," I tell him, smiling a little shyly when he cocks his head. "You're wondering what I'm thinking," I explain.

He brushes his thumb over my lips before kissing me again, pushing me back against the window as his mouth claims mine with that same unexpected softness.

I like him hard and rough, but I also like him soft and yielding. It's a nice change of pace, because it feels like it means something more when I get this side of him.

No one else does get this side of him.

I've witnessed it for over a month now.

I get the man no one else sees. The guy who holds me all night and staves off the nightmares. The guy who kisses me softly when he doesn't do anything soft.

The guy who watches me because he's constantly trying to figure me out.

The guy who watches no one else.

When I clutch his shirt in my hands and start pushing it up his body, he breaks the kiss and bends, giving me the chance to remove it and toss it aside. He quickly returns the favor, whipping my shirt off before his lips come back to mine, and he starts backing me toward the bed.

Just as we get laid down and he comes down on top of me, I shove at his chest. He rolls over, his eyebrows pinched together in confusion, until I start undoing his jeans, staring him in the pale eyes the entire time.

He lifts his hips, and I work his pants down his body, tugging his boxers down with them. When I get him fully naked and I barely graze his very hard cock with my hand, I smile up at him as I move between his legs.

He stares down the length of his body at me, his face blank but his breathing a little fast.

With careful movements, I lean over, brushing my lips across the worst leg. He stiffens as I start kissing along the scar, and his jaw tics as he stares at me.

I move my lips up slowly, not wanting to make him uncomfortable, and start kissing around his pelvis, grinning again when his cock jumps and thuds against my neck.

"I know you don't like showing emotion, but you're going to grin big and goofy when I finish with you. Just let it happen, Axle," I say with my grin returning.

He arches an unconvinced eyebrow at me. "Had plenty of orgasms before, Maya. I think I can control myself."

Funny guy. And so naïve.

"But you've never had a blowjob," I point out, wagging my eyebrows a little.

He fights a grin, determined to stay straight-faced.

"Can't be that big of a difference."

I smile to myself. "It's probably not, but there's something incredible about getting a new experience and an orgasm all in one breath that makes it impossible not to grin goofy."

"I'm sure I can—" His words cut off when a breath hisses from his lips when I decide to suck as much of him into my mouth as possible, surprising him.

Grinning around a very large mouthful—*attractive imagery, huh?*—I start working my way up and down, feeling my smile fade away with each curse or pant of air he releases.

His hands go to my hair when I tease him a few times, swirling my tongue across the tip. But when I hollow out my cheeks and start working for real, his grip on my hair grows painful.

His entire body is rigid, like he's fighting not to thrust up— *thank fuck.* I work him harder, using my hand on all the extra that won't fit into my mouth. No deep-throating skills here.

His stomach muscles ripple underneath me as my head bobs, and I know it's happening about two seconds too late.

I'm also not a swallower.

Unfortunately, I'm sort of forced to when my blowjob virgin shoots a little too forcefully into my mouth.

Only because I see his eyes crossing when they open, and I feel his body loosening and turning limp beneath me, do I decide to swallow without a fuss. I'd hate to steal his thunder right now.

His entire body trembles as I move my mouth off him, smiling as his grin starts to form and grow across his face.

His eyes narrow on me even as that stupid grin gets wider, and he covers it quickly with his arm across his mouth.

"No! You can't hide it from me," I say around a laugh, tugging at his arm.

He laughs, but fights me, not letting me see the smile on his lips that I can see in his eyes. When I start making some ground on prying that arm off, he spins, putting his face into the pillow, laughing a little harder when I curse him and straddle his back, trying to flip him over again.

"Damn it, Axle, I want to see that smile. I earned it!" I say, still laughing like an idiot.

He shakes his head, face still buried in the pillow, which only makes me laugh that much harder until I have zero strength due to all the laughter.

A squeal flies out of me when he suddenly flips, and I end up crashing to my back as he comes down on top of me. I'm still laughing painfully hard as he gazes down at me, amusement flickering in his eyes as a more respectable grin plays on his lips.

Jackass wouldn't let me enjoy the goofy grin.

As his expression turns serious and my laughter tapers off, he says, "Now I really will let you sit on my face."

With that, I burst out laughing again, and his grin spreads.

"Much better timing," I murmur, still grinning when he starts kissing me. I don't break the kiss until there's a knock at the door, accompanied with the promise of tiny condiment bottles.

Then I'm bolting off him, pulling my shirt on as I go, and leaving Axle to wrap up in a sheet or flash the waiter when I swing open the door.

I'm still smiling like an idiot the entire time I tip the guy.

I can't remember ever feeling this wrapped up in anyone. And I really like it.

CHAPTER 22

AXLE

"One more," Maya says, hovering over me and pretending she can spot me if I struggle with this set.

She couldn't even lift the ten-pound bar.

Obviously I'm not relying on her to keep me from getting crushed under the two-hundred pounds I'm benching.

Not that I tell her that, since she's delusional enough to think her adrenaline will kick in and she'll turn into Wonder Woman if the time calls for it.

Never thought I'd roll with so much weird shit.

But I like her weird shit.

She'd be easier to resist if she wasn't so damn bizarre. It makes her who she is.

"One more," she says for the twenty-eighth time as I continue on.

Rolling my eyes, I push the bar up, straining a little, and place it back in the holder as Maya frowns down at me.

"I said one more," she states firmly.

We spent an extra night in the hotel, and I decided it was fine to bring her to the hotel gym with me, thinking she could run on the treadmill or something. Instead, she's been annoying the piss out of me and acting like she's my relentless trainer.

Should have seen that coming.

"You say one more every single time," I answer, feeling winded. "Sort of makes it impossible to do just one more."

"But that's the point of exercise. It's called torture for a reason."

I snort, unable to help myself. "Torture is too dramatic, don't you think?"

"Nope. You think you're almost done, then realize you have another. And another. And another. Then the next day you're walking like you had bow-legged sex for fifteen hours, yet orgasms were never achieved. Good things bring orgasms. Bad things bring pain. Therefore, it's obvious exercise and torture are first cousins, at the very least."

When I move to the free weights, she follows me, making a show of checking me out, since I abandoned the shirt early on. We're the only two in here, so it's not like anyone is having to see my body besides her. And she doesn't mind looking at it.

"What if we had sex on the treadmill? Like, I could sit down on the top part, and you could run and thrust to—"

"Do you ever listen to the shit coming out of your mouth, or do you just talk until you get bored with talking?" I ask her, trying not to smile.

Never had to fight so hard not to smile as I do when I'm around her.

She grins at me. "Or we could totally do it on the pull-up thingy. I could hang there with my legs around your waist and you could—"

I cut her off when I kiss her, needing her to stop talking before I do something that will get us tossed in jail. Her damn mouth is constantly tempting me.

She sighs as I back up, smirking at how that always seems to subdue her.

Her eyes brighten like an idea lightbulb just went off behind them.

In case you haven't noticed, she can't be subdued for long.

"Gym selfie!" she says, confusing the hell out of me.

She turns before I can ask what the hell she's talking about, and she leans back while bringing up her phone, snapping a picture of the two of us.

"What the hell?" I ask on an exasperated exhale.

She just grins.

"If I could post pics to social media, I totally would right now. We could look like one of those sickeningly sweet gym couples, and you could do, like, sit-ups with me on your back or something."

I have no idea what she's talking about, so I resume working out, letting her continue to ramble all the while. We currently have an entire bag full of tiny condiment bottles for her to take back with us.

This is the girl who I can't get out of my head.

Not sure when or how this happened.

When we finish up and leave the hotel gym, she hops on my back and takes another selfie when she reaches out in front of us. She grins against my neck as I carry her, not even questioning her anymore.

A few eyebrows rise as I step onto the elevator with a selfie-taking fiend still on my back.

She giggles against me when I purposely act like I'm about to drop her.

She doesn't seem to notice when I tighten my hold directly after, needing her to keep her arms around me the way she is. She's like a fucking drug.

And I must be a motherfucking junkie.

Because I can't get her out of my system and I'm constantly taking my next hit.

Only with Maya, just breathing her in is like a damn good hit.

CHAPTER 23

"The progress is slow. Currently we're nothing more than an irritation in their side, but it *is* progress," I tell the other Families who have me on conference call.

"We knew it wasn't a fast game," Ingrid tells me.

I always feel relieved when they're not upset with the turtle-like speed of this plan.

"You have the wheels in motion, so we're confident that at this time you should be able to return home and oversee the rest from here," Ingrid goes on.

I could have easily returned home already, but I don't point that out.

We've come so far from the kids who joked about vajazzling moments before we watched our parents die.

"And the next time they kill off all of our retrieval team, I'd have to return. It's not easy finding guys with the skills required to pull this off, especially now that Phillip is onto the attack plan. We're having to space out retrieval hits so the security doesn't get too intense on his end."

I have a hundred or more names I'm still going through for the next-in-line team members. No doubt others will be picked off. And we're looking for people with the skills, and people who'd have a reason to never turn on us. Like for instance, their sister was taken and sold by Phillip, or he killed someone they cared for...that sort of thing. Or they simply hate the Cartels and are good with hitting them through a proxy like Phillip.

"You want to stay there?" Ezekiel asks like he's confused. "Why?"

"Because it's not so bad, and it's easier to oversee things from the ground level. And we agreed that it needed to be one of us to oversee it to cut out the risk of leaks, so there's no one else I'd feel comfortable leaving in my place."

I hear a sigh, and I know it's Ingrid. She wants me home to help her deal with the crazy level right now. Because she doesn't have a Smitty like I do who can run the Family and never miss a beat in my absence.

"You're at risk of being seen or captured every day you're there for longer than planned."

"I have a plan for that. Just had a salon girl leave my room, and I'm a whole new girl. But also, I have a very strong security setup. No one will look for me here, and I'm staying bunked down—not going into public unless necessary."

"Yes, your MC that's not technically a MC. Motorcycle clubs usually have cuts and charters. These guys are the rebels who broke off from the pack and think they can just start anew if they slap a name on a piece of leather," Ingrid says, annoyed. "I don't feel like they're a long-term solution for you to stay secure. This was a temporary deployment to begin with, and the unstable club doesn't instill confidence in its abilities to keep you safe. Besides, it sounds like they have their own war brewing, which is an unnecessary risk for you."

I check the door, making sure it's still shut, before I slowly stand from my seat.

"This is my plan. You put your trust in me to make it work. If I'm not here, then we run the risk of it going to hell. This club has ears to the ground, and they can hear things here that we can't hear there. You know how this works. I need to stay close to the action to ensure this wasn't all for nothing. My life is expendable, and we all agreed on that."

Ezekiel curses. "Your life may be *professionally* expendable, but not *personally*. Don't you feel as though we've all suffered enough loss? Staying there puts you at graver risk daily—"

"Lathan is looking for me in New York. He's not looking for me here," I remind him.

It's enough to shut him up. Well, for a second. Ezekiel always has a backup argument at the ready.

"If they see you, they'll know it's us and not someone who is after the Cartels. It could ruin the entire plan."

"But that's where you're wrong, Ezekiel. If Lathan sees me, he'll grab me and try his shit all over again. His problem with me is personal, and he'll likely believe my presence in Halo is solely related to him. Phillip doesn't think us capable of something this elaborate, so he'll think the same thing. I'm the *only* safe option to be here."

The door opens, and I look over as Axle walks in. His eyes widen when he sees my new hair, and I twirl a lock of blonde while winking at him. He starts moving toward me again, but pauses when he hears the phone on speaker and Ezekiel speaking.

"You know I hate this." Ezekiel sighs. "I want you back here. We're stronger together."

Axle, I swear, looks a little jealous all of the sudden, since he's hearing that out of context.

I like that look. It lets me know I'm not the only crazy one here.

It's been two weeks since we got back from the hotel.

In those two weeks, we've barely spent a second apart. And I get the private Axle every day the door closes us off from the rest of the world.

"I'm aware, but rest assured that I'm safe where I am," I say, watching as Axle glares at the phone. "We *are* stronger together, but I'm not gone. I'm just in a different state."

"We'll call in two days to see how the next retrieval went. You're logging the progress, I assume, and counting how many girls we've freed?" Ingrid asks.

Axle's angry expression changes, and he looks up at me, his face going blank. He starts to turn and leave, as though he just realized what this is, but I move in front of the door, blocking his escape.

I'm almost done, and he's been missing most of the day, which is something I've not had to deal with in two weeks. Today is the day I get my cars. Finally.

He runs his fingers through my newly dyed-blonde hair, eyeing it like he doesn't know what to think about it.

"Yes. And the costs are about to go down, along with some of the risks. I'm deploying the new vehicles in two days. It'll speed up the overall process of getting the girls home," I go on.

"We hope," Ezekiel adds. "Don't get too excited until it proves its worth."

Axle flips the phone the bird, and I bite back a laugh.

"Two days," Ingrid says again.

"Until then," I say, moving past Axle and to the phone, ending the call.

When I turn around, Axle has his arms crossed over his chest. "You ready to see what you spent a small fortune on?"

I nod, trying to play it cool, but desperate to see what they've been working on all this time. Understandably, I'm not allowed in their secret work space, so I haven't even gotten to peek at the progress as it's happened.

"But first tell me what you think," I say, twirling and fluffing my hair like I'm in a shampoo commercial.

"I think it's really blonde and I don't know why you did it."

I arch an eyebrow at him. "Because I'm less obvious with blonde hair, since I've had dark hair my entire life. It'll be a little harder for Lathan to notice me if I'm out for any reason. It's really nice to tell a girl 'it's pretty' when she asks for your opinion."

His lips twitch. "Blonde looks good on you," he finally concedes, and I glide over to where he is.

He tugs me to him, and then opens the door. It's hard to think when he's pressed against me, but he releases me and we start walking out.

"They want you back in New York?" he asks quietly, probably deciphering that conversation now.

"Of course. But I'm not going back just yet."

He nods slowly. "But you will be going back."

I'm not sure if he's asking me or telling me, to be honest.

"My physical presence in New York would be good on occasion, but it's not a mandatory or even a necessary thing. Ezekiel and Ingrid are just worried and tired. It's been a rough couple of years on us."

We reach the bottom of the stairs, and I frown when he doesn't move his gaze to mine or touch me.

"Ezekiel and you close?" he asks.

Totally jealous, and that makes me smile like a fool. "Not like that. Like I said, we all grew up together, with the exception of Sarah, so there's a true familial bond there. Our parents wanted that bond forged early, so when we one day would have to take over, we'd look out for each other. As I've mentioned before, we're not monsters. We're just warped versions of normal people."

He still doesn't look at me, and he pockets his hands, which tells me he has no intentions of touching me.

"If you stay here, then you're tucked away, out of sight, all day, every day."

I say nothing to that, because I feel like I know where he's going with this.

He continues, his eyes still averting mine. "If you go home, you can be out and about with your life."

"No, I'd be dead. Lathan is scouring New York for me. Or he has men scouring New York for me."

"What if he tells them your identity?" he asks me, his eyes finally meeting mine.

There's something there—concern, maybe.

"Can't. I think I've already told you he has as much to lose from that confession as I do. The Families have a large number of enemies. If he outs me as Blackbird, then he outs his own affiliation, if anyone even believed him. Same for Jenkins. He'd rather not have that hell rain down for him. That alone would be a death sentence from the powerful enemies our Families collected over the years."

His lips tighten as he looks ahead.

"What's going on in your head?" I ask him as we move toward the second garage they keep locked.

"Trying to figure out what's best for you, but also wondering if I'm just being selfish for wanting to keep you here," he confesses.

My grin grows involuntarily, and I stop walking. He realizes I'm not following him and turns to face me, his brow pinching like he's confused. Happens a lot around me.

"What?"

"Sounds like you might actually like me, Axle. Must be the blowjobs I've been giving."

He rolls his eyes. "If I didn't like you, you wouldn't be in my bed."

I move to his side, wondering how much freedom I have with his body. Usually I'm careful to always let him initiate physical contact. Even though he's never acted bothered by my touch since we started having sex, Sarah's warning is always in the back of my mind, and I try to respect his needs.

When my hands open on his chest and slide up to the back of his neck, he simply watches me, not tensing or acting as though my touch is unwanted.

"You like me for more than sex," I add, grinning at him even as he stares at me blandly.

What I expect is for him to say nothing to confirm or deny, but instead, he says, "As I said, if I didn't, you wouldn't be in my bed. I don't need my bed for sex."

I cock my head, riding the high. "That's dangerously close to sounding like a declaration of love from you."

This time, he does turn and walk away without saying anything, as that annoyed look takes over his expression. I laugh to myself as he punches in the code to the door.

"I'm not sure why you seem surprised that I like you for more than sex," he says quietly.

"Mostly because you're still a mystery, which makes me feel like you don't trust me with your secrets. It's mostly me telling you about me, and you telling me nothing in return."

His hand pauses on the doorknob, and he glances over his shoulder at me. "I don't tell anyone my secrets."

"You told Drex," I remind him, since he told me that in the beginning.

"Drex and I met in juvie, and he was in the same group therapy session I was in. And he had my back in that place, so I had his and kept him from getting killed. He overheard what was said in group when they basically told me to start talking or I wasn't getting out until I was eighteen." He shrugs. "He kept his mouth shut about it, and I came to live here."

He gestures around the warehouse.

"Now it feels like I live here again, since going home hasn't been safe in a while," he adds.

"Why were you in juvie?" I ask curiously.

"My foster home had a prick kid five years older than me, who slammed me against the wall. It was one of those times I didn't want to be touched," he tells me with a cold smile. "By the time they were able to pull me off him, he was unconscious."

"Why did—"

"Enough twenty questions, Maya. We're here to look at what you paid for, remember?" he asks, interrupting me.

"Why does it feel like you told me something and nothing at the same time?" I volley, crossing my arms over my chest as I grin up at him.

Frustrated—*with me*—he pushes open the door, and I follow him into the garage. When I see all my party vans, I move to the first one, and Axle opens the door, letting me inside.

Quickly, he shows me the numerous hidden compartments, all of which don't knock hollow and have secret levers to open and close them. He breaks down the x-ray blocker—not that they'll have that, but I like his preparation—and the body heat hiders for me.

I listen to him be…really fucking genius as he explains all this. Don't get me wrong, I've known he's clever, but this is brilliance at its finest.

And seriously hot.

When he's finished, he moves me around to the other fifteen, though I'm only halfway inspecting them, since I know they're up to par. Axle wouldn't leave me with something that would screw me over.

He has too much integrity for that.

Yes, even criminals have integrity.

I lean against the back of a van, cocking my head as we finish up, and Axle explains what's next.

"We'll drop these off at the drop point, and leave the code for the doors on the burner phone number you gave us. They can pick them up with a list of instructions that explains every detail," he says to me.

"So do you really like the blonde, or were you just telling me what I wanted to hear?" I ask him.

He rolls his eyes, something he's done a lot around me. And only at me, I've noticed.

"We're discussing the vehic—"

"We've been discussing them for two hours. I know what happens next. It's the third time you've walked me through it, and I know you'll handle it without fail. It's business, and you handle your business. What I want to discuss is if you like the blonde. Because I almost went red."

"It's your hair," he states dryly.

"I don't have to see it unless I look in the mirror, but you have to deal with it all the time."

It always makes me smile more the more exasperated he gets with me.

"I like the blonde, but I'll have to fuck you facing me for a while. It'll confuse me if I'm behind you and think I'm fucking someone else." He says this with a straight face. Yep.

"No wonder you brood so much," I say on a sigh, causing him to tilt his head in confusion. "You really are terrible at making jokes."

A small rumble of laughter leaves him, and he presses against me, kissing me as I lean into the back of the van. The obnoxious motors roaring outside are the only things that break up our moment.

Axle steps back, taking my hand in his.

"Party is about to start. You just put us back in business with your large order," he says, smirking at me. "So, tonight is a celebration."

"I'd rather just celebrate with you." I start walking toward the door, but he tugs my hand, pulling me back to him as he kisses me again, backing me against the wall.

I smile against his lips as he lifts me up, dropping my ass on a steel table before stepping between my legs.

He shoves my skirt up and jerks my panties down. I lift up, letting him work the annoying underwear down, and they drop to my ankles. I'm vaguely aware of them falling off as he runs his thumb over—

"Yo—*whoa.* My bad," someone says, causing Axle to jerk my skirt down as he turns a glare in the direction of the voice.

I clear my throat, glancing over as well to see Dash staring at the ceiling, a big-ass grin on his face.

"I guess that means she likes the merchandise," the dick says.

"Fucking comedian," Axle says dryly, bending to pick my panties up and shove them into his pocket.

I'd sort of like to have those on again, but I'd rather not discuss that at this exact moment.

I hop off the counter, and Axle laces his fingers with mine, pulling me with him as we head toward the door. Dash laughs as Axle shoves him aside, and we walk into the throngs of people who weren't here when we went into the garage.

Cases upon cases of beer are getting stocked in the long row of glass-door coolers behind the bar. And liquor bottles are loading the shelves, guys opening boxes full of them.

Glad to see their priorities are in order.

"You gonna get inked?" Dash asks me.

I open my mouth to speak, but Axle beats me to it. "I'm not Drex, and I'm not putting my name on her body."

I arch an eyebrow as a slow grin curves Dash's lips.

"Then you need to make it known she's with you to every-damn-body. Drex had a hell of a time with Eve."

Axle doesn't seem bothered. "Herrin's crew was here then. They're not now. These guys are assholes, but they won't cross that line."

He looks at me like he's reassuring me, but I remember the dipshit he had to punch after he got too insistent. I decide to stick close to him all night just in case.

"Looks like that fucker got him a blonde now. What the hell, Axle?" a guy with a long beard asks.

"Same girl. New hair," he tells the beast of a man who winks at me, but not in a creepy way.

Drex walks up, three beers in his hand, and passes two off to Dash and Axle. I take it upon myself to lean over the bar and grab some tequila and shot glasses, while they discuss party central.

As I start taking a few shots, I feel Axle's eyes on me, even as Drex speaks to him.

Eve saunters over with Colleen, and I nod at them in greeting, since Colleen did just make my hair awesome earlier. It makes me less inclined to slap her for the way she balked at Axle's scars that day.

I lean into his side as I take my third shot, and his arm goes around my shoulders as the group talks about fun stories from the past. A lot of girls are here, and the other guys are all lounging around, watching them as they dance to the music that is pumping throughout.

I prefer skating to dancing, but with all these people here, it's unlikely I can skate.

"You want to dance?" I ask Axle, nudging him with my elbow.

He looks at me like I just asked him to run through a row of hot coals.

"I don't dance."

"Don't worry about looking stupid. It's just fucking with your clothes on," I say, patting his chest. "You can handle that."

Dash turns his head, laughing into his hand.

"I said I don't dance. Not that I couldn't." Axle returns his attention to Drex, resuming the conversation I apparently interrupted.

Obviously I don't mention the sweet swaying we did at the hotel. I'm sure they'd take away his surly card if I did.

"I'll dance," Colleen says to me.

She's been...nice lately. Maybe because she knows she pissed me off, and that I'm *someone* who just ordered a shit-ton of vehicles and that I run a crime family.

My bad. Next time I skate and rant, I'll keep the music off so I can whisper-yell at them.

"Me too," Eve chimes in.

Drex grabs Eve by the arm, but I note that the hold is gentle. "Stay close."

She nods like she doesn't mind being bossed around. Drex is freaking bossy.

Is Axle that bossy?

I don't think so. I'd have a problem with a bossy guy. Though he does have his bossy moments. Maybe I only find it hot when it's Axle. No other guy is allowed to be bossy because they're not him. Totally not hypocritical of me at all.

"Shots first," Colleen says, moving to my abandoned tequila.

As she pours three shots, I eye Eve's tattoo. *Property of Drex.* No joke. That is tattooed on her shoulder.

"You let him put that on you, or you wanted it on you?" I ask her.

She tosses back a shot, and so do I. Colleen pours us another round as Eve answers me.

"You weren't here when Herrin was. The guys were just as dangerous as they are now, but there were a lot of sickos, too. Some of them didn't hear *no* for an answer. This kept me safe. The other girls have tats on their wrists to keep them safe from other clubs."

Colleen's wrist has a dark rose above a DC tat. Apparently the rose is to cover up the old DD tat. Or so I assume.

I glance over at Axle, wondering if he'd shit his pants if I got his name tattooed on me. Then I grin. I'm almost tempted to permanently slap his name on me just to watch him freak out a little.

I'd totally put it on my vagina for ultimate shock value.

CHAPTER 24

AXLE

Jude is drinking a beer, standing beside Dash and talking about the new girls who just came in from the strip club. I'm barely listening to any of it, because I'm on the verge of being drunk.

For the first time in a long damn time.

Hell, I forgot I could get drunk.

"How'd she like the final product?" Drex asks me, gesturing toward Maya when he sees me staring.

"Her panties are in his pocket, so I'd say she was impressed," Dash says with a fuck-wad grin on his face.

Drex arches a questioning eyebrow at me as I shake my head. "She liked the haul," I state dismissively, trying *not* to think about the fact she's wearing a skirt with nothing under it as she dances with Eve and Colleen.

Fortunately, she's not twirling. That damn skirt would fly up if she was twirling. I almost hauled her out of here when she leaned over the bar and I saw the bottom curve of her ass.

"Axle?"

Drex's voice has me snapping out of my trance as I turn to face him again, my movements sluggish. I'm pretty sure that grin of his is mocking me, but...well, what was I saying?

"I don't think he heard the question," Dash says, snickering lightly.

"I asked if Maya is going to be sticking around for a while," Drex tells me.

"Yeah," I say, looking back at her. "She is."

177

I've decided it's the safest, even if it's also for my own selfish reasons.

"How're the hits on Herrin doing?" Dash directs that question toward me.

"Good so far. Most of the surrounding clubs had no idea what went down, although there were several rumors floating around. So planting the seed that it was because Herrin turned and started informing the FBI was easy enough. It's starting to take root. Drug bust downtown worked out in our favor, since Herrin's guys were going to run the drugs for those junkies. Junkies are the easiest to convince, because they're already overly paranoid," I state flatly. "Just a matter of time before more people start believing it."

"Which means someone will eventually take him out for us or turn him over to us," Jude says, joining the conversation. "Especially since part of the equation is adding in Benny's son. People believe Ben and Herrin are linked, since it all went down at the same time, which is why Herrin is probably working so hard to remind people there's an alliance between his crew and the Hell Breathers."

Like a lightbulb went off in his head, Drex's slow smile spreads. "What if we could convince Benny Pop *was* working with his fuckwit son during all that shit?"

I start to speak, to tell them we already have too many rumors in the mix and this is just drunk talk, when Sledge walks over, interrupting us, a broad smile on his face.

"Just got word from a friend of mine that the Bloodhounds are out for Herrin's blood. Please ignore the accidental pun in there," Sledge tells us.

Bloodhounds are a fairly new, but completely ruthless gang in Dallas.

"Herrin was supposed to make a run for them," Sledge goes on, "and distribute their drugs to their dealers along the west coast. Two days after their meeting, the feds showed up and did a raid— confiscated close to three million just in heroine. Either someone is helping our little rumor gain some merit, or our rumor is true, and

Herrin really is giving the feds some info to keep the heat off his back."

Maya crashes against my side, just as Eve returns to Drex, and that ends the conversation. As Maya smiles up at me, Jude says something about getting a lap dance from any brave strippers.

They have to be brave because…well, his ex is someone they know will slit their throats. But a couple of new girls don't know Sarah, so he might have a little luck.

I lose all interest in everything surrounding us as I lift Maya, dropping her ass on the bar and stepping in between her legs. With the bar being so high, her head is a little above mine, and she gets the higher angle on the kiss for once.

She grins against my lips like I just did something right, and I tug her closer, making sure no one can see past my body to where her skirt has her exposed. Her nails softly graze my scalp as she wraps her ankles around my waist.

"I think I like you drunk," she murmurs against my lips.

"Not drunk. Just getting there." I tug her bottom lip between my teeth, but before I can take things farther, Drake's voice is busting up the moment.

"It's not a purse," he's telling someone as I turn my head to the group, staying put between Maya's legs. "It's a satchel. You cumstains try to carry shit when you're working with crutches. You get inventive."

"You mean you get a purse," Drex deadpans, amusement dancing in his eyes as Drake glares at him, reaching his hand into the green bag that does look suspiciously like a purse.

"You fuckheads probably need to deal with this pronto. It's never a good thing when someone drops a package on my doorstep and tells me to deliver it to you."

Drex reaches out, taking a manila envelope from Drake and ripping it open, pulling out a thumb drive.

"I'll grab a fucking laptop," Dash says on a sigh as he puts his drink down.

I glance over, seeing Drex tear Tiffany — the newest girl to join the ranks — off Jude before leaning down to his ear. Tiffany tries to step into Jude before he walks off, but he just lifts her and drops her ass to the chair he vacated, before following Drex back to us.

"What's going on?" Maya asks, biting on her lip.

"Stay with Eve." I jerk my gaze to Drake and point at him. "You stay right here. Anyone fucks with her — "

"I can handle babysitting detail. I have Eve with me almost daily," Drake interrupts.

"I work there. You don't babysit," Eve drawls.

I get what Drake is saying even if she doesn't, and I turn and follow the others into the meeting room as Dash finishes setting up the screen, linking it to the laptop.

Drex hands him the drive as I shut the doors, sealing everyone else out.

Sledge props up next to Jude on the wall, and we all wait really impatiently as Dash takes forever. "Sorry," he grumbles, finally getting it to play. "Little fucking too drunk for this."

"At least you're not — "

Drex's words die as a scream rips through the room, coming from the screen. My stomach roils as I stare at Liza being held down on a table, fighting and struggling as Herrin's laughter comes through the speakers.

My eyes dart to Sledge to see his eyes wide, his face pale, and his knees wobbling.

Liza screams again, and I realize Hershel — Herrin's right hand — is fucking her as Herrin ducks his head into the screen, grinning at the camera.

"If you can't keep your women safe, then it's just a matter of time before I finally get my hands on you." Another scream interrupts him, as Liza begs for them to stop. I swallow down the bile as Herrin chuckles, his eyes returning to the camera. "One down. More to come, son. Keep telling people I'm a fucking rat, and there will be far worse than this."

The screen goes blank, and Sledge darts to the screen, ripping it off the wall and smashing it against the ground. Dash leaps back to avoid the flying debris, and I lean against the table, feeling my heartbeat drone in my ears.

Jude slams his fist into the wall. Drex is shouting something, barely reining in his own temper. Dash is on the phone, trying to get a beat on Herrin.

"Someone thinks Herrin is hiding out two towns over at the old factory we used to own," Dash says. But he's wrong. That's probably a fake lead planted by Herrin himself.

He wants us to go to that old factory, because that's a lot farther away than he is.

"He's at the Royal Inn right outside of town," I say, silently seething as I straighten. The buzz from the alcohol is gone. All that's left is that never-ending rage that loves to come out and play.

"What?" Drex snaps.

"I've been to all sorts of motels around town for business meets. That peacock paper in the background; it's only at the Royal Inn. They shut down six months ago and the place is set for demolition. That's where Herrin is."

"I'm getting a message from a guy swearing he's holed up at the factory. They saw him ride in there today," Jude is arguing.

Sledge looks at me, his body tense and tight, ready to break. "You sure it's the Royal Inn?" he asks, eyes on me.

I nod. "I'm positive. The factory is a smoke screen and probably a trap. That paper is, without a doubt, that hotel."

Sledge slams his foot into the monitor one last time before sprinting out the door. We all follow, and Drex barks out orders to the others that have every man tossing away a beer or a girl and rushing to the hangar.

Maya is looking at me questioningly as I stalk to her, shakily taking in a breath, and doing all I fucking can not to lose it. Sledge and Liza have been on and off for over fifteen years. I can't even fucking imagine right now.

"What's going—"

"Stay here," I say to Drake, cutting Maya off. "Stay with her, Eve, and the other girls. Keep everyone inside, and lock the place down. *Do not* take your eyes off the security cam until we return. Got it?"

He nods slowly, eyes wide as he swallows. "Yeah. Got it."

"You got a gun in that purse?" I ask him.

"It's a fucking satchel," he bites out. "And yes. There's a gun."

Maya says something, but I can't hear it right now. All I can see is Liza on repeat, the way her eyes teared up as she stared into the camera.

That could have been Maya. And that's the most selfish fucking worry. I've known Liza for years, and my first thought is that I'm so fucking relieved it's not Maya.

She doesn't follow, knowing this isn't the time, and I load up, hurrying the motions of revving my bike as Dash passes out guns.

Sledge tears out, leading the way, and I ignore the fucked up feeling in my gut that tries to get me not to leave.

CHAPTER 25

Eve immediately walks toward the room the guys ran out of and took every other person with a penis — besides Drake — with them. They're acting irrationally, running out half-cocked, and I'm too curious to find out why.

I've learned this is their routine — strike back immediately. No forethought. No planning.

Someone could easily be using it against them.

Eve doesn't bat an eye when I join her, and I hear Drake trying to calm the girls down as Colleen jogs into the room. "I'll handle all the girls if you'll tell me what the hell is going on," Colleen tells Eve.

Eve is typing a password onto the laptop, waiting for it to start. I move in behind her, and Colleen does as well. The second the image pops up on screen, Colleen gags, the scream from a woman sending her to her knees.

Eve cuts her gaze away, choking back a gag of her own. But I've seen worse. I've seen a lot worse.

"Who is that?" I ask them flatly, wondering why this woman's eyes are glued to the screen and who she is to them.

"That's Liza," Eve says through strain, still averting her eyes.

A man comes into view, making threats. Apparently that's the notorious Herrin.

"How could they do that to her?" Colleen asks, but I'm more focused on the woman I've heard about a few times.

"Liza is Sledge's girlfriend who runs the bar, right?" I ask.

Eve shuts the laptop, standing up and breathing in and out harshly as Colleen wipes her mouth and eyes.

"Yes," Eve says quietly.

"Somewhere they launder the money," I say to myself.

Outside of the box, I'm not attached to this woman the way they are. I'm also really paranoid, so I could be wrong about my suspicions, and know how bad this could turn out if I'm wrong.

"What are you doing?" Eve asks as I pull out my phone.

Axle's phone goes to voicemail, so I start typing a text, hoping he reads it.

"Liza's been with the club a long time, hasn't she?" I ask Eve.

She wipes her eyes and clears her throat. "Over twenty-five years."

Twenty-five years of loyalty.

Blowing out a heavy breath, I send Axle that text.

ME: I think you're driving into a trap!

This could go really, *really* badly. I call Axle again, hearing it go to voicemail. "Call me. I think you're riding into a trap!"

"What?!" Eve demands as her head lifts from where she's telling Drake what's going on. I didn't even know he was in here yet.

There's no telling what Sledge has told Liza. I know she's unaware of my origins, but hell, she may know a lot of other things.

That thought alone has my stomach plummeting.

"Would Liza know about the cars for today?" I ask Eve quietly, crowding her space.

She gets a quizzical look on her face. "Yeah. We're having a party because of the big order, because the guys always do that for a big order, and it's a show to the rest that the club is still in business."

I turn and walk out, texting Axle again. Herrin never gave any indication verbally as to where they were, and there was nothing too obvious in the image as a landmark. Something got them running out of here with a direction in mind.

ME: They're setting a trap for you and coming here!

ME: Please hear this message dinging. Please!

"Why are you asking about Liza knowing about the cars?" she asks quietly.

I didn't realize they celebrated business or I would have known the person who cleans the money wouldn't need to ask where it was. They'd just need to know when the merchandise was ready— in order to stop the money from ever coming in, unaware of my arrangement with the club.

"Maya, please, answer me," she says, following behind me as I send another desperate text to Axle.

"Axle said all the women get escorts to and from their businesses," I say without looking at her. "Who were Liza's?"

"It varies. Liza just picks a couple of guys out at the club to escort her home, since there's always a group of them there. She closes most nights. Why do you keep asking questions about her?"

Telling her would be stupid. Because she'd tell Drex. And he's going to want to kill me for issuing that level of disrespect toward someone of Liza's stature within the club.

If we live to tell anything, that is.

"Of course she does," I mutter to myself as I jog upstairs to Axle's room.

The door is locked, and I silently curse as I jog back down.

"Do you have any weapons at all?" I ask Eve.

She blinks at me, and Drake snorts a little as he uses his crutches to carry him across the floor. The strippers—hate to refer to them as merely that—are in the seating area, watching us with guarded expressions, trying to stay calm.

Drake lifts a false panel, and the wall becomes a hollowed out shelving unit that is loaded with every type of gun I could ask for.

Only problem is, I've never actually had to shoot at someone. I hope the target practice I've had has actually prepared me for real life.

I'd love to see AJ right about now — not Sarah. Because in my head, she's two different entities, and I need the badass killer version.

"Why?" Drake asks me as I pick a gun and make sure it's loaded.

"Axle and the guys are driving into a possible trap. And we're likely to get hit. Please keep trying to call him," I state calmly.

"Colleen, get the girls underground. We'll come too," Eve tells her.

Colleen curses at the same time Drake does, but they both launch into action.

"This is why I simply tattoo people," Drake says on a grumbled breath. "So that I don't get shot at. So why the hell am I so close to flying bullets all the damn time?"

He glares at his phone next.

"Answer your phone. I'm a man on crutches and bullets are coming, damn it!"

The brace is still necessary, since he's struggling to learn to walk on it again. Apparently the injury was really nasty.

Colleen is ushering people into the back passage, through a secure door that Eve gives her the combination to. The girls follow her without asking questions.

Just as Drake starts barking at Axle's voicemail again, I hear the first shot burst through the glass, followed by what seems like a thousand other bullets. Drake dives on Eve, tackling her to the ground and covering her body with his near the door.

I drop, landing on my stomach, trying to crawl toward the doorway as glass bursts way overhead, near the top of the warehouse, and rains down on us. Ignoring the multiple stings, I continue to crawl over the broken glass, keeping my body low to the ground.

Eve and Drake manage to make it, but before I can get there, a loud, rumbling explosion bursts open the hangar door to the warehouse, and I scream, curling into a ball as the pulse wafts over me.

My ears rattle as smoke billows in, and I hear a ringing as gunfire continues to rage on. My eyes open, but I don't see what's going on around me.

All I can see is that building exploding back in New York. I can hear myself screaming for my parents, helplessly watching.

My breaths hit my ears, and I'm vaguely aware of two hands dragging me back until I'm shoved against a sealed door. Colleen is banging on the door, and I can hear Eve screaming at her through the other side, telling her the code, panicking when it doesn't open.

And slowly, I come back to the warehouse we're in, seeing the smoke. Seeing the scorch marks. Seeing the small flames that the overhead sprinklers try to snuff out.

But I can't move.

Frozen, I listen to the world around me, staring unblinking, as my throat tries to close up. Until I'm suddenly scrambling away from Colleen, curling up in a corner that makes me feel safer.

CHAPTER 26

AXLE

We stop at the end of the block, and I dig into my pocket to grab my phone that's been vibrating against my thigh since we left. We're only ten minutes out, which is pissing me off.

Herrin is taunting us by being this close.

"Hershel's bike is definitely parked out there, along with a few others I recognize," Jude says, walking from around the corner and coming back to his ride, while I listen to my messages, feeling my stomach sink.

"Answer your fucking phone!" Drake is shouting in the message that's just a few seconds old. "Maya says they're coming here. She's fucking positive for some reason, and—*fuck!*"

His voice cuts out as gunfire sounds against my ear—rapid, unrelenting gunfire.

Screams tear through the message, and I hang up, revving my bike. "The girls are under fire. You deal with this!" I shout at Drex, whose eyes widen.

"Go," Sledge says to Drex, his eyes on the Royal Inn. "Leave half with me."

Drex starts snapping out orders for which ones need to follow us, but I'm already driving, weaving in and out of traffic the second I get turned around.

My entire body is strung tight, and an old, very distant feeling I haven't felt in years almost chokes me.

Fear.

I haven't been this scared since I was a kid, but right now, I'm barely holding it together as I skid around a curve, almost colliding with a car that manages to hit a ditch instead of me.

It doesn't slow me down, because it's not my life that has fear settling on me like a tangible force.

It's Maya's.

Cutting a ten minute drive in half, I slide in sideways on our street, seeing the building come into view. Sirens wail in the distance, probably on their way to us, and my stomach drops when I see the smoke blowing through the window near the top.

It's not on fire, but I can tell they just blew the fucking hangar to pieces.

I leap off my Harley before it even comes to a full stop, letting it skid across the pavement on its side as I burst through the door.

Colleen is frantically pulling at the door near the back that probably sealed after the explosion, a safety mechanism. She's screaming, and ash falls down, landing everywhere like a blanket of gray snow. Wires hang and flicker with electricity. Glass is shattered everywhere.

The worst of the damage is closer to the hangar, leaving half the warehouse barely affected.

My eyes scan the place as Drex bursts in behind me, rushing to Colleen. More panic rises when I can't find Maya, fear ratcheting up more by the second.

"Maya!" I shout, barely getting the word out as my heartbeat echoes inside my own ears.

Drex is typing in the disable code to open the door, and I rush to it, looking for Maya to come out. Women pour out, including Eve. Drake hobbles out, grabbing and hugging Colleen as his eyes flick to mine.

"Where's Maya?!" I bark.

Before he can answer, my eyes dart to a corner, and I see her. My entire body is filled with so much instant relief that my legs almost give out.

"Don't!" Colleen shouts at me as I start walking toward Maya. "Don't! She's freaking out! Don't touch her!"

I ignore her, watching as Maya rocks, her eyes wide and fixed at the end where the explosion was. It's not hard to figure out that an explosion is rattling her, considering she watched her parents die in one.

Slowly, I kneel down, but when my hand reaches out to connect with her knee, she jerks, panic clear on her face. But the second her eyes meet mine, tears start leaking, and she reaches for me.

I lift her from the ground, carrying her toward the exit, getting her out of this hazard and away from the visual. She clings to me, her face buried against my neck.

Carrying her like a broken bride, I step outside, walking toward the back where SUVs are pulling up.

"I have to get her out of here before the cops arrive," I tell Byson as he glances at her.

"Take this. It was one of the few that survived in the other garage," he tells me, putting the keys back inside the ride as I open the passenger seat door for Maya.

She doesn't speak when I put her in the seat or buckle her up. Drex comes running out, Eve's hand clasped tightly in his as I shut the door on Maya.

Maya is just staring blankly ahead, possibly not seeing anything.

"Get her out of here, too," Drex says as he opens the back door for Eve. "Last thing we need to deal with is them asking questions about her, since her uncle is currently 'missing'."

I just nod. He'll know where to find me.

Maya says nothing as I start pulling us away from the warehouse, and Eve blows out a shaky breath.

"What now? That's where we were hiding out," Eve says quietly.

"We weren't hiding," I tell her tightly.

As I back all the way down the alley, I notice her in the rearview as her shaky hands swipe an errant hair out of her face.

"It all just happened so fast," she says as I get us turned around and head down the street. "The blast hit, we managed to make it to the door, but it slammed shut. Colleen had run out to help Maya, and we couldn't get it back open after it sealed shut. We were terrified Herrin's guys were about to burst in with Colleen and Maya stuck on the other side."

My hands grip the steering wheel as I glance over to Maya, seeing her motionless with that blank stare.

"Pressure sensor. If it senses an explosion of any kind, it's set to shut and seal to preserve the stability of the foundation, ensuring the blast doesn't cause harm. It's designed to be a panic room, so to speak. Or a panic floor, actually."

I cut the wheel, driving us toward one of the off-grid houses Drex owns. It's big enough to hold several of us. We'll scatter for a few days, then regroup after finding a new spot to call ground zero. Going home is sure as hell out of the question.

I reach over, taking Maya's cold, limp hand, noticing how she doesn't even react.

"How'd she know it was a trap?" I ask Eve.

"I have no idea. We watched that disgusting video Herrin sent, and suddenly she was asking questions and calling you."

"What kind of questions?" I ask her, turning down another road that takes us deeper into the desert.

"Questions about Liza mostly. Who escorts her home? How long has she been with the club? Other questions like that. And then she went into panic mode. Which I'm glad she did. We were all at the meeting room that was blown to bits. We'd be dead right now if she hadn't told us to go downstairs. Just attempting that put us all at the other end of the building."

I squeeze Maya's hand in mine, but I get only a small squeeze back in return. At least that's something.

Eve grows quiet and pensive, and I try not to think about what Maya must have meant with her questions. Sledge and I would be in a fight if she brought those up aloud, because Sledge would want her dead for an accusation like that.

And normally Sledge is the level-headed one.

A text comes through on my phone as I get stuck at a red light, and I release Maya's hand so I can text Jude back.

JUDE: Herrin is still in the wind, but we have ten guys, including Hershel. They were surprised AF that we showed up. Got Liza too. Sledge is gonna fuck Hershel up himself.

I glance at Maya from the corner of my eye, find her still staring endlessly, and text him back.

ME: We took a big loss too. Warehouse is fucked. The idea was to get us out so they could drive by and blow our shit to pieces.

JUDE: Yeah. That sucks, but no one was hurt or taken.

ME: What was Liza like when you found her?

JUDE: Not physically hurt, but you know. Probably emotionally fucked.

ME: But how was she? Were there guys holding her at gunpoint? Was she surprised or scared when you busted in? Did she act like she was emotionally fucked? Give me the details.

There. I fucking asked. And it's Jude, so he'll get pissed, but he'll keep his mouth shut about me asking that.

JUDE: I'mma pretend you're not asking this. And you're gonna pretend I'm not saying this. But she was alone in a room with no guns trained on her. Looks like she'd just gotten out of the shower not long before and was watching TV. And definitely surprised to see us, but she rushed to Sledge. Thing is, she was unguarded, but that doesn't mean she could have run and risked them seeing her. I mean, right? Careful, Axle. Don't poke this one.

ME: Just pretend like it's nothing? What happens the next time they use her against us? It'd be a stupid thing to forget.

JUDE: Fair point. Poke it delicately then. Like a virgin.

I'm not even sure if I'm reading into this or not. I didn't see her with my own eyes, and I don't know what made Maya so suspicious. Obviously, I'm worked up and getting ahead of myself.

One more text comes through as I pull up to the isolated house in the middle of nowhere.

JUDE: Take it from someone who knows, it's really fucking hard to believe your girl betrayed you.

Eve pushes her door open as I park, and I put my phone away and do the same. Maya weakly pushes her own door open, and I go to lift her from the passenger seat, cradling her against my chest as Eve goes to the front door of the house.

As I tell Eve the code, Maya puts her arms around my neck, nuzzling her nose along my jaw. At least she's coming out of her catatonic state.

We step inside, and Eve shuts and locks the door. The house is large, with seven bedrooms and even more bathrooms. Eve looks around with her hands on her hips.

"Whose is this?"

"Drex's," I tell her.

"Why the hell didn't I know about it?"

I shrug, carrying Maya to a bedroom I've only ever seen once.

"No one but me knew about this property. Drex bought this years ago, but kept it a secret. He only came out here when he needed a break from all things Death Dealer. And he thought if his sister ever needed a place to lie low, he'd put her here until he could figure out her next move."

Eve grows quiet, and I turn to see her eyes fixed on Maya in my arms. "Let me know if you need any help," Eve finally says, offering me a small, tight smile.

I nod before ducking into the bedroom, and I gently place Maya on her feet. She sways, but leans against the wall, her eyes on me.

Brushing her hair away from her face, I take inventory. Her face is smudged with ash, and her clothes are just as dirty. I'm just glad the blast was contained enough to not hit the other end of the warehouse. I'm sure those weren't Herrin's intentions, but the hangar is tougher than it looks, and it took the brunt of the hit.

"I'm okay," she finally says, though she has to clear her throat afterwards.

Moving away from her, I clench and unclench my fists, feeling fucking useless as I move into the bathroom and turn the water on for the tub.

As it fills up, I move back into the bedroom. She's already pulling her clothes off without having to be asked, and I shut the door to the room, giving us privacy.

As soon as she's bare, she moves into the bathroom, eyes on the tub.

I rifle through the damn sink cabinet, hoping the woman who tends to this house for Drex has left some supplies. All I find is a bottle of shampoo and conditioner, so I dump a big glob of the shampoo into the water, letting the faucet make a few bubbles with it.

"It's clean," I grumble. "Drex has a housekeeper who comes once a week and cleans everything to keep the dust away. He hasn't been out here in over a year, but he keeps her on payroll, even through this rough patch we had."

Maya gives me a small smile as she steps in.

As she gets seated and leans her head back over the edge, her eyes close. I use the opportunity to run my eyes over the small, barely-there cuts on her arms and legs from where she likely crawled over the glass, trying to make it to the door.

Her blood looks like flakes of paint on the small cuts, but it's still enough to send the anger simmering close to the surface.

"I don't know what happened," she finally says quietly. "I just froze. Colleen started trying to shake me out of it, and I screamed. As soon as she gave me space, I froze again."

I crouch next to the tub, putting my hand in the water and testing the temperature, even though she's not complaining.

"I had a gun in my hand, just knowing they were going to come in. I'm glad they didn't. After that blast, I just...*froze*. I've never had that happen," she goes on, her voice barely carrying over the steady stream of the water that's filling the tub.

Spotting a pack of sponges, I open it and pull one out, busying myself and trying to rein in my rage. She could have been fucking killed.

"I should have checked my phone sooner." The words come out gruff, my own voice strained right now.

It's like I can't take my eyes off her, worried if I do, she suddenly won't be here anymore. It's a fucked up feeling I've never experienced before.

"I'm glad you checked it at all," she says on a sigh, the tension leaving her body little by little.

I drench the sponge, using the shampoo to soap it up, and start washing some of the ash off her neck.

We stay silent after that. Her eyes remain closed as I sponge off the rest of her body, turning off the water when it's high enough.

She leans up, her back to me, and I take the opportunity to wash it too.

"You could climb in with me," she says softly.

If I got in there with her, I'd fuck her. Not because I'm turned on, but because I would need physical reassurance that she's really safe and not an illusion. Son of a bitch, what's wrong with me?

"I'll stick to the outside of the tub," I say under my breath.

She catches my hand, her eyes on mine. She's been in there for so long now that her fingers are pruning and the water is getting chilly.

"Thank you," she says hoarsely.

She leans in to kiss me, but a loud banging on the bedroom door halts it from happening. I straighten and walk out, though it's hard as hell to do, and close the door behind me.

Opening the bedroom door, my eyes collide with Drex's. His jaw is tight, his eyes are lethal, and I can tell we're finally going to get some blood on our hands. I couldn't be fucking happier to hear that, because I feel like I'm drowning in uncharted territory.

Fear.

Worry.

Dread.

All of those are emotions I never feel. Anger? Sure. It's my best fucking friend. But I'm almost a novice with any of the other emotions.

"Drake is bringing the girls some clothes when he rides out with Dash. Sledge is here—"

"Is Liza here?" I ask, the question blurting out without hesitation.

His brow furrows. "No. She's at the hospital getting checked out. We left her with a group of guys ready to kill a Death Dealer if they see them. But we have Hershel in the shed around back. The other guys they got from the bust are already dead and hanging near the factory where they tried to send us for a fucking trap."

I nod, unsure if I want to get into the Liza situation with Drex.

"Sledge might kill Hershel too soon if I leave him alone out there for long with him. I need your help on this. You can calm us all the fuck down, and right now, we sure as hell need that."

I swallow the knot in my throat as I give him a bitter smile. "As of right now, I'm not so sure how calm I'll be. Maya didn't get behind that door. Glass cut her up—shallow cuts, but they're still there. If Herrin had known about her, she would have been taken. They'd have come in after her."

"If he'd known Eve was there with just Drake watching after her, he'd have come in. But he didn't. His target was the new vehicles, because he's unaware of Maya being a sympathetic client and assumes this is going to hit us hard and get us into a mess with said client."

Which makes me really fucking happy that Sledge kept Maya a secret from Liza. And I can't believe I'm seriously thinking that. But Maya saw something that had her convinced we were running into a trap and that the club was about to be hit.

The club was hit, and conveniently, several people spotted Herrin at the factory where they tried to lead us.

For a likely trap.

He runs a hand through his hair like he's frustrated. "I'm not cut out to be the P. I'm a solid VP, but running things is different. I'm still in the frame of mind that someone will reel me back if I'm ready to rush in, guns blazing, ready for a fight. And Pop is using that against me."

I lean against the doorframe, crossing my arms over my chest. "You're a good P. Stop letting him use his knowledge of you against you and start using your knowledge of him against him. Think like Herrin. You're the only one who can do that."

He runs a hand over the scruff on his jaw and nods absently, staring at nothing in particular.

I push away from the door and go back to the bathroom, poking my head inside in time to see Maya wrapping a towel around her body.

"I need to handle something. Stay inside."

Her eyes meet mine, and she nods, being too quiet. Usually by now she has something to say.

"Drake is bringing you some clothes."

"I hope he brings me some underwear," she says on a sigh. "Otherwise, you'll have to dig that pair out of your pocket and your pervy panty-sniffing will have to be put on hold."

A smile slips over my face unexpectedly as she smirks at me. Looks like she's recovered.

"Stay inside," I repeat before stepping out.

Drex is telling Eve basically the same thing when I step out of the bedroom, and she's berating him for not telling her about this house. My lips twitch as I pass them.

Eve is simply trying to take his mind off feeling like he's failed. Once again. So she's getting him riled up—something she's damn good at.

I spend the short walk to the shed trying to get my temper under control so that *I'm* not one who accidentally kills Hershel before time.

As soon as I step inside, I see Hershel's head snap to the side, blood spraying from his mouth as a seething Sledge shakes out his fist and takes a step back.

Hershel looks like he's already been worked over enough for the day. His right eye is swollen shut. His lips are bleeding and swollen as well. His face is one step away from being mangled.

But the sadist is laughing even as he spits out another wad of blood. Because he wants to taunt Sledge into killing him.

Sledge raises his fist, but I speak before he can strike. "You can kill him now, or you can make it last for months."

Sledge hesitates, his eyes darting to me as he breathes heavily, fury etching his features.

"Because if he dies right now, he doesn't tell us anything. If he lives, he lives to suffer another day. And another. And another."

I pull my shirt off—something I do when I'm ready to scare the hell out of people who *think* they're a badass. My back goes to Sledge, giving him the visual, as I speak again.

"I know how to make the pain tolerance grow little by little, until you can handle so much pain that you're incapable of passing out from it anymore. You're forced to endure every single strike. Every single cut. Every single ounce of agonizing torture without the reprieve of your body shutting down to spare you."

I look over my shoulder to see Sledge lowering his fist, nodding at me once.

"I know how to make him pray for hope to survive because death seems like an elusive dream that will never come true," I go on. "And I can assure you, that after six months of being put through this sort of hell, he'll forget his own name. He'll beg you for mercy. He'll cry and piss himself when you step into view. He'll be your bitch, in other words."

Sledge takes a step back, blowing out a breath as he gets himself under control. Hershel has paled a little, reluctant fear etching his face. All these years, he's never heard me speak about the scars. He knows I'm not bluffing when I tell Sledge I can coach him on how to completely ruin a person.

"Not only will you completely wreck his body, you'll destroy his mind," I go on. "He's too old to recover."

A dark smile graces my lips as Hershel cuts his gaze to Sledge.

"Liza was good. Especially when she was screaming," he bites out, trying to rile Sledge into a furious retaliation that will kill him.

Sledge's lips twitch, not at all rattled.

"Let's do this your way, kid," Sledge tells me, his eyes shifting toward Hershel. "Because I want to see him beg."

Not speaking, I lift my shirt, tying the sleeves together, as Hershel tries to rock the chair he's tied to, but it's nailed to the boards of the shed's floor. After constructing a makeshift bag out of my shirt, I drop it over Hershel's head.

And with that, I turn Sledge into my pupil, telling him the things that he can do to Hershel.

Telling him the things I know.

Because they were done to me.

CHAPTER 27

Maya

Eve and I are at the window, watching as Drex, Axle, and Sledge talk outside the shed. They've been out there for a really long time.

For some reason, Axle is shirtless.

"Will you hurt me if I ask how he got the scars? I understand I'm just being nosy, but I can't help myself. I feel like these guys know my life, inside and out, yet I barely know anything about them," Eve says on a sigh, dropping to a chair and looking at me. "*And* they act like it's their right to know everything about me."

"He got them as a child. That's all I know," I tell her, understanding the feeling of everyone knowing your life but knowing nothing of theirs.

The Demon's Child comment he made has sent a few theories into my head. Only one makes sense, but I keep it to myself, feeling like it's Axle secret to share.

"He sees red when rape is brought up. It makes me a little queasy worrying that's what happened to him as a child, and that's why it's such a trigger," she says quietly.

An uneasiness settles in my stomach, but I don't think that's what it was. Still, I don't share that with Eve, and she takes my silence as a sign to change topics.

"How did you know about the hit coming to us? What'd you see on that video?" she asks me seriously.

I slant my gaze toward her, wondering what Drex would do if he heard my theory. After having Axle be so attentive and concerned, I also wonder how he would react, only I'm not as scared of his reaction anymore.

"She looked at the camera," I tell Eve, my eyes moving back to the window.

"What?"

I shake my head, deciding against telling her. "I'm going to go lie down for a bit."

She looks like she wants to press for more, probably confused at what I said, but I turn and walk to the bedroom. I'm wrapped in a towel; there are no clean clothes to wear, since Drake hasn't arrived yet.

Dropping the towel, I climb into the bed that smells fresh, as though the bedding was just washed yesterday. No sooner than I get comfortable and covered up, Axle walks in.

His gaze meets mine as he shuts the door and starts undoing his jeans. As soon as he's down to his black boxers, he comes to the bed, pulls back the covers, and slides in next to me.

I don't hesitate to quickly shuffle over to his side. This day started out so damn good. And went south so damn fast.

"What's going on in the shed?" I ask him.

"We're torturing Herrin's right hand for information," he answers flatly, no hesitation at all.

"Okay," I state simply, hoping he doesn't elaborate.

Blowing out a breath, I peer up at him, and he looks down at me, his hand resting on the curve of my waist.

"Go to sleep. I'll stay in here with you until the others get here."

I shake my head. "I'm scared to go to sleep right now. I'm afraid I'll dream."

He runs his other hand through my hair, turning to face me a little better. "You froze because you were back there...back to the day your parents were killed in the explosion," he says softly.

My brow furrows. "How'd you know th—"

"I was in a hospital from ten to twelve while they worked on fixing my fucked up head. They kept me in a colorful room with the lights on all the time the first year, because when it was dark, I was back in my own hell. They spent a lot of time sedating me before the doctors made the suggestion."

I swallow the lump in my throat as he talks about this so dispassionately, as though he's not opening up his darkest secrets for me.

"So it stopped when you were ten?" I ask him quietly. Since he said he was in the hospital at that age, that's all I can figure.

"No," he says, sighing. "Only the pain stopped at ten. It took me a long damn time to get out of that place mentally."

Even though I don't want to push him, I still ask him, "What happened? Why were you in the hospital?"

"They realized I needed the psych ward when they were tending to my burns. I was begging them not to hurt me, screaming for the light to stay on. I never got much light in the hole."

"The hole?" I ask shakily.

He goes on, his tone still flat, as though this is just any conversation. "The hole is what I called it. It was a cellar with no windows. The ground was dirt, and I had a small hole I slept in for three years. At least on unchained days."

He heaves out a breath, his eyes moving away.

"Someone kidnapped you?" I ask, confused.

He slowly shakes his head. "No. My grandmother passed away from heart complications, and the state awarded my mother custody. She'd turned her rights over to her mother when she had me and ran away."

"So you did have a name?" My question comes out soft as I tilt my head.

"I did," he says tightly. "But the memory of that name has been gone for a long time. It was part of my punishment. When I tell you that name is gone, I mean it. I can't remember what my grandmother called me. Even though they later found out my name, it still didn't feel right to use it. Or even claim it."

My hand slides over him, trying to be supportive. "So your grandmother didn't do this?" I ask him, just to clarify.

He shakes his head. "I only have a few memories of a kind smile and a gentle voice. But I know my grandmother was loving, gentle, kind...everything my mother wasn't."

"Your mother did this?" I ask, anger and sickness mixing together in my stomach and souring it as I sit up, running my finger along the deepest scar on his face.

He catches my hand, his gaze meeting mine again.

"No. I did the ones on my face."

Admittedly confused, I study him silently, waiting on him to elaborate. When he doesn't, I ask, "Why would you do this to yourself?"

He shrugs. "I thought if I looked less like him, she'd be less inclined to punish me for what he did. So I took a piece of broken glass and cut until I couldn't bear the pain anymore."

The Demon's Child...

After another long exhale, he says, "I'm the product of my mother's rape."

I swallow down the knot in my throat. That's not what I expected. I expected him to tell me his father had done this to him because of radical religious reasons, given the name choice.

He goes on, his eyes averting mine again as he continues to clutch my hand, bringing it to his chest and resting it there with his over it.

"She was fourteen, and her family was strictly Catholic. The man who raped her was some thug who'd just gotten out of prison for the very same thing. He left her abandoned in the street, and when she found out she was pregnant, her mother refused to allow her to have an abortion, saying it wasn't my fault this happened and God wouldn't want an innocent child punished for a monster's sins. Like I said, she signed her rights over after I was born and ran away, hating her mother for forcing her to have me. But my grandmother never blamed me for any of it."

"You weren't to blame. You were just as much a victim in this as she was," I say softly, hating the pressure on my chest.

I feel violent, knowing where this story is going.

"Anyway, seven years later, my grandmother died, and my mother came back into the picture. She was so fucked up in the head by then the state never should have let her walk away with me. She'd been on the streets, getting abused on repeat, and taking shelter with junkies she fucked for food and warmth. She said she was going to hell, but she was taking the demon inside me with her."

He clears his throat, his eyes meeting mine again.

"Between the drugs and psychological issues, she honestly believed there'd been a demon in the man who raped her. She believed by impregnating her, he'd passed that demon along to me. She performed her own versions of exorcisms, dehydrating me for days. Every time she asked my name, I told her, but she'd punish me."

He gestures to some of the scars on his chest.

"These aren't as bad as the ones on my back because she was terrified to face me, worried the demon would leap out of my eyes and into hers if she stared at me. So she usually put a hood over my head. Then she'd burn me with hot metal crosses, cut me, whip me, dehydrate me. I was fed and watered once a day like a dog, because she was afraid if I simply died, the demon would escape and she'd have to worry about it coming after her again, planting a new demon child inside her."

My hand on his chest slowly curls into a fist as I fight back the tears in my eyes. He keeps his gaze off me.

"She believed if she inflicted enough pain, the demon would show himself, and then she could exorcise it," he says quietly. "One day, she went too far. She went to cut off my dick, saying if she couldn't kill the demon, she'd make sure he could never get out of me the way he got out of the last host. I wasn't chained. She was so out of it, that she'd forgotten it was a no-chain day."

The scar on the base of his penis comes to mind, and I hold back a grimace.

"Not sure why that particular thing prompted my survival instincts to kick in, but the second that knife bit into my flesh, I shoved her as hard as I could. She fell backwards, and I grabbed the knife, stabbing it into her leg, frenzied and terrified. I started to run up the steps, but she grabbed me as soon as I reached the top."

He laughs humorlessly, running a hand over his face.

"It was so bright up there that I couldn't see. I'd begged for light for so long, then the damn thing blinded me as though I needed to be kicked while I was down." His gaze comes back to mine. "She knocked me down, and I was crawling blindly, bumping into shit as she limped after me. I felt something wet hit me, and then I heard the strike of the match."

My eyes inadvertently drop to his legs that are covered by the blanket.

"The pain I felt next was some of the worst I'd faced. My legs were burning as I ran, falling on her. I heard her scream as I scrambled out, crashing into a door and falling outside. On instinct alone, I rolled on the ground even as I screamed."

His eyes find mine once more, staring intently as his jaw tenses.

"The first thing I was finally able to see when my eyes somewhat adjusted was that house burning rapidly, catching fire because of the gasoline she had doused me and half the floor with. And she was on fire with it. I heard her screams and I fucking smiled, knowing I'd finally hurt her as bad as she'd hurt me."

He releases his hand that's over mine as his look hardens.

"Then I went to the hospital, the psych ward, a foster home, and finally juvie before ending up running with Drex. My mother's rapist was caught and put back in prison. He died before I ever had to deal with him. And my monster wasn't the man behind bars; it was his victim who was turned into a monster. I was just collateral damage. Now you know all my secrets."

And my heart hurts.

"Don't show me so much pity. It's why I don't like for fucking people to know," he bites out. "It was a long damn time ago, so don't think I'm that weak little shit anymore."

My eyebrows go up in surprise. "Pity is for strangers you care nothing about but can't help but feel sorry for them. It's the side effect of being human," I say softly, leaning closer so that our faces are inches apart. "What you see right now is a range of emotions on my face. This is me being angry for you. Me hurting for you. Me wanting to go back in time and hurt her while saving you. This isn't pity, Axle. This is me caring about you. It's a side effect of loving you."

He cocks his head, but I hold his gaze.

"And that kid wasn't a weak little shit. That kid is the ultimate survivor," I add on a breath.

He searches my gaze for a moment before his lips find mine, and he kisses me like he's thanking me. Or needing me. Or just caring about me too.

It takes me a few minutes of being lost in his kiss to realize I just told him I love him.

I really have the shittiest timing ever for romantic notions.

CHAPTER 28

We're a tangle of naked limbs when I wake up and see the dark sky through the window. Loud voices beyond the bedroom draw my attention, making me think that's probably what woke me up.

The door is cracked, as though someone didn't shut it and probably peeked in to see if Axle was awake.

As if he hears it too, Axle jerks awake, his hand immediately tightening on me like he's making sure I'm still next to him.

"I'm saying it's a possibility," I hear Jude telling someone. "Hershel tells us where to find Herrin, and we'll just kill him."

"Hershel won't talk this quickly," Sledge growls.

"No, but he will eventually. Death will be the reward, since he seems to want to push you into killing him. Is Liza coming out here?" he asks.

A lump forms in my throat as Axle sits up a little, bending over to grab his discarded boxers from the floor.

"No. She's still at the hospital," Sledge says quietly.

"Yo, Axle, you up?" I hear someone asking, probably hearing him shuffling around.

"Yeah. I'll be out in a second," he says. "Are Maya's clothes here?"

"Drake put them just inside your door," Drex calls out.

I spot a pink bag that isn't mine, but assume that's what's holding my clothes. I suppose that's the real reason as to why the door was cracked.

207

"We're going outside. Join us when you get dressed," Drex tells him.

As soon as I hear the front door shut, I look over at Axle. "I don't think Liza was really a victim."

Word vomit, hello. That totally wasn't supposed to come out like that.

His eyes flash to mine, his pants hanging on his hips undone, and I rush to add, "She stared at the camera, and victims who know there's a camera always stare away—"

He darts to me, clamping his hand over my mouth to shut me up as he looks over his shoulder toward the door.

He listens for a minute, like he's checking to make sure no one is still out there, before his eyes finally come back to mine.

"You can't say that to anyone else," he says quietly. "Liza has been with the club for longer than any of us, including Sledge. You're an outsider. That will piss a lot of people off, and—"

"I know," I interrupt, pulling his hand down. "That's why I'm telling you. Just you. I've had to watch tapes like that more times than I care to count. Some of the heads of other Families aren't quite as civilized as we are. We had to desensitize ourselves to things like this so that we didn't cave against the demands. It was part of our training."

He looks behind him again, before redirecting his attention to me.

"What did you see?" he finally asks.

"She stared at the camera," I repeat. "Shame is a powerful thing, even though these girls are feeling unwarranted shame. It still keeps them from looking at the camera, refusing to allow their families or anyone else to see them so vulnerable and exposed. Usually, the captors force them to look at the camera, and you can see the way it kills them. Liza looked into the camera for almost the entire video."

He blows out a breath and runs his hand through his hair before sitting down on the edge of the bed.

"That's how you knew it was a setup," he says quietly.

"That and the fact she had access to at least one of your accounts, since she cleans the money at the club. She also knew about the cars being done today." I glance at the bedside clock to see it's two in the morning. "Well, technically yesterday. And she chose her escorts. Twenty-five years is a long time, Axle. Especially for someone as devoutly loyal as I've been told she is."

He looks back at me, and I expect him to tell me to shut up and keep my opinions to myself. Being an outsider doesn't lend me the right to have an opinion, after all. People get killed for accusations like I'm making against one of theirs.

If someone accused Smitty of this, and they were an outsider, there'd be hell to pay. Although I didn't get too pissed when Axle tried to suggest as much once. But that's because it's Axle. I'm hoping he feels the same.

"Get on some clothes," he says, reaching over to tuck a strand of hair behind my ear. "And come find me when you're done if you feel like it."

"What about what I said?" I ask him.

He studies my eyes for a moment, hesitating to answer. "I'll figure something out. I can't just accuse her of not being a victim and then her turn out to be a victim. It wouldn't end well for you or me. Understand?"

I just nod, blowing out a breath. I knew it was treacherous territory. Hell, they trusted her enough to give her their account information. Which means they're too loyal to her to question her loyalty.

Vicious little circle there.

He stands abruptly and finishes doing his jeans up, before he pulls his boots on and walks out.

And I drop back to the bed to stare at the ceiling, wondering if he even realized I told him I love him.

I almost died today. I suffered what can only be a mild case of PTSD that I wasn't aware I had. Axle told me his inner, darkest, most painful secrets.

And I'm worried about if he caught onto my little declaration of love.

I'm apparently the queen of inappropriate timing and thoughts.

CHAPTER 29

AXLE

Just as I shut the door behind me, I freeze to my spot.

Sledge is sitting on a chair across from me, his eyes cast downward, and his hands clasped together.

"Liza is loyal to the club," he says calmly, his eyes coming up at the end of that sentence.

Tensing, I step closer to him, but keep my body between him and the door that shields Maya.

"I know," I say cautiously, warily gauging his body language that would trick someone into thinking he's relaxed.

He glances at me then past me to the door, and I grow tenser. No doubt he heard all that. I assumed everyone was outside.

His gaze settles on me again.

"The way you're protecting her, keeping yourself between me and her, that's not something I've ever done for Liza. She would have kicked my ass for thinking she needed my protection," he states emotionlessly.

I say nothing at first, but finally find something diplomatic to respond with. "Liza is tough."

He nods slowly.

"She joined the Death Dealers at fifteen, worked her way into a respectable position at one of the bars. I was twenty when I joined the club. She was twenty-five, and she liked the way I looked. She wasn't my piece of ass; I was hers."

My arms cross over my chest as I try to figure out where he's going with this.

211

"Mean as a rattlesnake, she was. Still is," he says, smiling tightly. "Tough as a bear." He pauses as he holds my gaze. "And cunning as a fox."

Slowly, he stands, and I let my arms fall to my sides as we stand at almost even heights—me, just a little taller than him.

"She wouldn't have screamed," he says while looking down, confusing the hell out of me. "Even if they'd chopped her arms off, she wouldn't have given them the satisfaction of screaming."

His eyes come back up to mine, as I try to decide if he's saying what I think he is.

"She would have fought," he goes on, biting the words out like they're acid. "She would have had skin under her nails. She'd have drawn their blood. They'd have had to beat her almost unconscious to get their hands on her, but there wasn't a mark on her."

I nod slowly, letting him know I understand. And honestly, I agree.

"She's always thought me a fool," he goes on, clearing his throat. "Always thought me too soft. Even hated it when I took Rush in because she thought it made me look weak to care about some kid. She always treated me like I was beneath Herrin, but good enough to warm her bed."

He grabs a blunt that is idling on the table, lighting it and taking a long puff. As the smoke billows from his lips, he adds, "She's loyal to the club. Just not ours." His eyes move to the bedroom where Maya is. "And your girl is too smart to be fooled. She's outside all this, looking in. And she knows how to run an operation four times the size of ours."

"I'm aware," I state dubiously.

"She'll see shit we can't. Listen to her. Because she saw through Liza immediately...probably saved lives today. It took me some calming down before I thought about it, and I felt like I was a fucking asshole for considering it. I'm glad I overheard her talking to you, because now I know I'm not a reprehensible piece of shit for my suspicions."

That was a hell of a lot easier than I expected, but then again, I expected him to be emotionally attached. He seems resigned to the truth as though he's been defeated by it already.

"How much does Liza know about Maya?" I ask as he reaches for the front door.

"Not a thing," he answers, turning his head to look at me. "Never felt right telling her something that could be dangerous. But also...just didn't feel right telling her at all. I guess that should have told me I was in the wrong relationship to begin with."

"Herrin never meant for us to find Liza, but it's likely that he planned to return her," I tell him.

He gives me a tight smile. "I know."

"No one expects you to deal with this. You decide how we play this."

He cracks his neck to the side before answering. "She just played me. She was willing to watch me go to my death at that factory, which might have happened if we'd taken the bait. She was willing to put all those girls at risk just because Herrin asked it. I think it's only fair I return the favor and play her for all she's worth. Then we'll take a vote on what to do. This is Drex's show. He loves a good vote."

He cracks a smile, though I can tell how weighted it is.

As he opens the door to leave, I turn and walk back into the bedroom, curious if Maya overheard all that. The second I'm inside the room, I see her on the bed, her eyes trained on me.

"Sledge is only thirty-five?" she asks, her brow pinched in confusion. "Not that he looks older or anything, but I thought he raised Rush. And Rush is in his twenties."

"That's what you ask?" I swear I'll never figure her out or see her zigs and zags before they come.

She shrugs. "Seriously. Only thirty-five? Or is my math wrong? Liza was fifteen when she joined, and she's been with the club for twenty-five years, so that's forty, minus five—their age gap—and that makes him thirty-five," she says so earnestly.

"You're really fucking hard to predict," I grumble.

"Thank you," she states as though she truly finds that to be a compliment.

Rolling my eyes, I answer, "Sledge just turned thirty-six last month, same day Rush turned twenty-two. Rush was fourteen when Sledge found him on the streets. He took him in like a big brother, but turned into more of a paternal figure when he realized Rush needed that. He was twenty-seven or twenty-eight and wise beyond his years."

"This is going to sound absolutely terrible that I don't know, but how old are you?" she asks.

My lips twitch. I honestly think that's the first time a girl has asked my age. "Twenty-seven and nowhere nearly as wise as Sledge was by my age."

She glances down at her hands, idly picking at the hem of a skirt she's wearing—a red one that has the same flowy bottom as the last one. But there are leggings on underneath it. Or tights. Hell, I don't know the difference.

"He seemed so okay with all of that. But I thought he and Liza had been together for fifteen years." As the words leave her mouth, they almost sound sad.

"I'm not sure exactly how long they've been together, but it's been more off than on over the years. Liza didn't want to be tied down, and Sledge was the only one to give her the freedom she wanted."

I study her expression, wondering why she looks a little upset.

"This is good, Maya. Means I don't have to bust up a friend to keep him from wanting to bust you up."

She peers up at me, nodding absently.

"It is good," she agrees. "Just didn't realize how hard you had to be on the ground floor. Makes me wonder if they ever even cared about each other. I mean, truly cared. My father would have never believed something like that about my mother, even if he'd seen it with his own eyes."

She stands and joins me.

"Are we still going outside?" she asks abruptly.

How hard you had to be on the ground floor? What does that mean? I'm tempted to remind her she had her ex tortured and executed for siding with the wrong people when her Family was attacked. But it seems a little cold to throw in her face like that.

Instead of saying anything and prolonging this unexplainable awkward tension that's settled between us, I nod and put my hand on the small of her back, guiding her out. We walk out to join the others who have a fire burning as Drex writes in the sand with a stick.

It's rare they light up a joint, but tonight...well, hell. It's been a shitty time of things lately.

I wave it off as a blunt is offered to me by Drake, and opt to simply drink beer.

Maya joins Colleen, who I'm surprised to see, and she leans against the back of a SUV to talk to her.

One day, I'll fucking figure out what's going on in her head, but apparently that's not today.

Just as I take a seat by Drake, who is obnoxiously spilling out his own conspiracy theories about what went down today, I hear what Maya said earlier. I *really* hear it. As though it's just now sinking in.

The words echo in my head like a distant memory instead of something that happened moments ago.

This is me caring about you. It's a side effect of loving you.

Drake has the blunt in his hand, and I tear it away from him as I bristle. He starts to object until I take three long drags in quick succession.

"What has you chasing the dragon?" the prick asks with a grin.

I say nothing, my eyes on Maya as I take two final draws and hand it back to him.

"Nothing bonds two girls more than nearly dying together," Drake says, stoned as fuck, gesturing toward Maya and Colleen.

Eve is in Drex's lap, and I'm admittedly a little annoyed with the fact Maya seems so content so far away from me. Which is stupid. That's not who I am. That's not what this is between us either.

She's going back to New York, after all. After the shit-storm she barely survived, that much is glaringly evident.

That thought has me taking the blunt away again. Damn girl is fucking ruining me.

CHAPTER 30

Axle peers at me over the paper, his eyes narrowed and his body tight. I'm not sure what his deal is, unless he regrets sharing all his dark secrets with me.

For the past two days, he's basically avoided any physical contact and he keeps looking at me but looks away when I catch him. So I pretend not to notice he's staring at me right now.

Sledge walks in, his eyes meeting mine, and I tense. Axle turns his attention to Sledge, who just stares at me before moving over to the coffeemaker.

Axle goes back to pretending he's reading the paper, even though we both know he's staring over the top of it at me.

Talk about annoying.

Everyone else is gone right now, tending to business as usual. There's a trailer full of bikes that Drex and Dash brought back, including Axle's skinned up one. He went for a ride just this morning, but he wasn't gone for long.

Axle's phone rings, and he glances at the screen, grimacing. Standing, he answers it, walking away and heading outside.

For the first time in two days, I'm alone with Sledge, and I sort of hope this hasn't all been an act, because he could easily kill me. *Sledge* is an apt nickname, considering he has all the brute strength of a sledgehammer.

I watch him warily as he sips his coffee, taking a seat in the chair Axle just vacated. He doesn't pretend to study the paper; he merely stares at me openly.

"You want to say something, so feel free to say it," I tell him, my toes poised on the floor and ready to launch me up so I can run.

"I have to go back to Liza tomorrow, before she gets suspicious," he says gruffly, surprising me. "You're the only person in this bunch that's ever dealt with betrayal from someone you cared about. I need you to tell me how you did it."

Ice runs through my veins, and I take a deep, steadying breath. Apparently they all know about my scars.

Our situations are similar, even though a stark difference rests in there too.

"I trusted the wrong person. My brother used his knowledge about me against me, and he groomed Thomas to be the perfect boyfriend that he knew I couldn't resist. Thomas was relentless, and I loved being chased. He eventually won me over," I say with a grim smile. "He worked in my father's crew and had the balls to tell my father to 'fuck off' when he tried to intimidate him into breaking up with me. He earned my father's respect that day, and I fell harder."

As Sledge leans up on his elbows, listening intently, I stare down into my coffee, trying not to think of that day but unable to do so.

"I'm begging, please! Baby, don't let them do this to me. You know me," Thomas pleads, the gun to his head as I skate toward him, pretending to be aloof and cold, hiding the broken pieces inside me as the gold mask rests on my face.

He's not allowed to say my name or his tongue will be cut out. Too many others are here to witness this—people who don't know my name. People who need to see Blackbird is fucking crazy as hell.

"Ah, but then you forgot to tell me you and my brother were working together, didn't you?" I ask him with mock giddiness, skating backwards now. "You forgot to mention my brother at all. Now he's missing, our parents are dead, and you were curiously packing a bag for one. Not two. Trying to leave me behind, Thomas?"

"You love me," he goes on, not trying to argue the truth. He knows me too well to think a lie will swim the shark-infested waters and make it to me.

The video evidence of him speaking to my brother, telling him everything about the meeting my father never should have trusted him with...it's all there. Plain as day. On a camera he never knew existed.

"I don't," I state honestly, a cruel smile on my lips. "You weren't quite that good, sweetie. Though you did try. All I want to know is where my brother is. Where Phillip is. It'll be a swift and merciful death if you're just honest."

His cheeks puff up, his face turns red, and the anger he normally contains so well appears.

"Fuck. You," he bites out.

I slide to a halt, lowering my face to where his is. My guys keep him on his knees, the barrel of the gun still firmly pressed against his temple.

"You did fuck me. Then you fucked me over." I straighten, skating backwards again as my music gets turned up louder. "Now I'm going to return the favor."

I cut my eyes to Smitty as Thomas raises a protest, telling me I'm not capable of this. Swearing to me he knows me better.

He's entirely too wrong.

And Blackbird will be twice as fierce when the word gets out that a cold-hearted bitch in a gold mask and roller skates is running the crew. One so cold she killed the man she cared for. They'll possibly even assume I loved him.

"Kill the others. They shouldn't even know who I am," I say to Smitty.

His lips twitch as he nods, vengeance driving him as it drives me.

"And him?" Smitty asks, pointing at Thomas who glares at me, still thinking he knows me too well.

"He knows something. Don't kill him until you've made him talk," I say sweetly, watching as the blood drains from Thomas's face. I feel...nothing. I felt more when I came in than I feel now.

"As you wish, Blackbird," Smitty says, a dark smile on his face. "It'll be my pleasure."

"I never fell in love. That's the difference between our stories," I tell Sledge, looking back at him as I shake out of the memories. "When I saw the video proof that I'd been a pawn and I'd been played, I was ready for war. Something inside me was broken in that instant. I watched my father's oldest friend collapse and bawl like a child the night before. He sobbed as hard as I did. We sobbed together behind closed doors so that no one would see us as weak. The next day, we became monsters. Can you be a monster where Liza is concerned?" I ask him.

His lips thin, and he slowly nods. "Drex has stood by me, always respected me, and always trusted me. Same for the other boys you've gotten to know. Liza didn't just betray me; she betrayed them, too. It's not just for me that I need to do this. It's for everyone I care about."

"But you were together for so long," I say softly.

My parents' bond was unshakeable. It was the thing I strived for. Now it seems almost like a unicorn—nonexistent.

"Time doesn't make something realer. It's either real or it's not," Sledge says on a breath. "The way Drex and Eve are? Liza and I have never been like that. Hell, I envy the kid for having that. And he would have killed you on the spot for suggesting Eve was part of it, even if it was blatantly obvious she was suspect. Though you'd never have to worry about that, because Eve would rather die than ever hurt Drex. The second he fell for her—that's when our lives changed. That's when he saw his Pop for who he really was. The right person makes you stronger. The wrong person forever drags you down, making you weaker. Liza made me weaker. I already feel stronger just knowing it's my turn," he answers.

Understanding what he's saying, I just stare at him.

He leans back, his eyes still on me.

"So you had them executed and him tortured to death. Did you know all the others?"

I nod hesitantly. "We'd been with Phillip for a long time. But too many of his guys knew me, as well as the other Family kids. They all needed to die, and they died quickly simply because I wanted it over. Troy, Smitty's eldest son, was the executioner that day. He had tears in his eyes, and was ready for bloodshed. You don't realize how close we are with our loyalist families. My parents were like Smitty's siblings and Troy is like my adopted brother. Smitty's very young daughters are my goddaughters, and therefore my chosen heirs, should I not have children of my own. Smitty gave Troy all of the quick executions, while he took Thomas below to torture him for days, dragging out all the information he could."

We sit in silence for a few minutes, letting the heaviness of the conversation settle between us.

"What happens with you and Axle now? I'm prying by asking, but how serious are things between you two? Obviously things have gotten severely stickier here. We're not able to protect ourselves at this moment, let alone someone as important as you are. What's keeping you here? Sarah? Or do you actually care about him? Because I know he cares about you. I never thought I'd see him care for anyone the way he does you."

My heart does an embarrassing little happy dance in my chest upon hearing that.

My sexy brooder was supposed to be a fun time with a guy too loyal, strong, and jaded to be anything like the snake Thomas was. And so much stronger than the other two men who died just for being too nosy, finding out things they shouldn't have learned, and trying to use it against me when their ambition hit them hard.

My father had no tolerance for that.

Our enemies were too great to risk my name because of idiots who saw an opportunity.

I'm sick of opportunists.

Axle was like a reprieve from everything. Far enough away to know everything, but smart enough not to get too close, and strong enough not to be so weak as to see an opportunity with my name.

Then I went and caught an unexpected case of the *feels*. The strong feels, too. The kind I never thought I'd be capable of. And I vomited up that confession like an idiot teenager.

A confession he's yet to acknowledge. And since then, he's acted weird.

"He's right." Axle's voice is like a cold bucket of water pouring over my head.

Sledge's gaze flicks over my shoulder, eyes widening marginally, and I turn my head to see Axle leaning against the wall—mostly out of sight as he eavesdrops. No telling how long he's been standing there and listening to our conversation.

He pushes away from the wall and closes the distance between us, coming to prop up on the kitchen island.

"We're not the ideal protection for you right now. We've scattered, and we're in self-preservation mode. Everything is chaotic. Shit is hitting the fan. And the war is just getting started. We don't even know who is trustworthy in our crew," Axle goes on, his jaw ticking. "You're not safe here. It's just a matter of time before you pique Herrin's interest. It's not like it'd be hard for him to get to you right now, with so much going on as a distraction. He could have grabbed you the other day if he'd known your value. If he learns who you are, he could easily team up with Phillip, using you as a bargaining chip. And together, they'd wipe us out completely."

In other words, it's dangerous as fuck to be together.

"I'm putting your life at risk by keeping you here, since I can't trust everyone around us or offer you the protection you need," Axle says softly, clearing his throat. "And you're putting all of us at risk by staying."

The worst part about it is that I know how right he is. I also know how selfish wanting to stay, despite the risks, sounds.

Sledge stands, leaving us alone to talk, probably feeling a little awkward for witnessing even this much.

"So you're saying you want me to leave?" I ask quietly, the tremor in my voice betraying my attempt to sound impervious.

He's a blank, expressionless man before me, concealing all his thoughts with such an ease that makes me twice as envious. My poker face only works on people I don't care about.

"I'm saying it's the safest for everyone. We have our own war. You have yours. Our styles keep clashing, and it's only a matter of time before it ends badly for everyone. I'm saying it's the smartest move." He blows out a breath and clears his throat. "Doesn't really matter what I want."

His eyes are down. His hands are in his pockets.

I remember the first time I saw him; his inky black hair, his scars, his scathing pale eyes that didn't know whether to kill me or dismiss me. Dark angel was the description I used.

It's still apt.

I reach for my phone, digging it out of my pocket, as Axle's eyes come back up to meet mine.

Saying it doesn't hurt to hear him be pragmatic would be a lie. Petty as it is, I wanted him to tell me he wanted me to stay, that we'd face the risks together.

Deep down, I know it's just a matter of time before we get ourselves and everyone else killed.

Feeling the weight of his gaze on me, I stare at my phone, clicking on "White Knight" in my contacts. My vision is blurred by unshed tears, so I don't look back at Axle as I make the call, since a text won't work right now.

"Please tell me it's time for pickup. That's the only reason you'd be calling instead of texting, unless there's someone you need taken care of," Smitty drawls, bypassing common pleasantries.

"Yes," I say in a rasp tone, then clear my throat. "Time for a pickup."

"You okay, kiddo?" Smitty asks seriously. "Give me the word if you are."

"Lathaniel," I say tightly.

He blows out a breath of relief, and I look up to see Axle frowning at me.

"Text me the coordinates. I'll have a team pick you up. I'm just glad you're finally coming home," Smitty goes on.

I feel like I can't speak. For whatever reason, there's a huge knot in my throat. Then again, I guess it's not *whatever reason*. It's about 6'4, lean, and staring directly at me—that's the reason for the emotion.

But I'm an expert at faking strength. It's just been a while since I felt weak enough to have to fake it.

"Will do," I say to Smitty, hanging up before he can ask me questions.

As soon as I put my phone down, Axle asks, "Lathaniel?"

"My father's name," I answer on autopilot. "It's my safe word to Smitty that lets him know I'm not being held at gunpoint or something. Precautions and all that. It's required."

His glaze flicks over my face, then his eyes meet mine again. "And the word that tells him you're at gunpoint?"

I smile weakly. "Blackbird. It's the only word I could squeeze in that wouldn't be an obvious panic word. When I speak over the phone, I refer to my family as Bluebird instead of Blackbird. Again, protocol."

He nods, both of us talking about anything but the giant elephant in the room.

"If you'll send in more vehicles, we'll redo all of the interior work again. Obviously free of charge," he says so matter-of-factly.

Things between us have been an array of things, but this is the first time it's been uncomfortable.

Deciding not to slip into formal bullshit chitchat, I pull up my GPS, looking at everything that's around, and isolate one place that will work. Then I send Smitty the coordinates of the extraction point—that is pretty much in the middle of the desert.

He texts back immediately.

SMITTY: Five hours. Be ready.

"What does it say?" Axle asks, his voice a little raw.

"They'll be picking me up in five hours. I should probably conference in the other three Families and let them know I'm coming home. Then, if you don't mind, someone will have to give me a ride."

Standing, I put my phone back in the pocket of my shorts, and I move toward the bedroom, batting away a few fallen tears. As soon as I'm inside, I lean against the door, trying my damnedest to hold myself together.

But the tears keep coming.

My chest feels like a building is pressing down on it.

Every swallow is painful.

Every breath is hard to catch.

Trying to pull myself together, I move to the bathroom sink and start splashing water on my face and the back of my neck.

I can see him again. It's not like this has to be it. Our individual wars will be over eventually. Calling is perfectly acceptable, even if Axle doesn't like talking on the phone very much.

There's also video chat, right? I mean, it's not asking too much for a criminal biker who is currently dodging constant, life-threatening attacks to find time to video chat.

After toweling off my face, I look back at the mirror, and jump a little, because Axle is also in the mirror with me.

Confused, I turn around, and almost immediately, his hands are in my hair, and his lips are on mine, kissing me like it's paramount above all else. Kissing me like it's the last time.

Kissing me like it's goodbye.

Damn it. More tears.

So, this is it?

He lifts me, and I wrap my arms around his neck while winding my legs around his waist, and he carries me out of the bathroom, devouring me the entire time.

The second he has me on the bed, I help him push my shorts off, then tear my shirt over my head. He leans back, stripping his shirt off, then comes back down to me.

With one hand, he undoes my bra, and everything slows down.

"Five hours," he says roughly.

Since my words are completely pointless, I nod, feeling a few more tears slip out with the motion.

Tossing my bra to the side, he leans down, and my back arches as his mouth closes over a nipple, sucking it. Whimpers...moans...I give him all the sounds, not holding anything back.

My fingers twist and grip his head, pushing him lower. Smart guy that he is, he takes the hint, pushing my panties down and not wasting time. His mouth fastens over my clit, and gibberish bursts out of me when I try to tell him how good it feels.

I swear he's grinning. Not sure I've ever had anyone grin when their face was right *there*.

The smile fades, and he starts holding my hips down when I try to move. It feels *too* good. And he makes me take it all.

It feels like minutes and hours in different ways, until I'm suddenly crying out his name.

He tears his mouth away, but his lips find mine before I can even catch my breath, and he thrusts in. I swallow his groan, feeling his chest vibrate against mine. When he breaks the kiss, he pulls back just enough to look into my eyes, his hips moving at an agonizingly languid pace.

And that's how he takes me.

Slowly.

Reverently.

Preciously.

With his eyes never leaving mine until I close them again, overwhelmed by sensation. He buries his face in my neck as his hips pick up a little speed, just enough to send him over the edge right behind me.

He kisses my neck—butterfly soft kisses. I run my hands over him slowly, sweetly, committing everything to memory as I keep my eyes closed, worried I'll cry more if they're open.

We lie like that, silently wrapped up in each other for what seems like no time, before someone knocks on the door.

"You said to get you in four hours," Drex's voice calls out. "What's going on?"

Axle tenses against me, his grip tightening on my hips. Yes, I start thinking he's about to tell me he can't do this. That he can't let me go. Or that he can't let me go without him.

Instead, he says, "Let's get you to that extraction team."

With that, he pushes up and off the bed, putting on his clothes, and he walks out, leaving me to get dressed alone.

CHAPTER 31

AXLE

"You have your roller skates?" Eve asks Maya, forcing a smile as I do everything in my fucking power not to break something. Or hit something. Or kill someone.

Those are currently my life goals.

Maya nods, not smiling in return, and I'm one step closer to risking everyone's lives when she quickly swipes at a new tear that has fallen.

She's crying over me.

Over. Me.

And I'm ready to kill over her. *For her.*

If it wasn't putting everyone else at risk, I'd say to hell with it all. But everyone else *is* at risk. And it's really fucking selfish to watch people who've had my back for years risk certain death because I finally found something I want in life.

"You know," Drex says quietly as he joins me at my side, his eyes on Maya and Eve as they talk near the vehicles, "I sent Eve away. Swore it was the best way to keep her safe. Didn't work out so well, in case you've forgotten."

He's careful not to touch me as he crosses his arms over his chest and continues to stare ahead at the girls.

"Eve didn't have an entire elite force at her fingertips when she went home. That team can't be here. It'd easily draw too much attention, and be too noticeable to her brother or Phillip. The guys she trusts are the guys they know."

He nods slowly.

"But you're not sending her home for her safety, are you?" he pries. "You're sending her home for ours. Which is, to be completely honest, really fucking insulting."

He quirks an eyebrow at me, and I blow out a breath while looking away.

"Not in the mood to fucking bullshit, Drex. We both know we're hurting right now. Too many loyalties are torn, and too many people are willing to fuck us over."

"At least until we make a statement," Drex says with a shrug. "Maya would be safe then, right? Since Pop's guys would be a little less brazen to just fuck with us? Right now, they still see me as his brat kid and the old man as the one with all the brains, but if we —"

"Drex," I say, feeling tired and really fucking sick of talking, "not right now. We've been strategizing to the point we're trying to make Herrin look like a rat to the feds, a traitor to Benny, and a thorn in Phillip's side. Today, I don't want to talk strategy. I don't want to talk at all."

My jaw tenses as the sound of a chopper nears, the desert sand stirring in warning. I don't look to the sky to see how far away it is, because I can't stop looking at her.

It's likely the last time I'll ever see her.

If I'd have known I'd fucking feel like this right now, I never would have let her skate her perky little ass into my bedroom. I'd have let Dash talk her into —

Fuck that. I would have beaten the shit out of Dash if he'd talked her into bunking with him and had her the way I did.

Then again, she never wanted Dash.

Just me.

Figures life finally pays me a debt to make up for the hell it has put me through, only to take it away the second I realize how much I want it. Guys like us don't get the sunshine and motherfucking rainbows.

We get the exhaust fumes and oil spills.

My eyes flick down to her rainbow shoestrings inside her white Converse tennis shoes, almost as if they're taunting me. She's all the good things, and I should have known it was too good to last for me.

The chopper gets louder and louder, and when I feel the first breeze of the blades, I turn and walk away, unable to fucking stand here and watch her leave. I told her goodbye with my body.

I've tasted her tears for hours.

I can't stay here and watch her leave, or I might not be able to let her. Or even worse, she might taste my fucking tears.

Even as they shout my name, I rev my bike and gas it away from them, driving back toward the temporary home I'm stuck in. Back to dealing with this life.

Back to being me.

Without Maya.

Yeah, blow me. I'm allowed a few hours of a motherfucking pity party.

CHAPTER 32

"You're finally here!" Ingrid shouts, squealing as she runs across my room in her five-inch stilettos, and throws her arms around me.

Weakly, I hug her back. "I'm back," I say on a sigh.

She reels back, her brow creasing. "Why does it sound like you hate the idea?"

"I don't hate the idea," I lie.

My new room isn't my room at all. It's a room secured and found for me through Ingrid and Ezekiel while I was away, since, you know, my brother is out for my head.

"You're definitely hating the idea," she argues, frowning. "What's going on? And stop lying. You know I hate lies, because it's just delaying the truth from coming out, and procrastination is my biggest pet peeve."

I huff out a small laugh, dropping to my chair, exhausted from all the crazy traveling to prevent anyone from back-tracking my pattern and figuring out where I've been.

First there was a chopper to the airport, then I boarded a private plane, then landed in Chicago. Then drove to an entirely too-small airport two states away, and boarded yet another private plane that dropped me off in Maine, then I was driven here.

It's been a long day, obviously.

Now...Ingrid.

"Can we do this tomorrow?" I ask her.

"No. Again, that's just procrastination," she states immediately, arching her eyebrow in challenge.

Rolling my eyes, I tell her, "There was a guy. I wasn't ready to leave, but here I am. Hence the attitude. I'll be able to smile too well for you to see through it once I get some rest," I assure her.

Unfortunately, that doesn't appease her.

"A biker who's part of a made-up MC?" she asks earnestly, not even realizing just how insulting that sounds. It's a lot different when you see the struggle and the determination. Hell, it's admirable.

"A biker. Yep. Can we leave it at that?"

"Hell no. You never mentioned you were dating one of them," she says, her grin growing as she gets more comfortable. "So then what happened? All I know is that you said you were coming home, even though you've fought us on that for however long now."

"They're in their own war, as you're aware. Axle decided—"

"His name is Axle? He couldn't have been a little more original than that?" she interrupts, mouth twisted in disdain.

"His name holds sentimental value," I explain calmly, leaving it at that, and trying not to get irritated. She has no clue she's bugging me with her condescension toward him. How could she know?

This was mine. I didn't share it with them.

"Fine. Proceed," she says, gesturing toward me.

"Anyway, he decided it was unsafe for me and for his guys if I stayed there. Which is true. If their adversaries learned of my identity and my intentions, they could join with Phillip. They'd be eradicated, along with me."

I say this as emotionlessly as possible, too drained to feel anything right now.

But when I stare at my tiny condiment bottles on a shelf, I'm reminded of the tiny condiment bottles I had to leave behind. The bottles we took from the hotel.

Together.

I reach over for the pretty—and not-so tiny—bottle of whiskey and pour a generous dose in a glass. Ingrid regards the whiskey like it's syphilis, because she thinks alcohol is the most disgusting thing in the world.

"He knows who you are. Do you trust him to keep it quiet now that you're gone?" she asks.

I snort derisively. "He threw himself on top of me when there was gunfire. He carried me out of a building that had exploded and washed away all the ashes when I couldn't bring myself to barely move. He punched a friend because that friend got a little too pushy with me." I give her a dry look. "I slept beside him every night—*really slept* beside him. He could have harmed me time after time, yet I was safe enough to actually sleep. How long has it been since you slept all night, Ingrid?"

She tenses, then I see her eyes glisten.

"You really cared about him," she finally says quietly. "Then why the hell did you leave? Or why didn't you bring him home with you?"

Smiling bitterly, I answer, "He'd never leave his friends when they're at their lowest, most vulnerable right now. If one leaves, they could all fall. And he asked me to go home. I understand it. I really do."

I drain the glass of whiskey and set it down. Ingrid stops me before I can pour more into it.

"Did you tell him how you felt?" she asks, genuinely concerned now.

"Yep," I tell her flatly, struggling to remove the whiskey bottle from her grip when she takes it from me.

"Did you love him?" she asks.

I sigh and glare at the whiskey. "Yep."

"And you told him you loved him?"

"For fuck's sake, yes. I told him I loved him. Why?"

"And he sent you home to help keep you safe, and wants nothing in return?" she asks, as though the notion is preposterous.

"Yes," I bite out.

"He's protective of you, then?"

"Yes," I groan.

"That means he cares," she tells me like it's a good thing.

"I never said he didn't," I grumble.

Her look softens, and she lets me take the bottle of whiskey. I pour the glass and drink it all down again.

"What'd he say when you told him you loved him?"

Sighing, I stare at the empty glass in my hand like it holds all the answers. "He didn't say it back."

I look up at her, seeing her eyes glisten more obviously now.

"Two days later, he decided I should go home," I add in a strained whisper.

Ingrid reaches past me, lifting the whiskey, and this time, she pours me a glass. Then, to my utter surprise, she pours one for herself as well.

"Well, then. I'm wicked confused," she says as she sips the drink, then makes a face. Then sips again.

I swear this is the first time I've seen her ever drink.

I hold my glass up, gently clanking it against hers. "Cheers to that," I mutter.

CHAPTER 33

AXLE

"The repairs to the warehouse will start next week. Cops had to get involved, since it drew too much attention," Drex is saying, while I clutch a tiny ketchup bottle in my hand for no fucking reason at all.

"The cops are just taking in the report and pretending to investigate, though," Sledge offers.

My eyes focus on the small condiment, and I try not to think of being back in that hotel room. It seems like yesterday and years ago at the same time that we were locked inside our own little world for two short days.

"Hershel is starting to talk already. Said Pop was coming after us with all he had once he weakens us a little more. But that's all he's given us so far."

"We need to find him and strike harder. But more skillfully this time. It feels like we're constantly playing defense, and are one step behind on offense."

"We're playing their games too much and letting our strengths become our weaknesses. We have to…"

The words are drowned out as I get lost inside my own head, unaware of who is saying what or what is even being said. It all just sounds like background noise as my mind wanders to Maya.

The only good memories I had as a child were stolen from me, wiped out by one psychotic woman. A different breed of a psychotic woman gave me new good memories.

Didn't realize that would affect me to this extent.

"Axle!" Drex shouting my name has my head lazily coming up to see all eyes are on me as I clutch the condiment bottle again.

"What?" I ask, bored with all this.

"Anything you'd like to add?" Drex asks me.

It's been four days since Maya left. Four days I've not given a damn about anything else. Four days since I drove back to the warehouse and risked a possible ambush by driving alone, all to retrieve those fucking tiny condiment bottles.

I know it sounds ridiculous.

I know it's pointless.

I guess it's as good a time as any to try to get back to me.

"We're running so many games to outsmart everyone that we're getting to the point we're outsmarting ourselves and losing track of the games we've started playing. We need to stop trying to be something we're not, and we need to remind people who the fuck we are. But we can't do that alone," I say as I lean up on the dining room table of our temporary safe house.

"The guys are scattered right now. It'll take a few days to bring them back—"

"I'm not talking about all the guys who could be compromised," I say in interruption to Jude, my eyes leveling him. "I'm talking about pulling in an Ace who would be worth fifteen men."

His jaw tightens, and I expect him to explode. I didn't understand the intense hatred before toward Sarah. Now I get it. If Maya had been lying to me all along, after getting me to trust her, it would have fucking gutted me.

But this isn't the time for grievances.

"You're talking about bringing in AJ," he states flatly, devoid of all emotion.

He looks around the table, noticing the way everyone is staring at him expectantly. Then his eyes return to mine.

"You sent your girl home to keep us all safe, even though it's clear she's the first thing you've ever given a damn about outside this club." His gaze shifts to Sledge. "You're still playing like you don't suspect Liza, kissing her instead of killing her like you want to do, after she betrayed us twice as hard as AJ betrayed me." He blows out a breath and stares down at the table. "I can put aside my own issues for the sake of the club if everyone else is doing their part. I'm not that fucking selfish or irrational."

His gaze lifts and goes to Drex.

"But only for shit like this. She doesn't get to be a part of us," he adds.

Drex nods once, his lips firm. We're still waiting on Jude to explode at any moment, since his eerie calm is creeping us out.

Jude simply leans back in his chair, keeping all his anger inside as his jaw tics and his eyes stay down.

"Then we'll see if we can reach her and see if she'll help us out with this," Drex tells me. "But what do we offer in return? She seems to mostly just ask for favors, but you never know what that favor might be."

"She won't risk Jude," I say hesitantly, watching as he stiffens. "Her favors won't be anything too extreme."

Jude cracks his neck to the side, blowing out a steadying breath, like he's staving off the explosive outburst he wants to release in rebuttal to what I just said. Instead, he stays quiet.

Much to all our surprise.

He stays in the room. Also surprising.

Usually any chat about his ex has him stalking out and finding someone to hurt or drinking himself to blackout oblivion.

"Where do we start?" Dash asks Drex.

Drex smirks, leaning up on the table, eyes trained on me. "We're already stuck in this fucking war with Phillip. No way does he not eventually come for us if he feels like we're in the way. And I don't particularly like any fuckwads just coming in and setting up shop without our consent."

Rapping my fingers over the table once, I squeeze that fucking condiment bottle a little tighter in my other hand.

"I say we take out that little fucking junkie bitch just to remind us who we are," Drex states.

"That will definitely put us in Phillip's sights. Are we ready for that?" Jude asks, still strung tight and tense, but finally being helpful.

"We don't do it balls-out," I say with a smirk. "We start subtle."

Drex and I hold each other's gaze for a minute, both of us smirking. It's been a while since this crew felt like we could handle shit. Things have been spiraling out of control. Somehow, in the midst of all the shitty luck, we forgot who the hell we are.

"Then we make a loud fucking statement after that," Drex says, turning his gaze to Sledge.

Sledge's grin is dark. "I want that pleasure. If I can't go through with it, I'll call one of you. But something tells me it won't be too hard."

I'm the first to stand and walk away from the dining room, going to get ready for bloodshed. Eve and Colleen are outside on the porch, and they both turn to look through the window at me as I head outside, moving toward the shed.

Hershel is strung up, his body resting on his knees as his arms are lifted above his head. He barely has the energy to peer over at me.

"If you want water today, you'll tell me all of Herrin's allies."

His cracked lips start to move, but then he narrows his eyes and looks away.

"Fine. Tell me tomorrow," I say with a shrug.

He whimpers as I exit the shed, and almost walk into Drake.

"No water for him today," I say as I eye the bottle in his hand.

Shrugging, he twists the cap off and starts drinking the water himself, turning to walk back with me toward the house.

"So Maya is gone gone?" he asks. "Like gone for good?"

My hand fisting again around the ketchup bottle, I nod. "I don't want to talk about it, Drake."

"Want to talk about why you almost ripped my head off for a tiny mustard thing I wanted to use on my sandwich?"

"Nope," I state flatly. "Don't touch my shit."

"Don't put your shit in the kitchen if your shit is condiments."

I barely take a calming breath, knowing I might break him if I hit him too hard.

"You should probably go get her back before you accidentally kill someone," he finally says, and I stop walking, standing near the porch the girls have abandoned.

"You don't know what's going on, so you should probably keep your opinion out of it," I bite out.

He cocks an eyebrow and smirks at me. "I know you're not going to land a girl like that again."

I narrow my eyes at him.

"What? You're not. Maya is pretty damn hot—at least a seven out of ten. You're maybe a five if you wear a bag over your head. Chances like this don't come around too often."

I just stare at him blankly as he continues to grin at me.

"You really do like to piss me off, don't you?" I ask dryly.

"I prefer pissing off Drex, but when you're brooding it's fun to jab at you."

Lifting a hand toward his throat, I take a step forward, then fist my hand, and just level the grinning bastard with a glare.

"Maya stays gone."

With that, I turn and stalk up the steps of the porch.

"Then I hope you like the hell out of your hand," he calls to my back. "Because, you know, you're not pretty like me and don't have all the unlimited options."

I can feel him smiling without seeing it, and know he's the type to only push your buttons for a reaction. Ignoring Drake is the only way to deal with Drake.

No one glances my way as I head into my room and slam the door behind me.

My eyes briefly flick to the bed. The spot Maya told me how she felt. The spot where I didn't tell her anything in return.

Carefully, I put the small ketchup down, take a deep breath, and slam my fist through the wall. Sheetrock crumbles around my fist, and I pull back, cracking my neck to the side as my skinned knuckles burn a little.

Feeling more like myself already.

Even if myself does feel like shit most of the time.

Picking up my phone, I dial the girl of the hour, not expecting her to answer. She surprises me by actually picking up.

"So you sent her home after I told you how important she was?" Sarah drawls. "Lovely. That was our get-out-of-jail free card, Axle. You couldn't play nice?"

My free hand turns to a painful fist.

"Long story short, Herrin almost killed her."

"I heard. I hear everything, remember? So why are you calling me?"

Leaning against the wall, I smirk. "I need a favor."

CHAPTER 34

Maya

"Ah! I've been wondering when I'd see you!" I glance over as Penelope—Smitty's wife—comes to the edge of my skating rink, watching me as I glide backwards.

I force a smile as I skate to the edge.

"How are the girls? I'm trying to keep my distance for the time being," I say to her.

She beams at me, unaware of my current situation—heartbreak and all that lovely shit.

"The girls are fantastic. Both are doing so well in school, but they do miss you. Smitty thinks we can arrange something so they can see you. I'm just glad you're back home."

I frown. "You knew I was gone?"

She rolls her eyes. "I've been married to Smitty for almost thirty years. Of course I knew you were gone, even though he never told me as much. He gave me the same story about you returning months ago, just as he gave everyone else. But I know him too well, and I could see the worry on his face. He wouldn't be worried if he had eyes on you."

I glance over, seeing John, one of my father's favorite bodyguards, as he pretends not to listen in on our conversation.

"I saw Troy yesterday, and he filled me in on Lathan's guys crouching near your brownstone," I say on a sigh to her.

She rolls her eyes. "Lathan can't touch us. He can't touch you either. And we've moved to our Manhattan apartment since then. Good luck getting through those doors without access. Not even the elevator works to our floor without a passcode."

She bats a dismissive hand, always the optimist.

"Oh! I meant to tell you, I got you some of those tiny condiment bottles you love so much! All sorts of different ones. Including hot sauce. I'll go grab them and be right back."

Considering this small rink is on the top floor of a large building, it will probably take her a while to return. So I resume skating, closing my eyes and turning the music up with my remote.

I've been trying to unwind for five days now. Ever since I returned.

Not even skating is freeing me.

Not screaming lyrics and shaking out the nerves either.

Nothing is working.

Giving up, I go to put my shoes on, my head down as I swap my skates for sneakers. Just as I stand and my head comes up, a scream flies out of my lips as something rough wraps around my face. My eyes open to darkness, and I struggle, when an arm comes around my throat, choking me.

I suck in air, and fabric goes into my mouth. Air barely squeezes through the threads, and I grow dizzy when the massive arm strangles me tighter, cutting off the small bit of air I was getting.

I try to scream again, wanting the men outside the doors to rush in with their guns, but a garble is all that escapes my lips.

Colorful dots sparkle in the darkness as I continue to suffocate, and my eyes grow heavy until...

CHAPTER 35

AXLE

"Where's Sarah?" Drex asks me as we all linger by the entrance of the warehouse.

Jude is fucking antsy, like he wants to be anywhere else right now. His eyes don't meet any of ours.

The second I open my mouth to speak, there's suddenly a knock at the door.

Jude walks away, and I pull open the door to see…Sarah. Or AJ. Or whatever.

This double name thing just gets more confusing by the minute.

She beams at us as she stands there all dressed in leather with her blonde hair straight and hanging around her shoulders.

"When does the killing start?" she asks a little too giddily.

"Five minutes ago. You're late," Drex says with an arched eyebrow.

She rolls her eyes, then turns and bends. My smile etches up when she starts dragging a body inside.

"I was busy getting you a gift," she says, dragging in a struggling Ben, who has been on the run for a while. After kidnapping Eve.

Drex's eyes widen and then narrow as his features harden.

Ben is tied up like a fucking calf at a roping exhibition or whatever it's called. And he's gagged as he sweats, panicking as he continues to struggle uselessly.

"And Cecil—your little rat—is in a body bag in my trunk. One of you boys can handle that," she says, patting Dash on the shoulder suggestively.

He groans while going outside to handle the body, and I smirk as I think back to Maya's comment about Sarah.

Sarah's like a cat. She gifts you dead rodents as a show of affection.

Is there any-fucking-thing that isn't going to trigger a memory? She wasn't in my life that damn long.

Drex's fist slams into the side of Ben's face, and Sarah whistles the tune to *Jeopardy*.

"We can reschedule this hit for tomorrow," I tell him as he shakes out his fist, while Ben cries on the ground.

"Agreed," Drex bites out. "I have plans for tonight."

Jude walks back over, his steps hesitating when he sees Ben on the floor. His jaw grinds.

"Need help?" he asks Drex, intentionally avoiding looking in Sarah's direction.

"Why the hell not? Everyone should get a turn," Drex says, smirking when Ben sobs around the gag, tears pouring from his eyes. "Drag him below," he adds as Dash walks in and drops the small body bag that is carrying our ex-tattooist and rat.

Jude and Dash grab Ben under the arms and legs, and the two of them carry the writhing snake toward the basement. Drex cracks his knuckles while looking back over at Sarah.

She forces a smile, jerking her gaze away from Jude's retreating figure to eye Drex.

"What do I owe you for that?" Drex asks her.

"Simple. Bring Maya back and do what I asked you to do in the first place. It's crucial she stays here. It means the other Families won't just come in guns blazing and wipe all of you out."

Trying not to strangle her, I say, "Maya is a liability. And we're a liability to her as well. It's not safe for her or us to be around each other. If Herrin—"

"Spare me the details of your reasoning. I've already heard it all," she says with a shrug.

My eyes dart over to Drex, and he curses Eve under his breath.

"Don't be mad at my girl. To be fair, she sort of owes me a debt as well. And she pays it by feeding me information that may keep you assholes alive."

"We can handle ourselves," Drex tells her with narrowed eyes.

"You can't handle what's coming without help," Sarah says seriously. "Trust me. I know the depths of depravity that follow Phillip's reign. Believe me when I say you pray for death once he sets his sights on you. And he will. Eventually. He'll wipe out all the MCs in the area, because they'll be in *his* territory once he finally settles in for good. You either work with him, or you're against him. Unless you want to be a set of bitches for him, you *will* need my help. And Maya's. And the other Families' help as well."

Drex runs a hand through his hair. "Deal with this and go scout the site again," he says to me. "Take Sarah and make sure we didn't miss anything."

Sarah follows me out, and Drex turns toward the basement, ready to have some fun and release some pent-up frustration.

Sarah straps on a spare helmet as we walk out, and she climbs onto my bike without touching me.

"I have to hold onto you," she says, clearly not touching me without permission.

I just nod once, and her arms slide around my waist. My entire body tenses, and I feel her tense in return.

"Should I just ride separate?" she asks me as I undo her hands from my waist, and pull my helmet off. I don't answer.

Instead, I walk to her car that is parked against the alley wall, and she follows me, sans helmet. Wordlessly, we get into her car, and I hold my hand out. The second she hands me the keys, I crank the damn car and drive us toward the massive warehouse that is just a few towns over.

"Want to tell me what all that was about?" Sarah asks flippantly after a long stretch of silence.

"Guess I wasn't in a mood to be touched."

"Have that problem with Maya?" she chirps.

I glare at her for a second before returning my attention to the road.

"Touchy. Touchy," she says around an amused drawl.

"Drop it," I warn.

"Or you know, you could just go get her. You're going to be at war no matter what. She's going to be in danger no matter what. You can be at war and in danger together."

"Not until we have Herrin handled," I say while bristling.

"Herrin is of no consequence. Even with his best sources, he'd never figure out who Maya is. And the Families would obliterate him before he even found Phillip to strike up a deal. He'd know that. If anything, Herrin would fear you more if he found out Blackbird was teamed up with you."

I say nothing as we drive, because I refuse to let her twist this and make me feel as though sending Maya away was pointless.

"This is it," I say when we're parked a safe distance away. "We walk from here."

She follows me out of the car, and because we need to be stealthy, she says nothing as we hike through the patch of desert that spans for almost a mile, and finally come out behind a few sheds that offer us coverage.

We both peer around, and I mentally curse. There are twice as many men here today. If not three times as many.

I jerk my head back, avoiding being seen. I half wonder if they saw us come through the desert, even though it's night. It's doubtful I can spot all of them.

"Lot of security," Sarah whispers.

"Possibly triple the amount here last night," I say just as quietly.

I peer around the edge again as a guy walks out of the warehouse with a cigarette lit and hanging out his mouth, an AK-47 hanging off him like it's just any other day.

Sarah backs back up, shaking her head.

"Why would they triple security?" she asks in a hushed tone.

I shrug, because I'm not a fucking mind reader or psychic. I don't just *know* these things.

I glance around, noting the spotlights seem to be trained toward the sky, weirdly enough. Not the desert.

Sarah and I both silently start trekking back, waiting for guns to fire at any moment. That side was clear last night. Seemed to be a blind spot. Tonight, not so much.

Fortunately, they never detect us, and we make it all the way back to her car that I crank immediately.

"Something had to have happened for him to amp up security since yesterday," she says in a normal tone as I drive us back toward Halo.

"Regardless, it's going to be twice as hard to get in there now and make this plan work," I growl.

"And you told no one outside your circle that you were doing this, right?"

"That's why we called you in. We don't know who else we can trust right now, so only the circle and you know about this."

She heaves out a frustrated breath. "Then obviously something else is going on. We need to find out what. I'm going back later tonight, because I'm like a ghost when it's just me."

"Too dangerous, and if—"

"Axle, I've taken on jobs that were ten times more complicated than this one. I can handle scouting solo. I need to see if I can't get a closer look at what's going on inside that place and what has them armed to the gills, shining spotlights on the sky instead of the desert."

When we make it back to the warehouse, Sarah is the first to exit, ending our argument prematurely.

She bursts through the doors, and we find a few of the girls from the strip club lingering near the bar for some weird reason. Tiffany, Simone, and Darla.

Sarah walks right up to them, and Simone and Darla throw their arms around her, hugging her tightly.

"What're you girls doing here?" she asks as she pulls back.

Darla wipes a tear out of her eye. "Herrin's guys shot at the club when we were in there. We didn't know where else to go. But the guys were killed. A bunch of Grim Angels were there. They drove us here to meet up with Drex."

"Always something," I groan.

But then a smile graces my lips. Herrin just fucked the hell up.

The Grim Angels on our side just killed any chance he had of beating us.

About damn time he fucked up. I was starting to get tired of him winning.

"By the way, who is Tiffany?" I hear Sarah asking as I walk away.

"I am."

I'm not sure what else is said—nor do I give a fuck. I jog down the stairs that used to be restricted to anyone outside the circle, but given it's the only place not in need of some construction right now, it's obviously where we're conducting business.

Nicholas—President of the Grim Angels—is casually propped against the wall, arms crossed over his chest, when I reach the bottom of the stairs. He and Drex look over at me, both of them wearing the devil's smirk.

"Nicholas has some guys tracking down where Pop is staying right now. He's all too ready to help us take them out."

"Good. Because we may only be able to focus on Herrin for a minute or two. Our other problem just got a little extra security."

Drex's lips thin, and he turns back to Nicholas. They clasps wrists and shake once.

"We'll be in touch," Nicholas says. "I noticed there was no longer an FBI detail on Herrin. Seems a little odd they went from watching his every move to vanishing right when he wants to try tearing five different towns apart."

They don't know the FBI was pulled off to hunt down the notorious AJ after they found out she had been staying with us. Nor do they know she's sent them on a wild goose chase that has them stalking half the country for her.

We keep that to ourselves.

Drex's knuckles are a bloody mess when he runs a hand along his jaw. "Things are changing a lot in Halo. We're about to raise some hell to let people know that we're not weak just because we're split. Probably best those feds aren't around."

Nicholas snorts and winks at him. "Understood, brother. Let me know if you find him before I do."

Drex nods, and Nicholas walks by me, careful not to brush against me on his way out.

"Where's Ben?" I ask Drex when I hear the door closing topside.

"In a few pieces right now. Jude is rinsing out the room."

"That didn't take long," I point out.

"I don't have your patience. I just make it hurt really fucking badly all at once." He grins, but it falls quickly. "Now tell me what the hell is going on with the other place."

"It's covered with men and crawling with security. We should move forward with the other hit. Is Sledge up for it?" I ask him.

Drex pulls out his phone with his other bloody hand, and sends a text. When it chimes with a response, he looks up at me. "Message is being sent. Liza will be dead within the hour, and she'll be delivered through one of his goons that Nicholas brought to us alive. The guy was pointless—had no idea where Herrin is. New prospect sent to his death for tonight's little show that cost Pop a lot more than he realizes."

"If he doesn't know where Herrin is, how will he send the message?" I ask him.

Drex just smirks. "Because Pop will find him. And when he does, whatever guys are sent, we'll end them. Because we'll be following the little weasel until someone shows up."

"I feel a lot better about this fucking game," I tell him on a breath, leaning against the wall.

"So do I. We'll get back to the junkie, though. I promise."

I shrug like I'm unconcerned, and turn to head up the stairs again. The second I reach the top, I see Tiffany staring blankly, her body as pale as they come, as Sarah and the other two girls talk animatedly about the old days.

"You good?" I ask Tiffany, who blinks a few times before her eyes meet mine.

She practically scrambles away from me, and I roll my eyes. Forgot that the majority of women are terrified of me. Maya tended to make me forget.

And just like that, she's in my head all over again, leaving me to wonder if someone else is watching her dress, or skate, or do her bizarre other rituals.

I'd probably kill someone if that was the case.

This fucking sucks.

CHAPTER 36

Maya

Groggy, I hear a few voices that sound miles away, even though I'm pretty sure they're in the same room. My eyes struggle to open, and each peek I manage just offers me a glimpse of light trying to make it through the black, cloth bag over my head.

When the voices start growing more distinct, I get a little excited at first, hearing the voice of my savior. The excitement is fleeting, though, because the words he's saying register next.

In that blink of an eye, he goes from savior to traitor in my mind, and my stomach roils.

"This was never the fucking plan, Lathan! How am I supposed to explain my absence that coincides with hers? I just drove us from New York to fucking Texas, and my phone has been blowing up with calls from Smitty. I had to kill John. Fucking John! Because you swore he was one of your men, and he wasn't. He almost managed to kill me before I even made it to her. We're lucky she listens to her music so damn loud when she skates. You fucked this all up, and then didn't even bother to show up with a ride for her."

I hear a sniff, like someone is snorting something, then laughter.

"You're far too annoying. Sure you don't want some?" Lathan's voice has chills rising up my spine.

"Snort your drugs with your other junkies all you want. Just give me my half of the money, because there's no way in hell I can go back."

"As soon as my sister awakes from whatever drug-induced coma you've left her in—"

251

"I had to sedate her when I realized I was going to have to drive her out here myself," the traitor growls.

" —I can torture all the account information out of her, and you can take your money and run," Lathan goes on, pretending there was no interruption.

A phone ringing has the traitor cursing. "It's Dad. Again. I have to tell him something."

"He won't suspect you. Tell him your phone was dead and you were fucking that little whore you love so much. That little excuse has worked for you before."

Cursing, I hear the traitor answer, and tears cloud my eyes when he walks out, leaving me unable to shout. My lips move in a desperate motion, but my throat is so dry that only a tiny squeak slips free.

It's only then that I realize my hands are tightly bound behind me, and that I'm tied to a chair, both my legs fastened to a chair leg.

The bag is instantly jerked off my head, and I blink against the blinding lights overhead as a shadow falls over me. A grinning Lathan is staring down at me, and I struggle in vain against the binds that hold me to the chair.

"Hello, sister. You'll notice I take you a little more seriously now," he says, gesturing to me. "Last time I never expected you to pick a lock and manage to escape. How exactly did you escape, and where were you these past several, long months?" he muses.

I roll my eyes and cut my gaze away.

He turns and grabs a bottle of water, and I struggle when he grips my chin in his hand, forcing my mouth open as I cry out in pain. Then he pours the water down my throat, causing me to cough and heave.

The water splashes on my face, up my nose, and down my neck as he pours it until its empty.

"Don't say I never gave you anything," he says as he flicks the empty bottle to the ground.

Nowhere close to hydrated, I simply glare at him.

"How long have I been here?" I ask in a scratchy voice as Lathan takes a seat behind a table that has lines of coke on a mirror next to a rolled-up dollar bill.

"Two days. You sort of almost died. Had to have a doctor come out and check on you since that idiot dosed you with enough sedatives to take down a horse."

He laughs, because he's bat-shit crazy.

"But you've survived. Now you're awake. And it's time to talk about the money you inherited. See, I'm going to need access to all Blackbird's accounts. Last time, I was polite and asked. This time, I'm going to tear the information out of you."

I snort derisively, and his look hardens as he stands.

Before he can make a move, Troy steps back in, and my eyes water as my heart kicks my chest.

"How could you?" I bite out.

Troy looks from me to Lathan like he's surprised I'm awake, then his lips thin as his gaze turns cold and lands on me again.

"Troy got tired of his family always living in Blackbird's shadow. His father is like a puppy at Blackbird's feet, no matter who Blackbird is. And now he's stuck being the next one in line to be your puppy," Lathan supplies, clapping his hands together as his grin returns.

I laugh humorlessly, but the laugh turns into a painful cough because I'm so dehydrated that laughing is a terrible idea.

"Your father gets paid like a king to be Blackbird's right hand. Not Blackbird's puppy," I manage to say, a smirk on my lips as Troy glares at me.

"Bullshit. I've seen what you have compared to my family, and it's time to even things out," Troy snaps.

"Smitty always did want you to work for things instead of just handing you everything," I say with a dark grin. "Twenty years old and you got impatient, and now you're going to die when he finds you. Because the thing he hates most is a disloyal little fuck who helped another disloyal little fuck kill his brother. Kill his family."

And now you're going to kill me — the girl he loves like a daughter. The girl who loved you like a brother. Figures you'd be the traitor amongst us. I never did have luck with brothers."

I spit up some blood from my dry throat, and cast a glare toward Lathan, who is narrowing his eyes at me.

Then I return my gaze to a seething Troy as he says, "You never saw me as a brother, or I wouldn't have been kept out of all the meetings. All the secrets. I wasn't even allowed to know where you were these past few months."

I snort again, working hard not to laugh. "Says the traitor."

"I'm not a traitor," he growls. "I'm just the guy who won't be your doormat and bring in all the money that you spend while you do nothing."

See? Misinformation leads to sociopaths lashing out. I never understood Smitty expecting his son to work from the ground up the way he did, but I'm glad he did that now.

Otherwise, Lathan would know everything the Families have been up to. As of right now, he has no clue that it's been me behind all his little hiccups with the sex trafficking ring he's running for Phillip.

Obviously we'd be having a much different discussion if he did know.

"Thing is, Smitty has more money than he can ever spend," I say, focusing my attention back on Troy. "He just lives humbly because it sucks to have the IRS breathing down your neck and trying to figure out where all that cash is coming from. Well, sort of humbly. He has a brownstone and an apartment in two of the priciest areas of New York."

He darts a look toward Lathan.

"True story," Lathan says with a careless shrug.

"What the fuck are you talking about?" Troy seethes, glaring at Lathan. "You admitted my father got pennies for all he does. That Blackbird brainwashes faithful servants into doing its bidding, then reaps all the rewards."

"Not my fault you don't realize how much it costs to have nice things in New York. And you're the idiot who was easily convinced that you'd get pennies. Now go away before I shoot you, and send in Garren. I'm going to need his expertise. Obviously I'm not even sick enough to coerce information out of my sister the way he can."

A sick feeling pits in my stomach, and Troy glares at Lathan a second longer before stalking out, slamming the door behind him.

"Obviously his brains didn't come from his father's side. Penelope, however, has always been a bit dense. Probably got it from her," Lathan says conversationally.

"The Families will hunt you down and tear you to pieces for this," I say calmly, trying to keep my emotions in check so that my threats sound a little creepier.

"They've been trying to find me for months," he says dismissively.

A small grin plays on my lips. "We've known exactly where you were for months. We're just waiting for you to lead us to Phillip," I tell him.

"Not the same place I took you the last time," he says, gesturing around the warehouse before ticking the side of his head with his index finger. "I'm not that stupid. But I do have a welcoming party waiting for them if they try to rescue you from there."

"We know exactly where you are," I say again, my grin staying in place, even as dread uncurls. A welcoming party? That's not good, because they'll go there first. Unless they figure out Lathan wouldn't take me there and know it's a setup.

He studies me for a second like he's trying to decipher if I'm bluffing or not.

"Nice try, sister, but if that were the case, Ezekiel would have barged in by now and already reclaimed you."

Damn.

Bluff called.

Still… "If you say so," I say with a shrug, looking away as though I'm unconcerned. He's paranoid, so I'm hoping to play on that.

My head jerks to the side suddenly, and pain lances through my face, rattling my teeth, as a loud *smack* resounds through the room. My cheek stings, feeling like it's on fire, as my eyes blink, trying to steady my focus.

It takes me a second to realize my bitch brother just bitch slapped me.

"Don't try to get into my head, Maya," he says, his eyes finding mine with cold detachment. "It won't work. I know you too well to let you fuck with me."

The door opens, and a guy steps in.

"Thought I told everyone not to disturb me while I was down here," Lathan bites out.

"Sorry, but Nicholas is here with his guys to take the shipment. We don't know where you keep the cash, and he's not running the drugs without cash."

It's pathetic the drug-running operation is just a ruse to cover up the sex trafficking, in case anyone goes rooting around for what he's up to out here. People like Drex and them who had no idea.

People like this Nicholas guy, whoever he is.

Cursing, Lathan walks out, leaving me behind, since there's no way he'd trust handing money over to anyone else even for a brief moment. Still a little dazed from his slap, I look around the room, trying to find something that will help me.

Being tied to a chair limits my options.

The door opens again, and a guy steps in, his face a stone mask as he starts undoing his jeans on his way to me.

"What the hell are you doing?" I growl.

He smirks at me. "I've come to make you talk. Lathan sent for me."

Garren. He mentioned a Garren.

"Whatever he's paying you, I'll quadruple it. All you have to do is get me out of here."

His gaze rakes over me as he bites down on his bottom lip. "Lathan would kill me," he says absently. "And passing you up would be hard to do."

"Ten million might change your mind," I offer, arching an eyebrow.

That has his attention, and his gaze sweeps back up to my eyes, suspicion pooling in their depths.

"Ten? Just like that?"

"You're only down here to torture information out of me — apparently by really disgusting measures — because Lathan wants access to the unlimited funds I have at my disposal. Ten million is the kind of change you find in my couch cushions, if you get my meaning."

He runs a finger over his lips. "Fifteen and you have a deal."

"Twenty if you get me to Halo," I go on, and a grin spreads over his lips.

"Done."

He buttons his jeans back up, and he checks over his shoulder before pulling out a knife. I try to stay composed even as I stare at that knife.

When he bends and starts cutting my legs free, I blow out a breath of relief. He quickly moves to my hands, talking quietly as he frees them.

"Lathan will talk to Nicholas for at least an hour, filling him in on the various drops. He doesn't let anyone handle that part of the business. And Nicholas and his club will be all over the front yard. Once we get to the top of the stairs, we'll creep out the back. You have to stay silent."

My hands get freed, and I alternate between my wrists as I rub feeling back into them.

"I want the money wired to me by the time we reach Halo," he adds.

"Not a problem, but I won't connect the full funds until I'm safely away from your vehicle. I'll only give you half until then."

He looks at me skeptically.

"I'm not the one who is untrustworthy. You came down here to do terrible things, and I'm paying for my freedom. Keep that in mind."

Shrugging like that makes sense, he turns his back and moves toward the door.

Fingertips throbbing, I stand and grab another bottle of water, guzzling it as he goes to peek out the door.

He gestures for me to follow, and I do, putting the bottle down, even though I'm still thirsty.

I stay close to his back as we creep up the stairs, but as soon as he opens that door, a gunshot sounds, nearly deafening me, and I swallow down any sound that tries to escape me as something wet splatters against my face.

I look up, seeing a gross hole all the way through Garren's head, as he slowly starts to collapse. I barely dodge his body in time as he starts rolling down the stairs, and I look up to find my brother blowing the end of the gun like it's an old Western movie.

"Good help is so hard to find when your sister can pay them more than you," he says on an exasperated sigh. "Guess I'll just have to torture you myself. Obviously I'll use different methods, since I'm not quite *that* fucking sick."

I cling to the railing, wondering if he'd have the balls to shoot me and risk killing me before he could get the info. Dead sounds better than tortured, so I risk it.

With one hard lunge, I tackle Lathan to the ground, surprising the hell out of him. He cries out in pain when my knee slams into his balls with all the force I can muster, and I knock the gun away before pushing up and taking off running toward the back door, bending and scooping up the gun on my way. I never slow down long enough to try and shoot behind me, too worried I'll miss and end up shot instead.

"Fucking stop her!" Lathan shouts through the strain.

I hear what sounds like chairs scraping the floor and shit crashing to the ground before thunderous footsteps start chasing. I practically crash through the back door, running as hard as I can toward the small canyon-like thing I can barely make out under the moonlight.

Gunshots ringing out from behind have me dropping to my knees immediately and then belly-crawling as fast as I can.

"Stop fucking shooting!" I hear Lathan roar. "If I wanted her dead, she'd already be dead! Get her!"

With that bit of assurance, I leap to my feet and start barreling ahead once again.

Bet those fuckers chasing me aren't making fun of all my skating now — after building up my leg muscles and stamina. They might still catch me, but I'm going to make them work for it.

CHAPTER 37

AXLE

"Meet me out front in five," Sarah says, a strange look on her face as she walks by me.

"Okay, why?" I ask, but she doesn't answer before slipping out the back.

Shaking my head, I take a long drag off my drink, then lean back in my chair as I watch the TV from our surveillance on Lathan's place. Sarah already returned from her solo mission.

Lathan hasn't appeared even once.

Scratching my jaw, I take in the scene. No cars have been in or out, but the wide doors open often. There's nothing but cars in there. No loads of drugs stashed in the corner like the last time I was there.

This isn't where Lathan is. But for some damn reason, he's trying to make someone think he's there. He has so many enemies and shady alliances that there's no telling who he's setting up.

I glance down, realizing it's been exactly five minutes, and I walk toward the door. Reflexively, my gaze flicks toward the camera, and I pause.

The neon yellow pole has been moved. Why? Because that pole stays in the only blind spot on the camera. It's bright yellow, so that it's noticed if it's ever moved.

Just the tip of the pole is in view of the camera where someone smooth thought they'd be smarter.

Fucking Sarah.

She'd better not let whoever this fucker is kill me.

Or even shoot at me, for that matter.

Obviously, she saw the pole first.

Cursing, I reach behind the bar and grab the trash, giving myself an excuse to go out. Plus, a bagful of mostly bottles doubles as a weapon, if necessary.

"What's going on?" Dash asks, eyebrows arched.

I never take out the trash. That's for prospects.

I gesture for him to hang back, and he mutters a curse before drawing his gun and moving out of sight from the door.

As I toss the bag over my shoulder and shove through the door, I force myself not to look around.

The barrel of a gun is quickly jammed into the back of my head, and I consider killing Sarah with my bare hands just as soon as I survive this.

"Six days ago, Maya Black left this club in tears," a man says, confusing the hell out of me and stiffening my spine at the same time. "She never said why. She wouldn't talk about it at all. I let it go, because she was safe and didn't seem hurt in any way."

The gun digs a little deeper into the back of my skull, and I resist the urge to fight out of this before he tells me what the hell he's saying about Maya.

"Two days ago, she was skating in her personal, private, and very secure rink. Suddenly she's missing, and the only thing I can figure out is this club had something to do with it," he bites out.

My stomach lurches, and I spin hard and fast, grabbing his wrist and turning the gun on him before he can adjust. He stumbles back, about to reach for a second gun, when Sarah is suddenly there, a gun to the back of his head.

He closes his eyes before blowing out a breath, and I take in the fact he's a beast of a man. A man who looks like he hasn't slept in too long.

"Sorry, Smitty. Don't go shooting Maya's boyfriend, or she might just cut you a new asshole," Sarah says, sounding overly enthusiastic. "And since I kind of want to get *my* boyfriend back, I can't allow any of his friends to go dying."

Her attention is solely focused on the side of his face as she walks around him, her gun inches from his skull—which is how you should hold a gun on someone instead of pressed against the skin.

But this guy is Smitty, apparently. And he's old school.

He glares daggers at Sarah until she comes completely into focus. Then he pales.

Sarah leans sideways and stage-whispers, "Think he just realized who I am."

Smitty swallows, and his face is a stone mask again. "You know who I am, and you know I don't travel alone," he tells her.

"You know who I am, and I would have noticed an entire horde of you in a city where I'm watching everything going on," she says.

"Both of you shut the fuck up unless you're talking about what the hell you meant about Maya missing," I say, lifting his own gun toward him.

He narrows his eyes at me. "I haven't slept since she went missing. My wife was talking to her one minute, and she said John had eyes on her. She went to her car and returned, only to find them both missing. She immediately called me, because Maya wouldn't leave when she expected her back. My wife worries often for Maya, but I take each call seriously."

"Cut the fucking story in half and tell me who took her," I growl, moving closer.

"I thought it had to be you. No one is seen on the cameras. They were disabled minutes after my wife walked out. John was found dead in an elevator. You're the only ones I could accuse besides Lathan. And I wanted it to be you."

The tears teetering on his eyes and his lip wavering as he stares at us has me lowering the gun.

"I need to know everything. Now. Because I sure as fuck didn't take her, but I am going after her. Is it just you?"

He shakes his head, and suddenly seven guys on each side turn the corners and start approaching us with guns trained on our bodies.

Sarah grabs her phone from her hip, rolling her eyes when she reads the screen, never moving her gun away from Smitty's head.

"Well, I just got a text saying fifteen or more guys from New York just crossed Halo's borders a few minutes ago."

Smitty's lips twitch when he arches an eyebrow at her.

"I sort of hate you right now," she tells him, but I talk over them before they can say more to each other.

"Lathan isn't at his warehouse. He's got to be somewhere else near there, though," I say as I dart inside.

"Drex!" I shout down through the basement entrance of the warehouse.

"What?"

"Get every fucking drug dealer or drug runner we know on the phone, and find out where Lathan is, because he's not at the other warehouse."

"Can it wait? We've kind of got a lot of other shit going on right this minute."

I start calling numbers, not bothering to answer.

"Maya is missing. It can't wait!" Sarah calls down for me.

I don't even hear what's being said after that. I barely even notice Drex as he comes topside, a flurry of motion as he starts pulling out every phone number source we have.

My heartbeat is in my ears, making it a struggle to even ask questions to the guys I actually have good rapport with. No one knows a Lathan.

No one.

Everyone has heard of him, but no one knows him.

Smitty leans over a counter, looking as though he's trying to compose himself. The fourteen militant men all drape around the counter, waiting on us to put forth the next move.

That's the moment I lose it.

My phone tumbles out of my hand as I charge the asshole, and he turns just as my fist collides with his face. He's thrown to the ground as Dash and Jude tackle my arms, holding me back.

"You were supposed to protect her!" I shout at the fucking asshole on the ground, fighting like a caged animal to break free from their hold. "Two fucking days she's been gone, and now you come to me?!"

He wipes the blood from his lip, snarling as he stands. "I've been looking every-fucking-where for her. That warehouse was armed to the max, and we've been watching it for Lathan. I only came here to find out if you'd sold her out to him, and to pry information about where he might be."

Jude curses as he digs his feet in, and Dash yanks me back when I try to go after the son-of-a-bitch to rip his head off.

"I sent her there to be safe!" I roar. "You're her fucking family! You have men everywhere and money to buy even more! Why was one fucking guy supposed to be guarding her on his own?"

Smitty just continues to stare at me like he wants me dead as badly as I want to kill him.

"The entire fucking building is secure. It's her Family's building! Only one guy was in the rink, but twenty or more were on that floor. She doesn't like a damn audience when she's trying to de-stress. I force her to let one man be at her side. Twenty fucking men. There's no way they could have gotten out!"

"Unless someone trusted to be there didn't raise suspicion and he took her out during a shift change," Drex points out, phone still at his ear as he turns away and resumes his conversation.

"Get the fuck off me," I growl at Jude and Dash.

"Not until you're less murderous," Jude snorts. "War, and all that."

"There's going to be a fucking war if anything happens to her because you let some half-ass loyal son-of-a-bitch that close to her," I say to Smitty.

"Everyone on that floor was born into this world," he defends, his face turning a furious red. "Every one of them is tied to her from birth. Either they saw her born or they grew up with her."

I stop fighting, breathing heavily as I think back to anything and everything Maya said when she was with me. She mentioned all the names of her closest protectors. The men she trusted with her life. None of them stand out.

"No one went missing?"

His jaw grinds. "Only my son went missing, but he has a small addiction of his own. Women. He was holed up in some hotel with one of his whores. Per the usual."

My veins run a little colder. "Where is he now?" I ask him, but Sarah plucks his phone out of his pocket before he can answer.

"What are you —"

"Where is he?" I interrupt Smitty as Sarah does something with his phone.

Smitty faces me again, his jaw set. "Troy loves her. He'd never do this. They've been like brother and sister their entire lives."

"She has terrible luck with brothers," Dash points out.

"They tend to get jealous," Jude adds.

"Where is he?" I ask again through gritted teeth.

"He wouldn't be that stupid if he did something like that," Smitty goes on. "He'd know better than to disappear, too. Someone would be setting him up. He's still in New York."

Sarah walks back over, her creepy chipper-smile gone, and a dark expression on her face as she hands Smitty his phone. "Troy is twenty miles away," she says tightly.

Smitty just stares at her for a minute, before he has to stagger back.

"No," he says hollowly. "Even if he was that horrible, he wouldn't be that stupid," he goes on, talking more to himself than anyone else.

"I don't care if it starts a war. If I get my hands on your son, I'm killing him," I bite out, then turn to Sarah. "Where's the signal from?"

"My guy is trying to pi it down, but I have a general location. He had to turn the phone on via remote access, then turn on the GPS via remote access, all from the number I got from Smitty's phone. He did it fast. It won't take—"

"Got him," Drex says, jogging up to us as he pockets his phone. "Nicholas is his runner. He only told me where to find him because I told him Lathan took Axle's old lady and explained the highlights of the situation, minus the mafia thing."

He starts jogging out, and we all follow. Smitty's men follow, but Smitty struggles to get up. I don't have time to fucking wait on him to absorb it, so we leave without him.

Drex yells at Drake as he pokes his head out of the tattoo parlor, telling him to keep an eye on shit. Then we're gone, driving like hell through the mostly quiet streets as fast as we can go.

Sarah is on the back of Dash's bike as I pass them, racing to get beside Drex. My stomach is in knots, my heart is in my throat, and everything on me is throbbing.

If she's dead because I sent her back...

I can't even think about it. I just need to focus on finding her.

Alive.

CHAPTER 38

Maya

Half of them have given up, the other half must work out a lot.

Doubled over and heaving for a few bursts of air, I look around, seeing my small canyon-like crater coming to an end, stealing all that coverage with it. I keep tripping over rocks or bushes, and my body feels like it's been banged to hell from the unforgiving ground, but I'm not ready to give up just yet.

Lungs protesting, I start running again, ignoring the burn in my legs. Why couldn't they have been in the back? Then I could have ran through the front and stolen a car instead of making a run for it.

ATVs sound in the distance, coming for me. They can't drive through the canyon, but they can sure as hell drive above it, looking for me. I duck behind more coverage, just as I've done on each of their sweeps.

Once they've moved on, I start running again. I can see the solid, steep wall just ahead, and I whimper a little. How the hell am I going to get out of this mess?

Loud, rapid gunfire echoes through the canyon, and I curse, diving to the side. It sounds too far away for the shots to be firing at me. Are they just hoping to make me scream so that I'll give myself away?

Lathan told them *not* to shoot at me, damn it.

He needs my money before I'm allowed to die.

More and more gunfire has me questioning what's going on. Especially when the ATVs suddenly take off in that direction.

After several long minutes of a lot of gunfire, I peer around the edge, wondering how many are still chasing me.

No one is there.

The gunfire sounds like it's coming from the direction of the house, and I look around, finding some roots poking through the canyon wall.

Hoping like hell those extra five slices of pizza I've been having all week don't break the damn roots out from under me, I start climbing them. Technically, I was starved for two days, since they sort of almost killed me, or whatever.

Admittedly, the more height I gain, the more I start cursing the pizza. I also curse Lathan for how weak I feel. That running wouldn't usually bother me. This climbing wouldn't normally be an issue.

But I'm hungry and thirsty, and my legs feel like gelatin right now. Half my stamina isn't as good as all of my stamina when I'm at one-hundred percent.

All at once, the gunfire ceases, and I peer over the top of the canyon, seeing it clear before hauling myself out. I'm tempted to go back and see if everyone is dead, but decide to keep running like hell.

I'd rather get picked apart by buzzards than risk returning to capture.

Lying on my back, I pant for air, ignoring the shooting pain through my side from the constant sprint for my life. Sheer determination has me pushing myself back up to my feet and stumbling my way into the desert.

But then pain explodes against the side of my face with no warning, and the taste of blood fills my mouth as I cry out, falling hard to the ground.

Weak from hours of running, and drained from exhaustion, dehydration, and hunger, I don't have the strength to push myself up to my feet. I hover on my knees, digging deep for strength, when I feel a boot collide with my stomach.

Pain lances through my core, and I get nauseous as I roll across the ground, my eyes closing and opening as I watch the black boots draw closer.

"Maya is so strong," comes a soft, taunting voice. "Dad always said that," Troy tells me on a sigh. "She's going to be an excellent Blackbird."

I spit out the blood, even though more merely pools in my mouth. I bit the hell out of my tongue when the dickhead punched me.

"How strong are you now?"

"Strong enough that I won't beg for my life," I say as I peer up. "Strong enough that I won't ever tell you how to steal my Family's money, no matter what Lathan does to me."

I spit out blood and wipe my mouth, my head swaying a little as I try to keep my attention trained on him and not allow myself to pass out.

"Strong enough to run for hours after being drugged for two days," I go on.

Though, I think I can thank adrenaline for that. I've apparently exhausted my supply, because I'm *reeeaaalllyy* feeling that shit hardcore now, and there's that whole dizzy and queasy thing just to put the miserable cherry on top.

Not that I'll tell him that.

"And strong enough to look your father in the eye and tell him I had to kill his son for being a traitor."

He laughs humorlessly as I continue to hug the ground, waiting for another burst of adrenaline to save me at any damn time it feels froggy.

Unfortunately, no such luck, and I see two laughing Troys, then one, then two again. My head feels like a big ball on a tiny stick, completely unbalanced and ready to tip over.

I drop it back to the ground, unable to find another ounce of strength.

"There's that spunk Dad always boasts about. You know, you're nothing more than a little girl with a big mouth. You amuse the men who actually matter. That's all you are—a court jester."

A small smile toys with the edges of my lips. "You know as well as I do this court jester will be avenged. Just picture what Ezekiel or Ingrid will do to you when they find out you betrayed me."

I get to see his bravado doubly falter when he splits into two Troys again.

"Not just that, Troy. I have other friends. Friends who might very well make the pain last for days. Friends who only know how to deliver pain. Friends who will make you wish you'd been born loyal instead of an entitled little prick."

He kicks me hard in the side, and I flop over onto my back from the force, grinning up at him as I start laughing.

"What the hell is so fucking funny?" he roars.

"I was so weak, that I couldn't get the gun out of the front of my pants." His eyes widen as I hold the gun up, concentrating on both of him. "Until you knocked me over. Thanks."

Since I can't decide which fuzzy blur is actually him, I shoot both of him, hearing a cry of pain that tells me I hit the real one with one of those shots.

But my head is spinning too hard, and I shoot again, trying to listen to where the sounds are coming from.

Another cry of pain is forced out of *me* when he's suddenly wrenching the gun away and kicking me hard again in the ribs. Definitely cracked some of those damn things.

"Fucking bitch. You shot me!"

"You betrayed me," I bite out, hissing out a breath of pain.

He grabs me by my hair, and I try to claw at his hand as he starts dragging me, cursing his bleeding wound—that apparently isn't freaking fatal or too damaging—as he uses my hair like a handle.

"Betrayal is cut and dried to you. Never mind what you do to all the people you step on to sit on your throne," he growls.

The pain in my scalp is borderline excruciating, and I struggle harder to free his hand from its death grip.

"I didn't step on anyone! Everyone knows what they sign on for!"

He snorts. "Unless their father is my father. Then you get a doormat for the queen and act like you're happy to do all the hard work, while she takes all the glory." He pauses and stops walking. "What the hell is that sound? Is that a golf cart?"

"No glory for the anonymous, you stupid son-of-a—"

A loud shot silences my words, and the hand on my hair slowly releases its grip. Troy drops to the ground beside me, or at least I think so. Everything is still so blurry.

I heave, retching as the nausea and dizziness finally win, and someone gingerly pulls my hair away from my face, running a soothing hand up and down my back.

"Easy," Sarah says, causing my entire body to relax when I hear her voice. "Couldn't have been easy to make it this far. Just take a few deep breaths. I've got us a battery-powered, quiet golf cart less than fifty feet away."

I snort, sob, and laugh all at once, creating a terrible sound, but relief continues to pour through me.

"I've already picked off all the ones who were still following you. Come on," she says when I stop shaking and the retching ends.

"If I could walk, I wouldn't have been flopping around on the ground as he dragged me around by my hair," I mumble as she helps me to my feet, grunting under my weight as I struggle to keep my legs from becoming jelly.

"On second thought," she grumbles, putting me back down gently. "I'll drive the cart to you."

Again, I make that weird combination of sounds, every emotion determined to come out at once as she kneels in front of me, pushing my hair out of my face again.

"Stay here," she jokes, then winks as she darts off into the night.

271

I glance over at the still body of a boy I used to play video games with. The boy was my brother. The man was far less impressive.

Smitty will be devastated.

"At least tell me I shot him somewhere good," I say as Sarah pulls up beside me, the golf cart parked directly in front of me.

I see the blur of her rustling around, pushing his body from side to side, and I ignore the sick feeling in my gut as I look away from a man I once called a friend.

"Looks like you got him in the ass."

I groan, cursing the fact the first time I finally shot someone, it was in the ass. Bad girl problems.

"You okay?" she asks as she helps me into the seat.

"As long as I pretend this is all one really twisted punchline for an ongoing joke, I won't fall apart. It's a coping mechanism. So start making really morbid jokes while my tears dry, because no one can see me broken."

My voice cracks on that last line, and she blows out a heavy breath. She knows the score better than anyone. Weak girls in our business get dead real quick. The weaker you look, the more people think they can kill you.

CHAPTER 40

AXLE

The second we figured out Maya had made a run for it—made obvious by the amount of people scouring the land and shouting that they hadn't found her—we started blowing shit to hell.

Now Lathan is on his knees before me, blood smeared all over his face from the multitude of dead bodies piled up around him.

His jaw stays tight, but his lip trembles as I kneel in front of him, cocking my head to the side.

"You're going to start a war if you kill me," he snarls. "Phillip Jenkins will come after you. He will *destroy* you and your little fucking club."

I gesture around at his employees who are still being dragged in—all of them dead, or mostly dead, as they get dropped to random places. Couch. Chair. Dining room chairs.

"It'll be suspicious but not tied to us," Sledge whispers to me, his back facing Lathan.

I look up from my crouched position.

"Did you hear that?" I ask Lathan. "We can't cover up all these bullet holes. We'd be here for weeks with rotting corpses," I go on. "But junkies die all the time from meth labs exploding. Now, anyone wise enough would notice the bullet holes if any body parts survive such an explosion. But let's face it, no one would immediately consider us. Certainly not Phillip."

He narrows his eyes, knowing how right I am.

"Besides, you *Family* people think we're just brute strength and rough finesse," I say with a dark smile, parroting Maya's words from so long ago. "Why would we bother blowing the place up to cover our trail?"

He swallows hard.

"What do you want? Whatever she's promised you, I can double it the second I have access to those accounts."

I don't have to say anything before Smitty steps up, and Lathan pales. He knows he can't turn Smitty. I'm sure he's figured out we're all untouchable too by now.

"If you tell me how Troy got her out of the building undetected, I'll end your suffering quickly," Smitty offers.

Lathan's nostrils flare, and his jaw tics. "Nice offer. I'll pass—"

I blow a hole through his knee, the barrel of my gun still pressed against his leg as he wails in pain. Pulling my gun back, I stare at him expectantly.

He puffs out a couple of breaths like he's breathing through the pain, his hands cuffed behind his back as he remains seated on the ground with his legs stretched out in front of him.

"How did he get her out of the building?" Smitty growls.

Lathan grins, eyes jaded and hollow. "You're old, Smitty. You know you don't keep up with the times. Your son is just smarter than you. That's all I'm saying."

I shoot a hole in his other knee, hearing him roar out his pain as his eyes roll back in his head. When he falls backwards, I stand over him, and in quick succession, put two bullets in his forehead.

"I didn't find out how he stole her from the building yet!" Smitty snaps, yanking me back by my arm.

My eyes drop to where his hand is touching me, and I slowly lift my eyes to meet his. Smitty, the beast of a man, clears his throat and releases his hold as he takes a step back.

Sometimes the scary scars come in handy. Saves me from finding out if he's too old to fight.

"Doesn't matter how he got her out. She's not going back with you. It's fucking clear to me that I can keep her safer."

His eyes narrow to slits. "You almost got her blown up."

"You let her get kidnapped and didn't find her for two days. Who fucking knows what has happened to her by now?!" I shout, getting right in front of him.

He starts to do something or say something, when Drex is suddenly there and pushing us apart.

"Sarah has Maya," he tells us, but his eyes are on me. "She's bringing her back right now."

I drop my gun to the ground and race outside, kicking my way through the door we mostly broke on entry. My eyes scan the area, searching for them, and the second I see the white golf cart coming toward us, I sprint to meet it.

"She passed out halfway here," Sarah tells me, jumping out and coming around as I take in the blood and bruises all over Maya's face.

"They knocked her around, but nothing on her face seems broken, Axle," Sarah says like she's trying to keep me from losing it. "Her ribs might be a different story."

Swallowing the knot in my throat, I carefully lift Maya into my arms. Her bleach-blonde hair is no longer there. She went back to dark hair during our time apart.

She doesn't even stir as I cradle her to me, trying not to put any pressure on anything that seems damaged.

"She's going to need fluids," Sarah goes on. "And soon would be good. She said they over-sedated her, and she's been out cold this entire time."

My entire body is strung tight as I walk and stare down at her at the same time. The closer we get to the lights shining from the house, the more I can see every bruise, red mark, and cut on her face.

Her lip is split and bleeding generously, and her cheek is swollen and cut.

I let her go to keep her and the guys safe. Yet, she almost died right down the road from me.

Smitty is panting as he runs up, his eyes tearing up when he sees her bruised and battered body lying limply in my arms.

"Troy did most of the damage," Sarah tells Smitty, her eyebrows going up when she provokes a reaction.

He turns away, gagging like he can't stomach the sight of Maya upon hearing that.

"I'll kill him," he bites out, back still turned. "He's not my son. He's nothing but a coward."

"He's already dead. I can show you where I left the body if you want to go collect it."

Smitty turns around, his face hard. "Let the animals feed off his remains. He doesn't deserve a proper burial."

He turns and stalks away, and I brush my lips over Maya's forehead, worried to death that I'm holding her too tightly.

Smitty opens the back door to his vehicle, and I just look at him like he's crazy.

"How is she going to ride on your bike when she's unconscious?" he asks.

"If you try to take off with her, I will hunt you down and kill you myself. Understand?"

His jaw grinds. "You keep making threats toward me when you know who I am. Watch yourself, biker boy. You're not playing with thugs right now. You're playing with people who can make you disappear from the face of the earth."

"Funny how Phillip and Lathan never disappeared then, huh?" I snap.

"Long game for the big ones. You're just a small fish in a massive ocean of sharks. No one will notice you—"

"Maya will notice him missing, and your personal family has already betrayed her once. Let's not make it a normal thing," Sarah butts in, moving to my side.

Smitty looks away, eyes glistening as he stares at the inside of his vehicle. "We'll discuss this somewhere else. Your friends are about to blow this place up, and I'd like to be far away from such action," he says much calmer.

"I can drive your big shiny bike if you'll commit the cardinal sin and let me," Sarah says, looking up at me as I stare at the backseat, Maya still in my arms as I refuse to put her down.

"Take the damn thing," I say without hesitation as I slip into the backseat, Maya still in my arms.

Smitty mutters something about brutes and Neanderthals, but I don't give a damn.

Maya sleeps all the way back to the safe house, and I carry her inside to the room we stayed in the day she had to leave me.

Carefully, with every ounce of fucking delicate I possess, I put her down on the bed.

"Doctor is on his way," Drex says as he follows me in. "We'll take her to the hospital if we have to. She'll be fine, though. Her breathing is solid and her heartrate is steady."

Blowing out a breath, I gesture for him to go, and I follow him out, leaving the door open so I can see inside whenever I want to check and make sure she hasn't vanished.

Smitty is drinking scotch when I step into the living room.

"You and I don't get to decide, so let's drink and wait for her to wake instead of fighting like barbarians over a woman who will kill us both for making a decision without her input," he says, handing me a glass.

I grab an empty glass and pour myself some of the whiskey Drex hands me, knowing there's no way Smitty tampered with it.

Call it paranoid, but these guys are shady as fuck.

Smitty's lips simply twitch as he drinks the glass of scotch I rejected, proving to me he didn't just try to poison me.

His eyes flit to the bar next to us, then he looks away. When his gaze darts back and settles on a few tiny condiment bottles I've brought here, a sad smile graces his lips.

"Well, damn," he says on a sigh, his gaze returning to me as though he's deflated. "She should have mentioned she fell in love."

It's like a punch to the stomach to hear him say that, because I go back to the sad look in her eyes the day she had to leave. Almost like she was waiting for me to reciprocate what she'd said. Or acknowledge it. Or hell, act like I heard her at all.

I drink more of the whiskey as he studies me.

The others give us some space, moving outside to drink and wind down from the night. Jude and Dash are still on their way back, since they're the ones who volunteered to blow the place to hell.

"That's why she was crying," he goes on. "And you sent her away to keep your men safe from Phillip. Not that I blame you."

"I sent her away because we have our own shit going on and she almost got killed because of it. It was just a matter of time before someone realized she was my weakness and used her against us. Against me. I didn't want that happening, and I didn't want my friends dying because of my selfishness."

"Yet now you're willing to risk it all?" he muses.

"Now I see it's not just here that she's at risk. As for the rest, we'll figure it out. Even if I have to chain her to my side so that I have eyes on her at all times."

His grin is brief as he clears his expression and clinks his glass against mine.

"Good luck with that. Maya hates being around people for too long. She prefers her solitude a lot of times."

A smirk graces my lips, and he just studies me. She never minded me close by.

My moment of smugness evaporates with reality.

I sent her away. I was too fucking busy being pissed to even tell her goodbye. I didn't call. I didn't do anything but push her away.

What the hell happens when she wakes up and tells me to go fuck myself?

CHAPTER 41

Before I can even peel open my eyes, there are voices around me.

"Axle might kill you if he finds you lying on the bed beside her," Eve is saying from somewhere in the room.

"Like I won't hear him the second they all get back. I'll have plenty of time to move," Drake tells her, sounding really close to my side. "I want her to think we got married in Vegas and that now I'm the Blackbird king. Should be interesting."

I'd laugh, if it didn't hurt so much to even consider. Guess Drake knows who I am now.

"I worry about you sometimes," Eve says on a sigh.

"Only sometimes? I must be losing my edge."

Ever so slowly, my eyes blink open to the bright light filtering through the room.

"She's awake," Eve says, even as I blink again, trying to adjust my vision to the brightness.

"Is that what it means when someone's eyes are open? Always wondered about that," Drake says, grinning at Eve when I look over at him.

Then he turns that dazzling smile on me.

"Afternoon, sunshine. You look like shit." He says all this with a grin.

"I was kidnapped by a sociopath," I say with a hoarse, scratchy voice, forcing the words out. "What's your excuse?"

Drake just grins broader as Eve hands me a bottle of water. I thank her with a tight smile as I start drinking the water, trying not to drink too fast.

"Well, she seems fine," Drake goes on, then looks at me again and holds up four fingers.

"How many fingers am I holding up?" he asks seriously.

Idly, I take in the fact there's an IV running into my hand, presumably fluids.

I extend my middle finger to Drake. "More than me," I say, still flipping him off.

He laughs lightly. "I'd say all her brain cells are probably destroyed, but that likely happened before the blow to the head."

"*Blows* to the head," I grumble, wincing when I feel the pain in my side that reminds me of my ribs. Just cracked—not broken. "Plural."

I look around, taking in the room I'm in, and a pain catches in my chest.

"Where's Axle?" I ask Eve.

"They had something to do. They had already gotten the ball rolling on striking back at Herrin and making a statement when we found out about you, and—"

Her words cut off when a familiar face steps into the room, and tears blur my vision as Smitty looks over at me with sad, haunted eyes. He's almost too big for the doorway, and he ducks his head as he comes in completely and straightens again.

"We'll give you two a minute," Eve says softly.

"I'm not going anywhere," Drake tells her in a bored drawl. "Axle said he doesn't trust the Family right now, and that I'm to stay put or he'll make me look as un-pretty as he is." He shudders dramatically. "I'm too pretty not to be pretty."

I groan inwardly, rolling my eyes as I swing my gaze to Drake. "Go. We need a minute alone."

He looks between us, and all jokes aside, looks genuinely worried about leaving me alone with Smitty.

"I'll leave the door open," Smitty says tightly, taking a seat in the far corner. "And I'll stay right here."

Drake warily stands, and a tear slips from my eye. Smitty looks broken. The man who has been like a second father to me acts like he's worried I'll be scared of him. Everyone is treating him like he's the one who betrayed me.

"Don't be ridiculous, Smitty," I say with a stronger voice, the water already helping to soothe the dry throat. "You can come closer."

Drake glares at me, but I ignore him. Compared to Smitty, I barely know Drake at all. Not that I don't appreciate the protective vibe that makes me feel safe right now.

Smitty looks down, a tear falling from his eye, and Drake stands to leave. "I'll be right outside. Armed. I'm a decent shot."

I vaguely remember shooting Troy in the ass, but I definitely don't bring that up right now.

I also realize I'm very naked under this sheet. Why am I naked?

Clutching the sheet to my chest, I sit up a little, even though it sends a shot of pain up my spine from the pitiful ribs.

"Don't try to move," Smitty says, standing and hesitating to come toward me.

"I'm sorry," I finally say to him, tears choking me.

His eyes fill with more tears, and he shakes his head.

"I'm the one who's sorry, little one. My own son hated the Family so much he betrayed you and almost got you killed. And I was too blind to see it coming."

"You shouldn't be expected to choose between your family and our Family. I understand if you can't be a part of Blackbird, and you have my word nothing will happen if you decide to retire." The words are barely a broken whisper.

He smiles grimly at me. "I'll be honest. I thought about leaving after I learned of Troy's involvement. Simply because I don't trust my judgment anymore. Lathaniel died on my watch. You almost died at the hands of my son."

"My brother betrayed the Family, Smitty. Not just Troy. I want Lathan dead worse than—"

"Lathan is dead," he interrupts, lips twitching. "Your boyfriend killed him when we came for you."

My heart beats a little faster at just the alluded mention of Axle.

"But I understand what you're saying," he says on a long breath. "When someone betrays you, the blood running in their veins doesn't make you more likely to forgive them. If their plan had worked, Blackbird would have crumbled, and Troy would have sentenced us all to death for greed. Not just you. His own sisters. His mother. Me. He gets no loyalty from me. If it's okay with you, I want to stay at your side. You're more my daughter than he is now my son. Even in death, I will never claim a man who doesn't care about his family."

"Because family is all that matters," I say with a small smile, knowing that's why we even call our organization a Family.

"They're very protective and don't trust me very much," he says quietly, gesturing with his head toward the door. "They fear I will want retribution for Troy's death."

"That's because they don't know you," I say softly.

He nods, looking down. "I realize I spent a lot of time worrying about you for nothing when you were here. This club, though a little rough and barbaric, has iron-clad loyalty to each other that you don't find everywhere."

"Only the inner circle. It's a little shaky the lower down you get. Any tips you can leave them with to snuff out the leaks?"

His lip wavers, and I realize how stupid that was to say. "No. I'm afraid I don't trust myself to give advice in that area right now."

I nod in understanding and silent apology, as I clutch the sheet a little tighter to me.

"I'm naked under here. Any clothes around that I can wear so we can get out of here?" I ask him.

His brow furrows. "You want to leave?"

I spot the little ketchup beside the door, perched on the dresser, and emotion clogs my throat. "Nothing has changed, and I'd rather not see Axle and have to say goodbye a second time."

I look back over at Smitty to see sympathy in his eyes. What the hell is that about?

I blame it on the fact he just lost a son and his emotions are a little heightened. It's hard to be sensitive to his loss when Troy was willing to turn me over to Lathan to be tortured. And the fact he beat the hell out of me doesn't help either.

Clearing his throat, he stands, opening a drawer and tossing me a T-shirt that definitely belongs to Axle. Damn it.

Then he tosses me a pair of boxers.

"Really?" I ask, trying to lighten the mood.

He barely cracks a grin. "Unfortunately, I didn't have the forethought to bring clothes, and yours were rather ruined." He clears his throat again. "I'll let the guys know we're about to leave. It'll take a few minutes to—"

"Axle said no leaving," Drake butts in, poking his head through the doorway after clearly having been eavesdropping.

Chest pain.

"Tell him thank you for coming after me," I say to Drake, forcing a smile. "But I need to get back."

He narrows his eyes at me. "Too pretty to be un-pretty," he says, gesturing at his face.

"You'll still be pretty no matter what," I say with a wink, and he rolls his eyes while groaning.

"Damn women. Why do I always get put in charge of the vagina squad, when everyone knows the vagina squad never listens to me?"

As he stalks away, Smitty looks over at me. "Odd little assortment of friends you've made."

Smitty turns and walks out, shutting the door behind him to give me privacy.

With a wince, I pull out the IV, and massage my hand for a second. Then I bite back a litany of curses when I pull on the clothes, my entire body protesting the actions.

Fortunately, in just a few weeks, the pain will be more tolerable in my ribs. Yes, I've dealt with this before.

I glance once again at the small ketchup, and my smile tugs up. At least he's been thinking about me a little.

That makes it a little less awkward that I went and fell in love with him.

As the sheet falls away, I realize I'm not completely naked. There's a lot of Ace bandaging around my torso.

My eyes drift to the small mirror on the wall, and I grimace when I see all the bruises on my face. The swelling is minor, but Drake's words still ring true.

I really do look like shit.

CHAPTER 42

AXLE

Fifteen of Herrin's men should be a damn good start to making a statement. That was what we did this morning when our prospect lure took Liza's body with him, and two others came to pick him up.

We followed.

We killed.

We burned down the damn place.

Pretty straightforward message: Fuck with us, and we'll fuck you harder.

Now Benny — president of the Hell Breathers — who has sided with Herrin, is staring inside a small bag where part of his son is staring back at him. He cuts his gaze away, handing the bag off to someone else, as he vibrates with fury.

"I wanted him back alive. I said I would handle it!" Benny spits out. His gaze lands on us again. "You want a—"

"Don't say war," Jude drawls, feigning boredom. "We're sick of that word."

Drex smirks as Benny looks back to him.

"Apparently you forgot that Pop was the civilized one out of the two of us. You sided with him. You let your goons join his on a ride that shot up my club," Drex tells him, and Benny's nostrils flare as his eyes widen marginally. "You chose your side. I'd reconsider that choice. Because in case you haven't heard, we've started reaping debts in blood."

He gestures toward the bag.

285

"He touched my girl. He kept her locked away, torturing her. That was actually fairly kind. Notice Hershel missing?" Drex asks flippantly.

Benny's eyes widen a little more.

"He's not dying as kindly," I say with a bitter smile as my phone goes off with a text.

"Last warning, Benny. Your guys side with Herrin again, and I'll add you to the list of names we reap," Drex warns.

A guy beside Benny pulls out his gun as Benny shouts at him not to do it, but it's too late. A shot rings out across the empty parking lot, and the guy's body hits the ground.

Benny's guys look around, like they're searching for where that just came from.

"No more games, Benny. We've made a few friends along the way," Drex goes on coldly.

I can tell Benny wants to kill us, but he's not a complete idiot. He knows there's a sharpshooter. Hell, he figured we came here with some backup, which is why he didn't go for his gun himself.

I turn my back on them, only because I know Sarah is still on top of a roof, her sights set on anyone who reaches for a weapon.

Benny will cool down, then he'll weigh his options. We just shot one of their guys in front of them, and they couldn't do a damn thing. And we're just one circle of our new faction.

I pull out my phone, reading the text from Drake, and curse as I hurry my steps to my ride.

"What?" Drex asks me.

"Maya thinks she's fucking leaving."

CHAPTER 43

Maya

Smitty opens the back door for me, as I lean on Eve a little to help me down the stairs. My ribs are screaming at me to lie back down, but I pretend as though all is sunny inside me.

"I wish you'd at least stay here until I can bump up security protocols. No one knows you're here. More and more people seem to know who you are in New York," Smitty says grimly. "I need a specialist to come in and find out how Troy got you out of the building."

I shake my head, hurting too severely to walk and talk at the same time.

Just as I reach the SUV, the loud, distinct sound of Harleys has me turning my head as the guys drive toward us, barreling down the highway.

Axle is out in front, and he pulls into the yard, parking directly behind the SUV. My heart does all its usual girly things, even as it breaks a little at the sight of him.

Hard jaw set in anger and eyes narrowed on me like he's furious, he tosses his helmet aside as he moves to be directly beside me.

"I didn't say you could leave yet," Axle tells me in his gruff, commanding tone.

My eyebrow arches in challenge. "As a matter of fact, you all but shoved me out the door once already. I think, if it's all the same to you, I'll leave on my own accord this time."

Proud that my voice is steady, I start to brace myself for the pain that will come when I haul my ass into the back. A breath

287

rushes out of me instead, when I'm suddenly being lifted—very carefully.

It's my turn to narrow my eyes as I look up to see Axle staring straight ahead as he cradles me to his chest.

"What the hell do you think you're doing?" I ask, then wince when the force of my words jostles my ribs unfavorably.

"Be thankful I'm cautious of your ribs," he says stoically. "Otherwise, you'd be tossed over my shoulder right now."

He stalks up the steps and into the house, and I cast a helpless glance over his shoulder at Smitty, who is closing the back door like we're not leaving.

I start to yell at him, when Axle turns abruptly and carries me back into the bedroom before kicking the door shut behind him.

"Axle," I groan, exasperated.

I focus on my frustration instead of all the things my heart is trying to do.

He gently places me on the bed, like he's worried I'm a piece of glass and will shatter at any moment. The soft gesture is only temporarily distracting.

His shirt being tugged over his head is a little more distracting as he tosses it aside. I notice the blood on it, so don't ask what he's doing as he stalks back out and says something about a sandwich I think.

Talk about random.

Then he's back in, leaning against the door as he stares at me in that old familiar way.

"As much as I appreciate you risking your life to come save me, I still can't stay here until you suddenly remember how dangerous it is—"

"You're not safer in New York," he interrupts. "We're raising hell, reclaiming the fear we instill that people seem to have forgotten about. It's only a matter of time before we finally kill Herrin."

My brow furrows. "What does this—"

"You're staying here, Maya. You said yourself that you didn't have to be in New York, and it's proven that it's not safe for you. Someone can get to you too easily."

He pushes away from the door, undoing his jeans as he comes to me. The door opens before he gets them pushed down.

Colleen steps in with a plate and a sandwich, and my stomach growls as if it's calling dibs. Axle smirks like he expected that, and Colleen hands me the sandwich that I can't refuse.

"Thank you," I mumble around a mouthful, and she smiles tightly at me.

She deliberately avoids looking at his back as she walks out and shuts the door behind her. Axle drops his jeans the second she's out, and I shake my head.

"No sex for me. I'm too sore. And I need to be leaving," I tell him, biting another piece of the sandwich and telling myself to eat slowly so I don't get sick. "Right after I finish this."

His lips twitch as he climbs into the bed beside me, careful not to jostle it too much. Meanwhile, I eat like a starving lady.

When he leans over, my breath catches and the mouthful of food stops getting chewed, because his lips skim the side of my neck.

"You're not going anywhere," he murmurs, pressing a kiss just under my jaw.

I almost shiver. Almost.

"Axle, I have to—"

"You're not going anywhere," he says again, a little more forcefully this time as he kisses his way down the column of my throat.

I swallow painfully at the barely chewed food, putting my plate in my lap as I tilt my head to the side.

"See, I'm keeping you whether you want to stay or not. Because I'm not going to be able to be that far away now that I know you're not safe there," he goes on, his words not as seductive as his tone as he kisses another spot on my neck.

A small sigh passes through my lips as he drags his lips up my neck, nipping my ear when he reaches it. "And I don't do well with fear. I hate it. It doesn't have any room in my life, but apparently I'm going to fear losing you no matter where you are. I'd rather you be here so I can at least put myself out of my misery when I've got you in my bed."

I feel his smile against my neck, and it stupidly infects me, forcing my lips to reluctantly mimic the same motion.

"If I stay, you can't kick me out again," I say when he just continues to kiss my neck, trying to soften me to his will.

"I'll have you chained to my side as often as possible," he says as though that's a perfectly acceptable response.

I roll my eyes, wishing my lips weren't so sore. Or that I had a toothbrush.

He sticks to my neck though, so that keeps me from worrying about the latter.

"I'm trying to figure out if you're crazy or romantic," I murmur absently.

"Both," he deadpans without hesitation. "It's a side effect of loving a girl who likes tiny condiment bottles as collectibles and skates when she's waiting on a death tally."

My grin crawls up, but then it falls immediately as his words sink in. He draws back, eyes intense as he studies mine.

"Tiny condiment bottles are a perfect collectible," I state flatly, my heart still thundering in my ears as he slowly smiles that devastatingly perfect smile so few get to see.

His gaze flicks to my lips, and I start worrying about that toothbrush again. He stops himself from kissing me, his eyes probably assessing the damage there.

"Are you staying?" he asks, his gaze flicking back up to mine.

"Are you really giving me a choice?" I muse.

His smile only grows. "No."

"Then why bother asking?" I ask on a mock sigh of frustration, though I can't stop the smile that spreads again. "Besides, Mr. Surly just said he loved me. I suppose I need to stick around so I can taunt you for it.".

A small rumble of laughter escapes him, and he slides his hand up my neck, gently cupping the lower part of the side of my face that isn't beaten to hell.

When his lips brush over mine, barely ghosting them, a tear rolls down my cheek. I'm not sure why. There's no pain. And there's no such thing as happy tears, right? I mean, I've never actually cried from being happy.

But all I feel is—

"So if she's staying, does that mean I get a free pass if I make Blackbird my bookie and bet too much?" I hear Drake calling through the door.

Axle groans, and I sniffle as I bat the weird tears away. His lips move to my forehead, kissing me there.

"Go away, Drake," he calls out. "Before I make you look like me."

"You need to stop threatening my face. It's the only thing too pretty for ink, let alone a butcher knife."

Axle laughs lightly even as I scowl at the door.

"You just wish you were as pretty as him," I defend, then feel stupid when everyone, including Axle, bursts out laughing. I'm glad that door is shut, that way no one can see my red face after being a little overly defensive.

"My little protector," Axle murmurs, sliding his lips back down my neck. "Eat your sandwich. We need to get you healthy."

I turn and look at him, arching an eyebrow.

"It'll be a while before you can have another blowjob, because of the ribs and all."

A snort comes from the other side of the door as Axle just grins at me.

"But you might be able to sit on my face in a few weeks."

That has me biting into the sandwich just to keep from thinking about my favorite thing to do, and he grins as he lies back beside me.

"I'm going to drink myself into forgetting I ever heard this conversation," I hear Smitty say from the other side of the door.

And I almost choke on my sandwich as the laughter restarts.

A small grin plays on my lips when I see the light peeking through those pale eyes of Axle's. That light is reserved for only me.

And it's really freaking special.

EPILOGUE

Maya

Axle's lips move away from mine, as he collapses to my body. It's been almost two months since all hell broke loose. Things are quiet right now, but we know Herrin is plotting his next move.

Just the calm before the storm.

Hershel has started singing. He broke a lot quicker than most anyone expected, but I won the pool because I guessed it the closest. Betting odds are sort of my thing, and they're thinking about taking me out of the pools in the future.

Petty amateurs.

No backlash has found us for Lathan's death. From what little information Ingrid has been able to gather, Phillip thinks the Family came down and wiped out Lathan for taking me and trying to steal Blackbird's money.

Understandable.

Phillip doesn't want a war with the Families, and he doesn't yet know one is coming.

"I can't believe you fucking did this," Axle says, eyeing my left breast that has his name literally tattooed on it.

He didn't freak out, much to my dismay. He merely threatened to kill Drake for seeing so much of my ladies. No, those were nowhere nearly his exact words.

Anticlimactic as his reaction was, it was still funny to see him turn murderous and Drake hide in the storage room that day, swearing he never saw nipple, as if that made it all better.

"I like it. It's totally awesome to wear a low-cut shirt, too, because girls see it and know I'm crazy enough to get your name on me, so I might be crazy enough to stab them in the throat if they try to steal you."

He grunts, and I feel him roll his eyes.

"We could stay in here all day," Axle says against my neck as he kisses his way back up.

"But the warehouse has been fixed and modified to now withstand an outside explosion," I say as he slides his lips all along my chest, working his way down to tempt me.

I grab his hair, halting his descent, and feel him smile against the underside of my left breast.

"And I really want to see what I've paid for," I go on, grinning when he rolls his eyes.

"Drex will pay you back just as soon—"

"I'm not worried about repayment. Consider it my payment for the protective services I'm being given. Besides, if I'm staying there, I never want to have to worry about being exploded again."

He tenses subtly, not wanting me to feel it, but I find myself wishing to recant that terrible joke. I blame him. He's made me less funny because he's horrible at being funny.

"Besides, I also bought a gift for the club, and it's finally here. I want to see the unveiling," I go on, grinning when he looks at me curiously.

"You're making me feel as though I have a sugar momma at this point."

I burst out laughing, then wonder if he maybe stole my funny and left me with his non-funny humor. Totally an unfair trade.

We clean up and dress quickly, though Axle is reluctant to leave our bubble. He's always reluctant to leave it.

I ride on the back of his bike, my hands clutched around his middle. He's relaxed and at ease as we follow Dash and Sledge to the clubhouse.

Today is the dawn of a new era.

It's a big day.

And I feel excited to even get to be a part of it.

It feels as though my heart is with two Families now.

We pull inside the newly renovated and larger hangar, and Axle helps me off the bike before he drops his arm around my shoulders.

His name is visible amongst the cleavage I'm sporting, and he glances down at it, shaking his head as a small smile plays on his lips. Secretly, he loves the tattoo, but he's too proud to admit it.

His face turns to stony expression, giving nothing away, the second we step into the partying atmosphere, everyone celebrating the clubhouse's revival. Axle doesn't share smiles with just anyone.

They're special and reserved for people he finds special.

I get the most smiles. Not that I'm keeping score or anything.

The room inside has been made a little larger, perfect for skating when this place isn't full of bikers. Maybe that was on purpose.

There's a guy in a chair with a bag over his head, his hands tied behind him, and his body shaking with silent sobs. It appears I'm the only one who is even given any pause by the sight, because all the others are drinking and enjoying the girls who are happily paying them attention.

"Anyone know why Tiffany and the other new girls are giving me the same cold shoulder as the ones who worked with Sarah?" Jude drawls. "Been getting worse over the past two months."

"Probably has something to do with the fact your legendary assassin ex has started working with us on certain jobs," Axle says with no emotion.

Jude snorts and rolls his eyes. "She can cock-block me all she wants. It doesn't change the fact we're never getting back together."

"What's with the prisoner thing?" I ask, gesturing toward Mr. Bagged Head.

Jude glances over, gives me a careless shrug, but a wicked grin spreads over his face. "Demonstration day."

Frowning, I study the guy. "What sort of demonstration?"

Jude musses my hair, treating me less like an infectious disease and more like a tolerated nuisance. "You'll see, skater girl."

He turns and walks away, leaving that suspended in the air, and I cut my eyes toward Axle.

He shrugs, unconcerned, and I roll my eyes as Drex stands up on the bar. The music cuts out, and hushed silence falls over the room as the partying pauses.

"In case you haven't heard, over the past two months, we've made a hell of a lot of changes. The clubhouse is safer than ever as long as what's within the walls is loyal."

He walks over, taking a shot from Eve, who is sitting on the bar, and he tosses it back before continuing.

"Lots of changes," he says, staring down at the empty shot glass for a brief second. When his eyes come back up to see the quiet room, he makes a point of meeting every pair of eyes that he can.

"Ben Mars was delivered back to his father—well, most of him."

A few cheers and laughter follow that, and Drex smirks.

"Benny has abandoned Pop. He doesn't want to be in the middle of this war anymore. He's not the only alliance to cut strings. Pop's men keep randomly disappearing, and we have a little songbird selling out all the traitors within our club."

Everyone bristles, glancing around as though they're going to find someone with "traitor" stamped across their forehead.

Drex crouches, looking down at the man with a bag over his head. "If you're one of those who hasn't been sold out yet, I suggest leaving the state before I get my hands on you," Drex says coldly, looking back up. "It'll be the only way to save your hide."

Byson—yeah, he's sticking firm to that name—walks over and rips the bag off the man's head. I've seen the guy before, but his name escapes me.

A few hushed whispers stir as Drex takes a seat on the edge of the bar.

"Paul here is just an example of the latest one to confess his loyalty to Pop after he was outed."

Paul has tears streaking down his face as he looks at the crowd, silently pleading to be saved.

"Liza and a few others have already been dealt with. But since this is our first gathering in a couple of months, I thought it important to remind everyone here that I'm twice as dangerous as Pop. Twice as unforgiving. And twice as fucking brutal when I'm betrayed."

Drex hops down from the bar, moving to stand beside the gagged Paul who cries a little harder.

"And we've done all this with just a handful of us and one partially psychotic ally," Drex adds, smirking.

Everyone looks at Jude as if compelled to do so at the mention of the partially psychotic ally. The girl standing closest to him takes several big steps back, causing me to restrain a smile as Jude rolls his eyes and drinks more of his whiskey.

Gazes shift back to Drex as he talks again. "Imagine the hell we can rain when we're all together again."

Roars of cheers follow that, men saluting Drex with their beers.

"And, as a gift from our newest ally, we have something to give everyone. Now, normally there's more ceremony and tradition for such a thing, but we're breaking all the rules lately. Might as well fuck this one in the ass, too."

Laughter and hoots follow that, as though Drex is working the crowd. He smirks over at me before returning his attention to the numerous boxes on the ground. As he leans over and opens one, he pulls out a Death Chasers cut, and the roar of cheers almost deafens me.

"It's official," Drex says as the cheers die down. "We're official. Fuck anyone who wants to argue with that."

He studies the cut in his hand, a dark smile playing on his lips.

"And fuck anyone who stays loyal to Pop after they put this on." He turns to look at Paul, who is shuddering as tears stream down his cheeks. "Pop might kill you. But I'll rip your spine out before I let you die."

Grins are the answering reaction to that.

"Hell yeah!" one guy cheers, causing resulting chuckles to ignite.

Barbarians—I'll say it again. But it's sort of grown on me.

At least you know you lie with danger here. It's different from the hidden dangers that lurk behind designer suits. It's actually a little more honest and pure.

Weird as that sounds.

He gestures toward Jude, who puts down his drink and comes to cut Paul free.

"Viewing room will be in the basement for anyone who wants to watch the show. Don't want to get blood on our shiny new floors," Drex says with a sadistic smile as Jude starts dragging a struggling Paul toward the basement door. "The rest of you line up for your fucking cuts and bring your drinks. It's going to be a hell of a night."

This time when the cheers erupt, they don't die down very quickly at all. Sledge walks up, a cut in his hand and a smile on his lips, as he hands Axle his own cut.

"You could have told me you paid for this," Axle tells me.

"They're a lot more expensive than I realized. I didn't understand why all of you hadn't pitched in to get some yet. Now I get it. Why don't the members pay club fees?"

Axle takes the cut, looking over the Death Chasers logo and name, fighting his grin. He's like a kid with a new present at Christmas, but too cool to look like that in front of people.

"Because we're not a traditional club. We're not here just for shits and giggles and the joy of riding. In case you haven't noticed, we're sort of criminals and need all the hands we can to stay untouchable," he answers absently.

When he turns it around, he freezes, staring at the *Vice President* patch under his name. His confused gaze swings up to Sledge then shifts to Drex as he comes to join us.

"I don't remember voting on this," Axle says, his frown creasing his features.

"We voted without you so that you didn't vote against yourself. Pretty damn close to unanimous," Drex says with a shrug.

His eyes shift to Sledge. "This should be—"

Sledge waves a dismissive hand before interrupting him. "I'm not cut out for VP. I had the wrong woman in my bed for so long that my head isn't right yet. You're the clear choice, kid. We all agreed on that."

Before Axle can try to argue again, Drake struts over, eyeing the cut in Axle's hand. His walk is normal now—no brace and no crutches.

"Glad to see you fuckers are finally showcasing my beautiful fucking art. I was wondering if it was just going to waste away. Now you can go back to being matching boys with no originality."

Drex flips him off, shaking his head.

Drake winks at me when I grin, because I love it when he gives them hell. It's like they all tolerate it without giving him much thought. Unique relationship, but intriguing at the same time.

And he's technically an outsider, which makes it all the more intriguing.

"Rush still on duty?" Sledge asks Drex.

"For now. Herrin's next move would likely be something shady," Drex says, not calling him *Pop* for once. "My sister would be the most obvious target if he knows where she is."

"You want to send him some backup?" Sledge offers.

Drex looks over at him. "If it'd make you feel better, you're welcome to join him. But you know as well as I do that Rush is fully capable of handling anything solo. It's one reason I sent him. He's the most lethal with a weapon, and the most vicious under fire."

"I wouldn't discount Jude in that race," Dash snorts. "He's getting more vicious the longer he goes without sex. And Sarah is doing all she can to make sure his dick is a terrifying thought to any woman who steps foot inside the club."

My grin is huge. Not gonna lie. I find it hilarious that Sarah scares the shit out of other women who might touch her man.

"I want that sort of power. I really need to learn to shoot," Eve says on a sigh as she joins Drex at his side, and his arm drops around her shoulders as he kisses the top of her head.

Sledge laughs under his breath.

"The trick is to be really crazy in front of people," I tell her. "You don't have to know how to shoot; you just have to show people your inner psycho and hide all the sweet stuff behind closed doors."

She gives me a thoughtful look.

"I don't have a whole lot of psycho to show," Eve finally says.

"I can totally give you lessons," I offer.

Drex groans as Axle turns his head, his body shaking with silent laughter.

But Eve just gives me a conspiratorial grin. "I'll take you up on that as long as I don't have to learn to skate."

"You need your own gimmick. Skating around corpses is mine."

"I think I'll party with my girl over there before your girl gets her hands on her," Drex says to Axle, tugging Eve away as he guides her toward the rest of the party.

Cuts are still being handed out, everyone looking for their own names. It's a good day for the Death Chasers.

They've fought like hell for a good day.

The others break off to join the party as well, leaving me alone with Axle as he pulls on his cut. It fits him well, even though it needs a little breaking in.

"I want you shirtless with just that cut on later tonight," I tell him as I wag my eyebrows.

He smirks as he lifts me suddenly, and I try not to giggle like an idiot—because I'm supposed to be a psycho and all that—as he puts me down on the bar and steps in between my legs.

When his lips find mine, I wrap my legs around his waist, kissing him like I'm claiming him in front of everyone. He kisses me just as hard, gripping my ass and pulling me closer.

"I changed my mind," I murmur against his lips. "I vote we skip the party and party by ourselves in your room upstairs."

Grinning against my lips, he lifts me, and...then throws me over his shoulder.

Huffing out a breath of defeat, I flop around over the barbarian's shoulder, letting him haul me toward his cave before he clubs me over the head to keep me.

Then I grin.

Because, well, obviously I'm a little crazy.

And so is he.

And everyone loves a little crazy.

THE END

Adrenaline *Rush* is coming next for the Death Chasers MC Series. Rush's story.

ABOUT THE AUTHOR

C.M. Owens is a *USA Today* Bestselling author of over 30 novels. She always loves a good laugh, and lives and breathes the emotions of the characters she becomes attached to. Though she came from a family of musicians, she has zero abilities with instruments, sounds like a strangled cat when she sings, and her dancing is downright embarrassing. Just ask anyone who knows her. Her creativity rests solely in the written word. Her family is grateful that she gave up her quest to become a famous singer.

You can find her on Facebook, Twitter, and Instagram.

Instagram: @cmowensauthor

Twitter: @cmowensauthor

Facebook: @CMOwensAuthor

There are two Facebook groups, the teaser group, and the book club where you can always find her hanging out with her fans and readers.

CPSIA information can be obtained
at www.ICGtesting.com
Printed in the USA
FSHW011254090720
72013FS

9 781976 035876